Unmasked

An Evergreen Academy Novel

Ruby Vincent

Published by Ruby Vincent, 2019.

Prologue

"W-who are you?!" The tight band I had not felt in so long constricted my chest. I thought I knew fear, but nothing compared to the terror that shook me and tore my lungs. I couldn't breathe. I couldn't think about anything other than the horrors I learned that night.

Were these faceless monsters going to kill me?

"Let me go!"

"Let me make something very clear." That dreadful voice stopped me cold. "You're done at Evergreen Academy. Goodbye, Valentina Moon."

I opened my mouth to curse them when the hands reared up and sent me flying through the air. I screamed as I splashed down. Water rushed into my mouth and nose, choking me as I sank below the depths.

Chapter One

"**M**aybe we shouldn't go back."

I lifted my head and met Sofia's gaze over the computer screen. If I could see my face, I'm sure it would have the same anxious expression as hers.

"It's not going to get any better," she continued. "We're looking at the same hell as last year."

I lowered my eyes to the Evergreen student portal. It was time to pick our classes for our final year at the academy. No doubt Sofia had the same fleeting thought that I did. I should just put "screw you" in the comment box and move on with my life.

But I can't.

"I have to go back, Sof."

"Why? There are plenty of other good schools." I picked up a hint of desperation in her voice. "None of them are Evergreen, but they would still look great on our college applications. I was reading up on one—Breakbattle Academy. It's not far from us and—"

"Sofia," I cut in gently. "I have to go back."

Her shoulders slumped. Sofia dropped down until her forehead rested on the laptop. "I hate this, Val. It shouldn't be like this. I'm— I'm scared."

"I know you are. I am too." I rose from the kitchen table and went around to my best friend. She let me pull her into my arms. "That place has been a haunted house horror show since the moment I passed through the gates. You're scared. I'm scared. *Everyone* is scared. They are afraid of the Spades and always have been. That has to stop. It's time someone put an end to their reign."

She pinned me with a look. "That someone does not have to be *you.*"

"They made it me when they bullied, harassed, violated, and marked me." My grip on her shoulder tightened. "Ace is coming after me so I'm coming back just as hard."

"Val, Ace marked the Knights. That has never happened before. They are supposed to be untouchable. Last semester was... bad."

"It would have been worse if we didn't have each other's backs. We'll watch out for each other, Sof, and we'll take down Ace and whoever is left of the Spades so that they can't hurt anyone else. Alright?"

Sofia still looked unsure. Tears had collected in her eyes that threatened to fall with every blink. I suddenly had a vision of those tears mixing with dye and staining her red dress. The retribution that came down when Ace marked me and the Knights was swift. It hit just as hard for those that stood with us.

My heart broke thinking of that day. "Why don't you transfer?" I seized upon the idea as I grabbed her hands. "This is my fight. It was never yours and it doesn't have to be. You should leave Evergreen, Sof. You're a science whiz who invented a new shampoo in middle school. You never needed the academy to be successful. You'll have your pick of universities. You go to Breakbattle and—"

"Not if you don't come with me."

I blinked. The tears and desperation were gone. Sofia's voice was infused with steel.

"I'm not leaving you to face them alone. We both leave, or we both stay."

I tried another way. "I won't be alone. I have the boys. We—"

"We're a team, Val. We were long before the boys came around. You wouldn't leave if it were me, would you?"

I didn't reply, but I knew my eyes held the answer. Never in a million years would I abandon Sofia.

A look passed between us and, at that moment, I knew we understood each other.

Sofia took a deep breath, held it, and then let it out slowly. "Okay. Let's pick these classes."

I couldn't resist leaning in to kiss her cheek. "I love you, Sof."

"I know." There was a trace of teasing in her tone. "I love you too."

I stood as I heard the sound of barreling footsteps. I knew what was coming before—

"Mommy! Mommy!"

I turned in time to see Adam burst into the doorway. I took in the beaming three-year-old. His perfect head of wild curls, shining green eyes, and complete lack of pants.

A smile tugged at my lips. "Adam Moon. Did you use the potty?"

He threw his hands up. "Yes!"

"And then did you run away before Olivia could put your pants on?"

"He did!" Mom shouted down the hall. "He was so excited; he had to tell you before he did anything else."

I scooped my laughing baby up. "I'm so proud of you," I said between peppering his face with kisses. I saw Olivia enter the dining room over his head.

"You get his pants on, Mommy Tina. I'll start on breakfast." She tossed the thing on my head before I had a chance to reach for it. "Thanks, Mom."

"So what classes are you going to take?" Sofia asked as I sat down with Adam.

"I'd say any class that doesn't have the *new Knights* in it, but that's not an option. I miss when the classes were split."

"Any class that you don't have with me, you'll have with Zane, Kai, or the boys. You will never be alone with them."

"But we'll still be outnumbered," I replied under my breath. The thought sent my mind whirling. Even with my friends by my side, it was hard to face an entire school of people determined to take me down. They had destroyed me once and I swore the same wouldn't happen to my friends.

I gazed at Sofia while she tapped away at her computer. *I'm going to keep my promise. I have a plan, and this time, no one is changing my mind.*

"Mommy?"

I shook myself out of my thoughts. "Yes, baby?"

"I'm hungry."

"Olivia is making you breakfast right now, Adam."

He seemed to accept this. He rested his head on my chest and got comfortable.

"So now you're Olivia and Mommy," Sofia said. "Will your mom be Grandma soon?"

I snorted. "I tried calling her grandma once and ended up with a sore backside for my trouble. As for me, I call myself his mommy so he's been calling me that instead of Tina."

"Aren't you worried about... being called that in public?"

"I was," I admitted. "I was afraid of people asking questions about how I ended up as a fourteen-year-old mother, but now"—I dropped a kiss on Adam's head—"I don't care what people think. I'm his mom. I never want him to think he shouldn't call me that."

"I wish Madame Madeline and I had the relationship you two have. I called my nanny mom until I was four. I was really confused when she told me the lady that flitted in and out of my nursery every other day was actually my mother."

I winced. "Are things still awful with you guys?"

She didn't lift her head, but the tapping on her keys got more vicious. "There's a reason I packed up and came straight to your place after school ended. I never told you this, but Mom and I got into a huge fight after I was— after what happened. The nurse called her because I wouldn't stop crying. She asked me why someone would do that to me and when I told her it was because I stood up for people who were marked, she flipped out.

"She started shouting at me and demanded to know why I would do something so stupid. If I was marked too, they might come after the business and destroy what she's worked for. Everything I went through and the first thing she did was make it about herself!" The keyboard assault got worse until I was sure it would break under her hands. "The worst part is she was right. All of a sudden, Honey Hair products are being flooded with bad reviews saying they make your scalp itch, your hair fall out, and are tested on animals. Awful lies that are hurting sales. Mom is so consumed with damage control; she hasn't called once since the start of summer break."

"I'm so sorry, Sof."

"Don't be. It wasn't you. It was *them*."

She didn't need to define "them." I knew exactly who they were. The new Knights.

"They won't get away with it this year," I stated. "I promise."

"I know. We have each other's backs."

Not just that, I thought, but I didn't correct her.

"Girls." Mom's voice drew our attention. "Breakfast is ready."

We abandoned our class schedules in favor of eating. My mind was a tangle of thoughts while I fed Adam his yogurt. I knew what I had to do, but I had no idea if it would be enough.

There were a lot of people in my way now, but this battle was between me and Ace. Nothing would stop me from finding them. I would bring them down no matter what it took.

"MOMMY, WHERE YOU GOING?"

I paused with my hands on the suitcase. It crushed me that my son knew what it meant when I brought it out.

Adam gazed curiously at me from my pillow. I tried for a smile. "Remember I told you Mommy has to go to school?" He cocked his head. "Today, baby. Mommy is going to school today."

"I don't want you to go." He said it so matter-of-factly, but it made me feel worse. Leaving him never got easier.

"I don't want to go either." I climbed onto the bed and let him snuggle into my side. Pushing it and trying to convince him I had to leave would only make him cry, which would make me cry. We had to leave in ten minutes. I didn't want us both to be a mess when we rolled out of the driveway.

"Val, you're not going to believe this." Sofia's voice preceded her before she marched into my room. "They're coming. They are actually coming." She waved her phone at me like that was a clue.

"Who is coming?"

"My parents." Sofia tossed my suitcase aside and took its place. "After months of nothing, Mom just called to say they are coming to College Day. She said we need to present a united front." She kissed her teeth. "Again, she's making it about her."

"Maybe this will give you a chance to talk."

"We're going to talk alright." There was a glint in her eye that sharply reminded me of when Sofia punched the crap out of Natalie. "She sent Dad down to pick me up and I've got a lot to say to both of them."

Sofia dropped the look long enough to give me a sad smile. "He's going to be here soon so I've got to say bye now, but I'll see you at school. At least no one will try to pull anything on College Day."

I had to agree with that. Today would be the one day out of the coming school year that I should be off-limits. The same went for everyone who had been marked along with me.

We hugged one more time before she went back to the guest/Adam's room to pack her things.

Sofia's dad showed up while I was in the middle of getting Adam into his suit. She shouted goodbye at us as Mom came into my room.

"How do I look, kid?" She did a little spin. "Do I look like I'm about to send a daughter off to college?"

"Not at all," I said to Mom's crisp white pantsuit. "You look like you're about to go to college yourself."

She winked. "Good answer. I knew there was a reason I kept you around."

I laughed as I heaved Adam into my arms. "Is it weird that I'm nervous? I know we're just meeting the Somerset rep today, but still, I keep practicing what I'm going to say over and over in my head."

"Not weird at all. This is a big deal." We talked while we headed out to the car. "Somerset is your first, second, and third choice university. We're all praying you get in so you can be close by."

"I won't have to worry about tuition," I replied, thinking of the bank account Caroline Shea kept healthy. "But the price tag is the least of your worries when thinking of Somerset."

"When the rep learns about you, she'll confirm that you're a lock to get in. Trust me."

I held on to Mom's encouragement as we loaded the car and set off for Evergreen. Today wasn't just any move-in day. For the seniors, it was College Day.

The day when college representatives from all over the country came to Evergreen used to be later in the first semester. This fact changed when helicopter, live-through-their-children parents began harassing the former headmasters and demanding they be allowed to come. They wanted to be sure their kids spoke to the *right* reps and impressed them.

They made it open to parents, but that led to complaints about scheduling and getting time out of their boardrooms. The compromise was to hold the college event on the day when all of the parents and students were collected on the Evergreen campus.

If there was one good thing about this nerve-racking day, it was that no one would mess with me on College Day. Even if they didn't fear Evergreen's wrath for embarrassing the school, they weren't about to embarrass themselves in front of the reps they wanted to win over. The real hell would start tomorrow when everyone was gone.

Or they will try to start hell. I'm going to put a stop to it before they get a chance. I won't put my friends through this. I'll protect them and... my boys.

Thoughts of Maverick, Jaxson, Ezra, and Ryder flooded my mind as the distance between me and Evergreen grew shorter. I couldn't wait to see them. Texts and random visits when they could get away hadn't been nearly enough. I loved that I would get to see them every day now, but I hated that came with a dark cloud over our heads. A cloud named Ace.

When Mom joined the line of cars in front of the school gates, I scanned the sea of faces. Students in jet-black dresses and blazers mingled on the cobblestones. That was our color this year. Black for seniors. Black for our final year. Black for the painted bells on the joker hat that plagued my nightmares.

They are here somewhere, I thought as Mom drove past the entrance for the parking lot. *Ace is here.*

Mom pulled into a space and we piled out. I steadied my nerves as I settled Adam in my arms. The toddler munched on his cookies without a care in the world. I looked down at him and smiled. I hadn't told anyone, but there was something else I needed to do.

"Miss Moon?" I glanced up and landed on two of the school staff. "We are happy to take your bags up to your room."

"Thank you."

Mom handed them the keys on her way around the car. "This thing doesn't start for another hour, right? I'm going to hunt down a bathroom and those refreshments the email promised."

"Okay. I'll head up to the dorm with my bags."

We split up in the driveway. Olivia went in one direction while Adam and I followed the familiar path to my dorm. As we passed through the side gate, I could see the booths and stalls covering the front lawn. Parents and students streamed around them in their haste to get their things put away, load up on snacks, and get in a few tips before the reps arrived.

We reached the disused building that had become my dorm and one of the staff opened the door to let us in. A racket of noise smacked me over the face.

"What is going on?"

I stepped in and was met with chaos. Staff ran all over the front hall, yelling to be heard over the sound of drilling.

"There you are, Miss Moon." I turned as Gus came down the stairs. "I hope you had a good summer."

"What is going on?" I repeated. "What are you doing to my dorm?"

Gus held his arm out to indicate he wanted to go outside—a good idea considering the noise. I let the staff with my bags go on while the three of us stepped back into the crisp September morning.

"What's up, Gus?"

"There has been a change, Valentina. I'm afraid I got word only this morning." Gus spoke casually like he would to a friend, or to someone he had gotten very familiar with after the school turned on me for the second time, and his job as head security guard got even harder.

"What change?"

"The Knights went into Evergreen's office two hours ago and issued new orders."

I stiffened. Those were not my Knights, which meant this wouldn't be good.

"Eight students are to be removed from the senior dorm and placed in here. I was given a list."

Gus handed it to me but I knew what it said before I read it.

"This is a new method," I said, "but at least it didn't take flaming balls of duct tape to drive them out."

He shook his head. "Nothing like that will happen again under my watch. This will now be a coed space so cameras are being installed. You, of course, understand that I will be enforcing *all* rules in regards to all of you living here."

My cheeks warmed. I didn't want to think about what those cameras picked up before everything changed, but that was all over now.

The new Knights had screwed me again.

"I get it, Gus. Do what you have to do."

He nodded and then went back inside. After a minute, I followed with Adam.

"Things just keep getting more complicated, baby."

Adam nodded solemnly like he knew exactly what I was talking about. I took him up to the third floor and excused the staff putting away my things. When they were gone, I set my son on the bed and stepped back.

"Okay. Do you want to help Mommy get ready to speak to the rep?"

"Yes."

I cleared my throat. "Hello, my name is Valentina Moon. I—"

"I should hope he knows your name."

I whirled around as my door swung open on squeaky hinges.

"Ryder," Adam squealed. There was a soft thud and then the toddler streaked past and tackled Ryder's legs.

The older boy chuckled as he ruffled his hair. "Hey, little man. Did you miss me?"

"Yes!"

"Did Mommy miss me too?"

"Mommy missed you so much."

If I could see my cheeks, I was sure red would have glared back at me. "Adam, don't give away my secrets."

Adam giggled as Ryder hefted him into his arms. He raised a brow at me over the little boy's head. "Oh? Was it a secret?"

"Yes." I closed the distance between us, a smile playing on my lips. "I can't have you thinking I'm pining after not seeing you for two weeks. How was the rest of your summer?"

His forehead wrinkled. It drew my eyes above his brow to the faint scar that now marred his features. "Now that I'm eighteen, Benjamin's partners have been coming by the house and dropping non-subtle hints about my plans for the company. I've been in unofficial meetings with them the last couple weeks. Mom appointed someone to step in after he... disappeared, but the arrangement was only meant to be temporary."

"What are your plans?"

He shook his head. "I don't want anything to do with *his* company. He certainly never wanted it to be mine."

My skin tightened thinking of Adam.

"But it's not just about me. There are over a hundred thousand employees working for Shea Industries. I owe them something even though I owe that man nothing. Not to mention Mom. I have to make sure she is always taken care of."

The smile did come through now. I gazed at Ryder as warmth spread through me. "You're a good man, Ryder Shea. Who knew?"

He cracked a smile. "Don't tell anyone. The reputation I've been building as a cold, violent maniac may get us through this year."

Those words popped my bubble of good feelings like a balloon. My eyes snapped up to his new scar. "Ryder, I don't want you to have that reputation. Things are *not* going to be like last semester."

"They're not just going to stop, and we're not going to let anyone mess with you."

I reached up and pressed my fingers to his temple. I gently traced his scar. "I'm so sorry. I never wanted—"

"Stop." His hand flashed up and grabbed mine. "You didn't do anything wrong. Don't apologize."

I couldn't help but be sorry. After that horrible morning when the Knights woke up and found out they were marked, it all started up again. Another card was put in my locker and no one was hearing that it was fake.

My classmates came for me just as hard. The worst thing was they had the picture of me and Ezra in the library to use as ammunition. I found it everywhere—on my locker, my desk, my dorm front door, everywhere. The Knights were ruthless in defending my honor, and when one guy tried to corner me in the library, leering about "round two," Ryder socked him with a punch that cracked his jaw.

The two got into an awful fight while I screamed for them to stop, but I couldn't pull them apart. Not even when Ryder's head was bashed against the shelves and blood poured down his face. They both ended up in the nurse's office the day before school let out and I vowed right there that I would end this.

"You're all in this mess because of me," I replied.

"We're in this mess because Ace is psychotic. They flipped when the Knights they thought belonged to them chose you. They did this to punish us and show the school who is really in charge."

"The Spades," I whispered.

He nodded.

The breath whooshed out of me and took my strength with it. I dropped forward and rested my head on his chest. "How will we ever find out who it is? Or if there are more Spades? We thought it was over with Scarlett. The entire senior class could be Spades and how would we know?"

"We'll figure it out." A warm hand settled on my head. "Don't forget we've got that list of Ace suspects. Somehow all of this fits together. We'll find out who these people are."

"I'm not going through this again, and I'm not seeing my friends get hurt anymore. I told Ace I would find them and make them regret ever sending me that first text. I meant it."

His chest rumbled with his chuckle. "I know you will. When you set your mind to vengeance, you can't be stopped. Turns out its incredibly attractive when it's not directed at me."

The words flipped on the bubble machine in my stomach. *What am I going to do with this guy? He keeps me at arm's length all summer and then goes and says something like that.*

Ryder tugged on my short strands until I raised my head. Our eyes met in a spark of electricity that made my pulse quicken. Our lips could not have been more than an inch apart. It would take nothing for me to rise up and close the distance. So I did.

"We shouldn't," he whispered, stopping me when we were only a hair apart.

"Why not?"

Ryder twisted his neck to the side. I followed his gaze and we both landed on Adam. The toddler was fixed on us. A tiny pout was forming in the corner of his mouth.

"This is why," he whispered. In a louder voice, he said, "Adam, Tina is mine."

I had all of a second to ride the high those words gave me until—

"No! She's my mommy!"

Adam's pout was in full force now. He glared at Ryder when only a little while ago, he was pleased to see him.

"See?" Ryder went on, laughing. "Better not to do that in front of him. I don't want to get beaten up by a toddler again."

Mortified, I took my angry baby out of his arms. Ryder had been doing this all summer. He would come to Wakefield to visit, take me and Adam out for the day, and then end the night saying we couldn't go any farther.

"What are you going to do when you can't use Adam as an excuse?"

Ryder's smile hung on his lips as he looked down at me. "I guess I'll have to kiss you."

I lost my reply as I blinked at him. I was not expecting that.

I didn't get a chance to find my words as a voice sounded behind us. "Baby. Eugene. Let me end your suffering." Jaxson pushed Ryder to the side and planted himself in front of me. "I have arrived."

Jaxson ruffled Adam's hair. "Hey, D-man. Did you miss your uncle Jaxson?" Jaxson had taken to calling him D-man after Adam's middle name, David. Usually, he liked the name.

Adam twisted around and buried his head in my neck. I soothingly rubbed his back.

"He doesn't mean it," I assured. "Ryder set him off and now he's a little upset."

He nodded. "He has that effect on me all the time."

Ryder rolled his eyes as Jaxson walked past me and plopped down on my bed. "Can you believe it? We're all bunking together in this sweet dorm. Everyone said senior year would be awesome."

"It's not a gift, Jaxson," Ryder reminded. "I heard it from Gus. The Knights booted us from the main dorm. Plus, he's putting cameras in to make sure we don't do whatever you're fantasizing about doing."

"We still get to be closer to Valentina. I call that a gift."

I buried my head in Adam's curls to hide my smile. Jaxson Van Zandt could say the sweetest things when he was ready.

Adam snuggled deeper into my neck. The act sharply reminded me of what I needed to do.

"Guys, I know we're all getting ready for College Day, but there's something I need to talk to you about before we go."

"That's cool." Jaxson leaned back and folded his fingers behind his head. "But I'm not going to College Day. Higher education is not for me."

"I thought you said last month that you were thinking about it," I said.

"I did think about it. I pictured late-night study sessions, walking across the quad, and sneaking into your dorm."

"Did you now?"

"Yep. It was real dirty, mama. Can't talk about it in front of the kid."

Now it was me rolling my eyes.

"Anyway," Jaxson continued, "I'd love to be at Somerset with you, but university isn't for me. I talked about it with Papa Van Zandt and I'm going to work at the studio after I graduate. He is starting me as the lowest-paid grunt until I earn his trust, but eventually, I'm going to take over." He shot me a smile. "I know what I want to do. I'm going to start now."

"I think that's great, Jaxson. I'm happy for you."

"The best part is I'll still be close to you."

"That is definitely a bonus." I stopped flirting long enough to look at Ryder. "What about you? You've never told me your plans."

"I'll be going to a school nearby." Ryder looked straight ahead, not meeting my eyes. "I can't leave Mom."

He said it so casually, but those words struck right through me. "But... there's only one decent school near your mom."

"That's right." I think I caught a ghost of a smile. "Somerset University is my first choice."

I was saved from thinking of something to say by a knock on the doorframe. I turned to find Gus standing in the entrance.

"Now that you are all here, I'd like you to come down to the front room so I can explain the rules for the *new* senior dorm."

We tromped out behind him to find Maverick, Ezra, Sofia, Zane, Kai, and Paisley waiting for us at the bottom. The rest of the marked and all of those who stood by us when the new regime took over. Everyone looked amazing in their best suits, dresses, and shoes, but the grim looks on their faces didn't match.

Sofia took Adam off my hands when I stepped to her side and faced Gus.

"You know why you're here," Gus began. "I'm sorry I can't do anything to change your circumstances, but know that your safety is no less important to me. Cameras cover every inch inside and outside. The windows are shatterproof. The building has fire alarms on every floor." Gus met each and every one of our eyes as he spoke. "I was made aware of another security risk in regards to the courtyard. I intend to have a camera installed there too."

I didn't need to ask how or who made him aware. The boys had spilled about Scarlett's attempt on my life. If it keeps everyone safe, then it was a secret that needed to be spilled.

"The rules are the same for the main dorms. Opposite genders are not to be alone in a room. You have a ten o'clock curfew. Staff have the right to enter as they please. Any questions?"

A few people shook their heads, but otherwise no one moved.

"Alright. You have a big day ahead of you so go on. Your things will be put away and your dorm ready when you return."

I turned on the boys before the group could split up. "I need to talk to you. Will you go up to my room?"

The guys went up without a word while I took Adam back.

"Val, is there something up?"

"Yes."

She placed her hand on my elbow. "What is it?"

"Hey. Did you have that talk with your parents?"

Sofia blinked at my subject change. "Yeah, I did. I chewed them out for trying to make me feel bad for doing the right thing. Honey Hair is a great product and can survive a few trolls, but I let them know our relationship wouldn't if they didn't learn to support me."

"I'm proud of you, Sof. You stood up and told the truth." My eyes drifted up the stairs. "Now it's time for me to do the same."

She didn't ask me what I meant. Instead, she squeezed my arm before heading back outside.

I let out a breath. "Okay, Adam. Are you ready?"

"Yes," he replied, even though he didn't know what he was supposed to be ready for.

"Tina isn't ready. Will you give her a kiss for luck?"

Adam didn't hesitate in dropping a big smooch on my cheek. "Tina, I love you."

The words were a straight shot of warmth and confidence to my heart. I knew at that moment that I was doing the right thing.

The former Knights were waiting in my room for me like I asked, and they had made the space their own. Jaxson reclined on my pillows. Maverick sat on the edge of my mattress. Ezra took up the desk chair and Ryder leaned against my bathroom door.

Despite the rules, I stepped in and closed the door. I figured Gus would give me enough credit to not get up to any funny business with a three-year-old in the room.

"Let me guess," Ezra began before I could open my mouth. "Strategy session."

"We need one," Maverick responded. "They went hard at us last semester. It'll only get worse."

"It won't get worse," stated Jaxson, "because we're going to be smart. Ryder's end-of-the-year throwdown aside, they've been sticking to the rules and not getting physical. If we don't go anywhere alone—"

"Guys."

"—we stuck together last year and that didn't stop what happened to Sofia and Val," Ryder reminded them. "They've been targeting the girls and we can't be with them all the time."

"Guys."

"The hell we can't," Jaxson protested. "I'm perfectly happy to spend every minute with Val. I'm sure—"

"Guys!"

Four pairs of eyes flew to me as the conversation came to an abrupt halt. I took a deep breath. "This isn't a strategy session. I asked you to come here because I have something important to tell you."

Maverick rose to his feet. He was so tall he came up as high as the canopy over my bed. "What is it?"

I glanced down at my son. "It's about Adam."

The baby looked back at me with trusting green eyes. I kept my attention fixed on those eyes as I revealed the truth I had been holding back for years.

"Adam is not my brother. He's my son."

No one made a sound. Silence spread through the room, pressing down on me as I refused to look away from Adam.

"Val." Ryder's voice broke through. In the next breath, his arms were around us. "Thank you for telling us."

I lifted my head to give him a smile that wobbled. He knew of course. He knew everything. But his support meant more than I could tell him.

I finally chanced a look at the others. Maverick and Jaxson's faces held the shock I expected while Ezra's expression was carefully schooled.

"Guys, please, say something."

Jaxson broke first. "Is this what you meant when you said there were things I didn't know about you?"

I nodded. "Pretty much."

"Adam is your son."

"Yes."

"So you gave birth to him when..."

"I was fourteen," I finished. I held the toddler a little closer. "There is more I need to tell you about the circumstances of Adam's arrival, but I won't do that in front of him. All you need to know right now is that he's mine and I love him more than I thought I could ever love anyone."

To my surprise, Jaxson cracked a smile. "That's good enough for me. Honestly, I always thought it funny how obsessed with the kid you were. Everyone else can't stand their younger siblings. This makes way more sense."

I shifted my gaze to Maverick. The taller boy spoke the second he caught my attention. "This changes nothing between us. I love you and Adam's a great kid." He stepped forward as another smile found its way to my lips. "Thank you for trusting us."

I put my hand in his when he reached out. I couldn't believe I had been afraid to tell them. I turned my smile on Ezra.

He didn't smile back. "Can we talk more about this later? Just the two of us?"

"Oh. Yes, of course, we can."

"Great." Ezra got to his feet and made for the door. "We should get going before Gus comes down on us."

"Okay," I said softly as he brushed past me.

"Val, he—"

I slipped my hand out of Maverick's. "Don't. It's fine. I'll talk to him later like he asked. We should go. The reps will be arriving soon."

Maverick didn't say more. He bent, kissed my forehead, ruffled Adam's hair until he giggled, and then walked out. Jaxson did the same.

Soon it was just me and Ryder. "I know that must have been hard."

I swallowed around the lump in my throat. "It was, but I had to do it. If there is going to be any real future for us, then I have to be honest. Adam is my first priority."

I took his hand. It was cold to the touch and reminded me vividly of the granite I used to compare him to. "I should have told you I was going to do this. It involves you too."

"This isn't about me. You can tell who you want when you're ready, but... are you going to tell them everything?"

I was highly aware of Adam on my hip. "Not everything, but I'll tell them as much as I can."

He nodded. "I'll be there to support you if you want me. Just tell me what to do."

I gripped his hand tighter. "You're already doing it."

"Tina." Adam's voice brought me back to reality. "I'm hungry."

I quickly wiped away a stray tear before turning a big smile on Adam. "Of course you are, baby. Let's go find Olivia and the snacks."

I was in better spirits when I walked out of the construction zone and into the bright morning. The promised refreshments were laid out in the courtyard and I found Mom by the punch talking to Evergreen of all people. I picked up the pace.

"Mom?"

"Hey, kid." She held out her plate. "Have you tried these mini quiches? They're amazing. I've got some crackers for Adam too."

The toddler didn't waste time grabbing a handful. Evergreen looked down at him as he shoved the lot in his mouth. "So this is young Adam. Handsome boy."

"He is," Mom agreed. "Which is why it's a crime to be away from him. As I was saying earlier, I'd like you to rethink your 'only three weekend passes a semester' rule."

My eyes widened. "Mom, you—"

She held up a finger and I snapped my mouth shut. I had no idea she was planning to do this, and I would have stopped her if I had. I wanted nothing more than to come home every weekend, but Evergreen wasn't one to change his mind and Mom wasn't one to back down. The last thing I needed was for Mom to beat up my headmaster in front of the school.

"I can appreciate that you'd like to see your daughter, but it's imperative that Evergreen students are focused on their studies. As I understand it, Miss Moon plans to attend Somerset University. She can't afford any distractions."

My face twisted into a frown, but Mom beat me to it before I could reply. "Adam is not a distraction. Neither is her mother." Olivia's tone was chilly.

He blinked. "Of course. I did not mean to imply—"

"Yes, you did."

Uh oh. Can anyone else hear those sirens or is that just me?

I put my hand on Mom's arm, but she ignored me, plowing on. "It was because she came to see us so often last year that you changed the rules. You're aware that Val's situation is different than the other students. She has more reasons than most to come home."

Evergreen was stiffening up tighter than a bowstring. "I am aware and I have made more than my fair share of accommodations for Miss Moon, but there is a limit. I cannot keep giving her special treatment over the other students."

Mom folded her arms. "How about a compromise? You're worried about her studies so consider this: if she maintains her grades, she can come home on the weekends as she was allowed to before. If her grades drop, then take away her privileges. This can apply to everyone so it's fair."

Olivia said this in a perfectly even tone but bright splotches of red appeared on Evergreen's cheeks. "I'm not in the habit of having my policies questioned. I make decisions in the best interest of this school and its pupils. If you have a complaint, you can go through the proper channels."

"You mean I can donate a million or three to get you to open your ears?"

I sucked in a breath as Evergreen's eyes popped. "I-I beg your pardon!"

Olivia sniffed. She wasn't the least bit impressed. The woman had dealt with poverty, homelessness, single motherhood, and heart-breaking trauma. Evergreen didn't scare her. "You don't have to listen to me, but you should know, Mrs. Shea and I are united on this. She intends to come today and speak to you herself about Ryder coming home to see her. If you grant him more visits, then I expect you to do the same for Valentina. Her family needs her too."

"Caroline is coming?" I blurted.

"Our children are eighteen," Mom continued. "You cannot hold them hostage."

"Hostage? That is quite an exaggeration."

Mom's eyes narrowed. She closed the distance between them, putting her face up to his as alarm flickered across his features. "I want that ban lifted, Evergreen. I'll do what it takes to make it happen." Olivia lowered her voice until it was barely a whisper. "You won't deny my grandson his mother."

I looked between them with wide eyes, wondering who would break first. Adam just kept eating his crackers.

The air crackled between them as Evergreen straightened to his full height. "I will take your suggestion into consideration. Good day, Miss Moon."

Mom tsked after he strode off. "I never liked that man."

"Olivia," I hissed. "What was that?"

"I should have told you I was working on busting you out of this place, but I thought you'd try to stop me."

"I find it easier to get through school when I don't draw his attention." I snorted. "Not that I've managed that. But hold on. When did you talk to Caroline?"

"She and I have had a lot to discuss lately." Mom glanced around. "I won't get into all of it here, but after this year, the help she's been offering you is going to stop. I will pay for the college you get in to. I will be the one who steps in when you have problems at school."

"But, Mom—"

"No buts."

I blinked. This was one of the rare times I had seen my mom so serious.

"I stayed out of it before because I— I didn't think I had the right to—" Mom halted. She took a shuddering breath as she ducked her head. "It was all my f-fault."

"Mom, don't say that." I drew closer and put my arm around her. "It wasn't your fault."

"It was. I let that man near you. I didn't see what was going on." A tear dripped from her nose and splashed on the stones between us. "I didn't feel I had the right to say no when she stepped in to help you. I had ruined everything. I couldn't stop her from making it right." She shook her head. "Or at least, that was what I thought. Things are different now. I'm holding down a steady job. I've got savings and a home. I'm not that stupid woman who thought she could change her life by landing a rich husband. I've grown up a lot since then, and now, I'm going to take care of my family."

I was quiet as her words sank in. "You know," I began, "Somerset is one of the most expensive schools in the country."

She swiped her hand across her eyes. "I know that. I'll make it work. I can't force you, but I'd like you to give back all the money Caroline gave you. She paid your Evergreen tuition for all four years, but I made it clear that no more money will be coming."

I think it surprised her how easily I nodded. "Okay. I'll return the money."

"You will?"

"Yes." My eyes drifted across the courtyard to where Ryder spoke with Marcus Beaumont. "I've been thinking about the kind of relationship I want to have with Caroline and... her son. I'm starting over this year in a lot of ways. Giving the money back is the best way."

"Thank you, baby."

"And, Mom." I turned and looked her in the eyes. "I need you to know that I never blamed you. Not once. Not for a second."

The barest of smiles appeared on her lips. "I know, Val. You should have, but I know you didn't. You always were better than me. You're the one thing in my life I did right."

Tears prickled behind my eyes. "Mom, don't make me cry."

She laughed as she pulled me in for a hug. I hugged her back just as tightly until Adam complained.

"Livia," he whined.

"I'm sorry, little man," she said, slightly choked. "Come on. Let's get you more food."

I let Olivia take him. I looked around as they wandered off and realized the courtyard had begun to fill. The college reps had arrived.

In their wake, buttoned-up students and their overeager parents followed. They claimed their targets in the game of mingling and small talk. I decided on another tact. I couldn't wow the rep with stories of my summer in St. Tropez or tell them how I made my first million. It was better that I waited for the official event—when I could wow them with me.

I loaded up a plate with nibbles and took it out of the courtyard. There were dozens of booths taking up the lawn from every prestigious school in this country and a few from other countries. I bypassed them all as I looked for Somerset. I didn't care about anywhere else. I was staying home, close to my son. Nothing else was an option.

I spotted a flash of light blue and white out of the corner of my eye.

There. In front of the fountain.

I veered off, practically running as I descended on the Somerset booth. It was a simple setup. A plain pop-up tent and beneath it was a table loaded down with glossy catalogs and the school flag taped to the front. Two chairs had been placed before the table and boxes were stacked in the back of the tent.

I placed my food down and reached for one of the brochures. Somerset wasn't perfect for me just because of the location. It also boasted one of the best psychology programs in the nation as well as a minor in dance.

Smiling faces looked back at me as I flipped to the course section. *Getting in here would be—*

"Ah. Eager."

I jerked and the catalog went sailing out of my hands.

"I like the eager ones. It shows that you want this."

I raised my head to see a woman stand up from behind the stack of boxes. She pushed her wire-frame glasses further up her nose as she peered at me. "Decided to give the food a miss?"

"No," I said when I found my voice. "Couldn't say no to these mini quiches." I pushed my plate toward her. "Do you want some?"

"Don't mind if I do." She picked one up and popped it in her mouth. Up close, I could see her name badge read Andrea Towne.

She dusted her fingers off when she was done. "Well, since you're here. You can help me finish setting up. I've got more catalogs in those boxes, and school pens and pencils in that one."

"Okay." I walked over to where she pointed. "Sure you have enough? I heard Somerset on the lips of almost all my classmates last semester. They're going to clean you out."

She laughed. "Somerset is proud to have the highest number of Evergreen applicants every year. I'm assuming you're going to be one of them."

"That's right. Valentina Moon. Get used to this face because you're going to be seeing a lot of it on campus next year."

She laughed again. "I like the confident ones too. So, since you're here, tell me why you'd be a good fit for Somerset."

I took a steadying breath. This wasn't how I planned to give my spiel—while being used as free labor—but this was the perfect chance while I had her alone.

"Somerset is my first choice because..."

Andrea and I had a great conversation. She told me all about the courses I wanted to take and I even managed to make her laugh a few more times. Then she said the best thing I ever heard.

"I think you'll be a great addition to Somerset, Valentina. We could always use more smart, ambitious young women."

I bit my lip to stop me cheesing too hard. Over her head, I could see a mass of people leaving the courtyard. The unofficial mingling was over. It was time for College Day to start.

"Thank you. I've already started my application essay."

"I look forward to reading it." Andrea reached across and stuck her hand in one of the boxes. "Call me when you come to campus for a visit. We'll meet for coffee."

"I will." I didn't hold back my cheesing as I accepted the card. I stood and shook her hand just as Natalie Bard strode up to the booth. Flanking her was a heavily pierced man I had seen before and a woman that must have been her mother from the resemblance. Natalie didn't so much as glance at me as she planted herself in front of the booth.

"Hello. My name is Natalie Bard. Former chess grand master and fifth highest grade point average in the academy."

I slid away as Natalie launched into her resume. At least I was right about my classmates being on their best behavior while the reps were here.

I wandered around the lawn, eyes peeled for Mom and Adam. There was nothing for me to do now that I had impressed Andrea. What was interesting was seeing the parents of my classmates. They ranged from business people to celebrities to musicians to producers to models and everything in between. So many talented and famous people had given birth to these nightmares.

After a few laps around the event, I went back to the courtyard for some food. Our eyes met the moment I placed my foot on the stones.

Caroline patted Evergreen's arm. "I'll meet you in your office in half an hour. Thank you, Seamus."

Evergreen looked like he wanted to say something, but Caroline glided away before he had the chance. Her bodyguard fell in step behind her and blocked the headmaster from view.

"Good morning, Valentina." Caroline's smile was beautiful for how genuine it was. She was so kind and generous with me. I guess because we both knew what it was like to suffer under the hands of Benjamin Shea. "Will you walk with me?"

"Of course." I gestured toward the food table. "I was just going to get something to eat. Do you want anything?"

"I couldn't."

I accepted that without comment. I wasn't in her company often, but when I was, I noticed that she didn't eat much. Just like I notice her expensive clothes hung off her body and there was a gauntness to her otherwise lovely face. She looked like a strong breeze could snap her in two, but all the same, there was a strength to Caroline Shea. I saw it the morning after I killed her husband and found her at my dining table.

I quickly loaded a plate with food and then made my way back to her side. She held out a thin elbow for me to grasp. Jacob, her ever-present shadow, fell back a few feet without being asked. I glanced at him as we stepped out onto the lawn in the opposite direction of the crowd.

"Caroline, is it okay if I ask why you travel with a bodyguard?"

"My husband made enemies on his way to the top of the corporate ladder. Those that think his disappearance has left the Sheas vulnerable. There have been attempts made on my life."

"What?" Horrible thoughts flooded my mind. "Is Ryder safe?"

"He is when he's at home or here at Evergreen. Other times I employ a security team to trail him without his knowledge."

I gaped at her. That she trusted me was something I had known for years, but still, it was odd how easily she told me the truth.

"Jacob has been my close friend since I was a student here," Caroline continued. "There is no one I trust more."

I looked back at the stoic man and met with mirrored lenses. She said they were friends, but I had never once seen them have a full conversation.

"How is everything with you?"

I focused back on her. "I'm good. Looking forward to my last year at the academy. Speaking of, I know you and my mother talked."

"Forgive me for not telling you." She patted my hand. "We have our own relationship, but I did not feel right going against your mother's wishes."

"No, it's okay. Mom is right. It's time we stood on our own feet." I stopped and faced her. "I'm going to give back the money in my account and, if it's okay, I'd like to have a different relationship with you. I want us to talk and maybe I can come to visit when you feel up to it. I can sit with you and—" Doubt began to creep in. "But if you don't want that—"

"I'd like that very much." Her hand was still on mine, and my tension eased as she squeezed my fingers. "There will never be anyone who understands me as well as you do, Valentina. Do you know what I mean?"

"Yes," I said softly. "I know exactly what you mean."

There wasn't any more that needed to be said.

Caroline and I walked through the grounds until Jacob's pocket chimed. He placed the phone in her hand just as she lifted it.

"It's time for my meeting with the headmaster. If it goes well, you should have no trouble coming to visit me this year. Goodbye, Valentina."

I had a feeling it would go well. Caroline had secured me late entrance into school, a personal bodyguard, and who knew what else in the battles against the headmaster. I was reminded again that she wasn't as frail as she looked.

I ventured back to the front of the school after she left. Stepping onto the front lawn, I could see the event was starting to wrap up. The booths and tents were coming down. Students were walking the reps to their cars for one last attempt at making a good impression. College Day was over.

"Saw you at the Somerset booth, Moon."

Every muscle in my body went rigid.

"You don't actually think you have a chance of getting in, do you? They don't accept dark corner sluts."

"Then I guess you don't stand a chance either," I shot back. I didn't move or turn around to see, but I could sense they were all behind me. The new Knights.

"Clever. You always have a comeback. You never learned to keep that mouth shut."

I heard the sound of footfalls and then they were in front of me.

Natalie Bard. Airi Tanaka. Isabella Bruno. Darren Rosewood.

Proof that Ace hated my guts, the four people who despised me most in this school were put in charge of running it.

Isabella tossed her head. She had no hair to flip over her shoulder but she couldn't seem to help herself. "You should have some respect, Valentina. You won't last at this school for long, but during your short stay, you'll see we're making a lot of changes around here. If you keep it up, it'll only get worse for you."

I rolled my eyes. "You four are in my face every other second like deranged stalkers. It can't get much worse than that."

Darren's laugh made a shiver go up my spine. "Natalie's right about you and that mouth, but..."

He sidled up to me and draped his arm around my shoulder. Revulsion twisted my stomach. Darren had gotten more handsy with me since he became a Knight. The result of which landed him in the nurse's office with Ryder.

"If you take my offer and put that mouth to better use, I can make life a lot easier for you. Maybe even lift the mark again."

"You don't have the power to do that, Darren. Even if you did, you're fucking disgusting for dangling it over my head in exchange for sex." I roughly shook him off. "Besides, the last time you pulled that, it ended up on national news and Mommy tore you a new asshole. You really want to be trending again?"

His brows snapped together. "What? What are you— Are you fucking recording me again?!"

Darren dove for me. I let out a shout as he grabbed my chest, roughly groping my body.

"Get off me!"

"Adam!"

I reeled back to slap him when a tiny blur raced across my vision.

"Leave my mommy alone!"

I had enough time for my eyes to bulge before Adam raised his fist and hit the only thing he could reach.

"Argh!" Darren doubled over, clutching his crotch. "What the hell?! Where'd this kid come from?"

He lashed out and seized Adam's wrist.

"Don't touch him!" I surged forward. Darren released him just as I placed my hands on his side and shoved. He stumbled over his feet and went down hard.

I scooped up Adam and held him securely to my chest. My heart pounded against my rib cage as I lifted my eyes. The former Diamonds looked at me with twin looks of shock, and one look of glee.

Natalie's face twisted into a horrible expression as she feasted on Adam. "What did he just call you?"

I trembled. I wanted to come clean, but not to these people, and certainly not right now. I clutched Adam tighter. They could do what they wanted with me, but I wouldn't let them mess with my son. If they did, I would be responsible for three more deaths.

"You heard what he said," I rasped. "You have a problem with it?"

"Problem?" Her smirk grew wider. "Why would I have a problem?" I could see the pieces clicking in her mind. "You're that kid's mother which means you had him... in middle school? Am I right?"

Isabella and Airi just kept staring like they were doing the math themselves.

Natalie shook her head. "That's quite a secret you've been sitting on, but I can see why. Everyone was right about you. You're nothing but a sl—"

"Stop." Airi whipped out and caught Natalie in the stomach. Her expression was blank as she said, "Not in front of the kid."

Airi turned her back on me and walked off. Isabella was right behind her. Looking confused, Natalie was slower to follow her friends.

Mom ran up to me just as Darren scrambled off the grass and took off. "Sorry, Val. He got away from me. Is everything okay? I saw the little scrapper got in a shot."

"He did. Even though we do not hit, do we, Adam?" I smiled at him, taking the sting out of my scolding.

The toddler pouted. "He was mean."

"He was very mean."

Olivia looked after the new Knights. "Did Adam call you..."

"Yes, he did. It'll be all over the school in an hour."

"I'm sorry, Val."

"Don't be. I don't have anything to be ashamed of. If anything, I should be proud I have a son who has my back." I snuggled into Adam's cheek. "Don't you? Don't you have Mommy's back? Don't you, baby?"

Adam's giggling chased his pout away. Our little scrape would have no lasting effect on him which I cared about a lot more than the effect it would have on me.

"I think that's enough excitement for one day," Olivia said. "I should get him home."

"You're right."

Together we crossed the lawn for the parking lot. I could have imagined it, but I swore I felt the weight of a hundred pair of eyes.

Apparently, it takes less than an hour for news of a teenage mother to spread around the school.

I was glad Olivia was taking Adam away from all of this.

We went out to the car and I buckled Adam into his seat. I kissed him a dozen times, told him I loved him a dozen more times, then I hugged Mom goodbye. It was good that I had full faith in Caroline because I was going home to see them whether Evergreen liked it or not.

I waved them off until their car disappeared down the hill. There was no way I was going through the crowd that lingered on the lawn so I took the back path for my dorm. I sat down on the steps with a strange feeling hanging over me. It settled into my bones as I noticed someone had the same idea to get away.

"Hey."

"Hi, Ezra."

The dark-haired boy took a seat next to me on the stoop. We were quiet for a moment as we watch the last dredges of the seniors leave for their new dorm.

"They know about Adam."

I shifted my gaze to him.

"Natalie was down there shooting her mouth off," he continued. "I'm sorry. If you were keeping it a secret—"

"I'm not. Not anymore. I don't like that Natalie is the one sharing my business, but people were going to find out one way or another. I want things to be different from now on, Ezra. I want to tell the truth. It's the only way I can move forward with... the people I love."

"So what is the truth, Val?"

"I feel like you've guessed," I whispered. "That's why you're so upset."

Ezra's expression didn't twitch. "Do I look upset?"

I reached out and took the hand resting on his knee. "I know you, Ezra. I know when you're angry. Your mother did a great job teaching you to be the unbiased reporter, but you can't hide from me anymore."

He was quiet for so long I thought he wasn't going to reply. When he did speak, his voice shook. "It may be a good thing in this case that I'm holding back my feelings. What is the truth, Val? What couldn't you say in front of Adam?"

Tears collected in my eyes. They weren't for me. Somewhere along the way, I had begun to heal from the trauma of what was done to me. These tears were for Ezra. For how I knew this would hurt him. For all the healing he still needed to do after what Scarlett did.

"I was raped, Ezra."

A horrible keening noise ripped from his throat. It wrapped around my heart and squeezed as he sank his head into his hands.

"Please." The tears spilled from my eyes. "Please, Ezra. I'm okay. It's all o—"

"Who? Who did this?" His body shook violently. "I'll k-kill him."

I threw my arms around him. "Ezra, he's gone. He's dead."

He jerked his head up. The mannequin blankness was gone. Everything he felt was shining in his eyes for me to see. "Dead?"

I nodded. "The man who did it is dead. He can't hurt me or Adam or anyone else. Please, don't let him into your thoughts because I've made up my mind to do the same. I'm focusing on the good in my life. I have Mom, Sofia, Adam, Maverick, Jaxson, Ryder, and you. No matter how bad it gets, I'm okay as long as I have all of you."

"You're so strong, Valentina." Ezra brushed the tears from my cheeks as I pulled him closer. "I never understood how you could be so strong."

"I told you. It's because I have you."

Ezra slid an arm under my legs and put me in his lap. We sat there for a long time, holding each other in a perfect, quiet moment before the chaos could descend.

That strange feeling clung to me as we sat on that porch, but it told me I was doing the right thing. All of those people had given me a piece back when I was broken. They helped put me back together.

I would destroy Ace and the Spades before they could hurt them.

Chapter Two

I stayed in my dorm for the rest of move-in weekend. I didn't want to hear what people had to say about me being a teenage mom. I'd get enough of it during the school year.

On our first day of classes, I was awake before the sun broke the horizon. My phone's buzzing woke me from a light sleep. I felt around in the dark until I found it.

The light blinded me at first so it took me a minute to register what I was seeing. When I did, the haze disappeared.

Ace: I warned you. You'd better not blame anyone but yourself for how things have turned out. It's because of you that I had to mark the Knights. It's because of you that they betrayed the Spades.

I shot up in bed, fingers flying across the keys in the dark.

Me: So you finally admit that you're a Spade.

Their reply came in seconds.

Ace: I am not a Spade. I am THE Spade. There is no point in hiding that fact. We both know who I am. My only regret is that I didn't mark you again at the start of junior year. I let the Knights get away with defying the Spades and they got bold. That won't happen again. Now all five of you are in your place and you'll stay there because I still have the video.

Me: What's in this for you, Ace? Do you have a clue why I was marked in the first place? Do you understand what was

happening in that video? Did you ever think that the Knights defied the Spades because THEY HAD NO CHOICE?

Their response did not come back right away. A minute passed. Then two. Then ten.

I leaned over to put my phone on the nightstand when it vibrated in my palm again.

Ace: What is that supposed to mean?

Me: You say you're THE Spade so either you knew what Scarlett was doing and why she wanted me out, or you had a traitor in your ranks and you had no clue. Either way, it's your fault how all of this turned out. Not mine.

With that, I powered off the phone and tossed it on the pillow next to me. I wasn't losing sleep because Ace either supported a predator, or they were clueless of one. Either way, the Spades were the enemies in my story.

Hours later, I was awake, dressed, and speaking to Kai from the landing.

"To think I didn't believe you when you said how insane this place is." Kai leaned against the banister, watching me from the open door. "You know Mom and Dad almost didn't let us come back."

"Really?" I quit throwing things into my backpack long enough to look at him. "What happened?"

"Zane was raging after what happened to Sofia. He let it slip to Dad and it all came out. The marks. The bullying. The Knights. The Spades. They had no idea about any of it. They wanted us to transfer, but Zane refused to leave Sofia alone, and I refused to leave all of you." He picked himself off the rail and came to stand in the doorway. "But they did call up the headmaster and threaten to sue him and the school down to the last eraser if anything happens to us. Maybe that will help."

"It's great to have anyone on our side," I replied as I hitched my bag on my shoulder. "But I don't know how much it will help. I've been thinking about it, and the genius of the mark is that the real people involved never get their hands dirty. You can sue the students who hurt you or the teachers who didn't get involved, but you never touch the Spades."

"That's why people are so scared." A small voice behind us made Kai turn. Paisley stepped to his side. "Not to mention the silent war they wage against your family, businesses, and you. You see what is happening to Honey Hair. There's a reason people obey the Spades rather than fight back."

"But *you* fought back," said Kai.

She cracked the tiniest smile. "That's another thing people don't know. How much you hate yourself for being a bullying coward. I did it once. I couldn't do it again. Not after Valentina forgave me when I didn't deserve it."

"I wouldn't call you a coward." Kai clasped her shoulder and her lips blossomed into a full smile.

I hid one of my own. "You guys are super cute right now, but I need to get out of my room."

They sprang apart like I caught them doing something naughty. Paisley mumbled under her breath and took off down the stairs.

"I've got to watch you, Moon. You're bad news."

I laughed. "You're just figuring that out?"

"Come on. Everyone is waiting for us downstairs so we can walk in together looking all tough and cool like one of those slow-motion movie scenes."

I gathered the rest of my things, smoothed down my black skirt, and trailed Kai out of the door. The good thing about my friends being kicked out of the dorm was that it was easy for us to sit down and plan how we would face this year. They didn't know all of my plans, but they were confident about theirs which was good. I didn't want to lose any of them to the mark and the bullying. They had to be strong enough to face what was surely coming our way.

Together, the nine of us crossed the grass for the courtyard. We weren't alone. Gus's staff swarmed the place installing cameras. I still felt like he could do more—much more—but at that moment, I was glad that he always did what he said he would do. Though Scarlett wasn't around, I would hate to think of someone else ambushing us in the courtyard like Darren had tried to do to me in the library.

The main building was awash with noise when we walked in. Freshmen scurried about the place looking like chickens with their heads cut off. We skirted the chaos and headed for the elevators. Paisley pulled out her badge and waved it in front of the scanner.

It flashed red.

"That's weird." Paisley tried again. "Mine isn't working. Kai, use yours."

Kai scanned his badge and got another red light. It quickly dawned on me what was going on.

"I have a feeling none of our badges will work," I said. "We'll have to take the stairs."

Ryder and Maverick tried anyway and got nothing. We'd be spending our senior year hoofing up and down four flights of stairs.

"This reeks of Isabella," I said when we hit the second landing. "This is how she operates. Get your passcode to destroy everything in your room. Steal your towel and make you walk around naked. Put up flyers saying you'll give out two-dollar blowjobs. She's all about the mental torture. Making you feel helpless. She's gotten you booted from the dorm and I have no doubt we'll find out she has used her power to take away more privileges."

"This is her dream come true," Sofia added. "She's been trying to elevate the status of the Diamonds and now she, Airi, and Natalie are as high as it gets."

I nodded. "She told me yesterday that there would be changes."

"And we won't like any of them."

We fell silent as we continued up the stairs and then paused in front of the double doors.

"There's no going back now," I said. I stepped forward and pulled them open. We weren't hit with a wall of noise this time around. After three years of finals, breakdowns, expulsions, and quitting, this was the smallest class in the school. A little more than three dozen people in the senior class, and except for those next to me, they were all coming for me.

"Where are your lockers?" I asked as we walked into the hall. The hostile eyes turned on us immediately.

"I'm 219."

"367."

"498."

"523."

"600."

"710."

"845."

"999."

"I'm 1027," I finished. I balled my fists when I realized what was happening. "None of us are close to each other. They are splitting us up."

"It's not going to work." Ryder stepped to my side. The back of his hand brushed against mine making goose bumps erupt on my skin. "We stick together like we planned."

In groups, we went off to our lockers agreeing to meet back in front of homeroom. Ryder had been assigned locker 999, so he came with me.

The walk to our lockers was loaded with filthy looks, but no taunts. Somehow, that was worse. I didn't like it when they were quiet. It made me feel something worse was around the corner.

We stopped at Ryder's locker first.

"Give me good news," I said as I rested my back on the cool metal. "Did your mom manage to persuade Evergreen?"

"I think she did. She didn't give me all the details, but she said she got him to bend."

I scoffed. "Evergreen is as bendy as a steel pipe, but if anyone can change his mind, it's her."

"Sheas have donated a lot of money to the school over the years. We are the largest financial backer."

I blinked at him. "You are?"

"Yes." Ryder spoke without looking away from what he was doing. "I told you I've been in meetings for the past few weeks. The partners have been filling me in on our holdings and asking which investments I'll continue to make. The donations we've made to the school are nothing to sneeze at. I'm pretty sure we're responsible for the building of the stadium and the sports complex."

"Wow. No wonder Evergreen refuses to upset her." A thought occurred to me. "You know, Kai said getting the parents involved might help us, but it seems Caroline is in the best position to do that. She could—"

"No."

There was a hard edge to his voice that pulled me up short. "No? Why?"

"My mom isn't going to fight our battles for us. She's not well. She needs to rest."

"She'd do anything to protect you, Ryder. She's well enough for that."

Slam!

I jumped as his slammed locker drew more eyes to us.

"I said no," he forced through gritted teeth. "And don't you dare go behind my back and talk to her."

My face twisted into a frown. "First: you don't tell me what to do. Second: I wasn't going to go behind your back. It was just an idea."

"Good."

"Fine!"

I spun around and gave him my back. My body was vibrating with anger. I heard him behind me cursing and roughly throwing things into his bag.

"Is it always going to be like this?" he burst out. "We'll never stop fighting and pissing each other off."

"No," I shot back, "because you're irritating as fuck."

I was shocked to hear him laugh. "Then why do you want to be with me, Moon?"

"Don't try to get me to say nice things about you right now. You're annoying. You've always been annoying. But you're stuck with me, and lucky you. You won't find anyone else like me willing to put up with your crap."

Suddenly, his body was pressed against my back. His heat seeped into me as his chuckles reverberated through me. "You're right." Ryder rested his chin on my head. "I won't find anyone else like you..."

A flush crept up my neck. I had been waiting a long time for Ryder to say things like this and touch me this way. He was all the things I said, but still, I wanted to get through those walls.

"...just as irritating as me."

Heating up, I elbowed the asshole and took off to the sound of him guffawing. Why I liked him was a good fucking question.

Ryder ran to catch up and strolled next to me looking pretty pleased with himself. I rolled my eyes every time I looked at him.

We got to my locker and I put away my things. Next stop was Professor Roundtree's homeroom class.

The rest of the group was waiting for us before the classroom. We shared a glance, bracing ourselves, and then Ryder opened the door and walked in.

A tall man in a pressed suit leaned against the desk. I stared at him longer than was socially appropriate as my brain made sense of him. He was our professor, he had to be, but he did not look a thing like the professors I had come to know.

His suit was perfect and obviously expensive, but everything else looked out of place from the tattoos peeking out from under his collar to the spiky hair, and the piercing in his ear. If this guy was older than twenty-seven, I would eat my textbooks.

"Ah, more young vessels waiting to be filled." He looked right at me and grinned. My cheeks heated up like a Florida sidewalk. This guy was also seriously attractive. "Don't get comfortable. I'm assigning seats."

"Professor Roundtree." Natalie half rose out of her chair. "None of us are going to sit next to them. *They* are the ones we were telling you about."

"Really? So you're the ones who were marked?"

My eyebrows shot up my head. He said that so easily. I had yet to hear a single professor acknowledge the mark except for Markham.

He frowned. "There are a lot of you. When I was a Knight, we never had anyone get marked, let alone nine."

"Five of them are marked," Natalie corrected. "The rest are just stupid."

Roundtree didn't reply or look at Natalie.

"You were a Knight?" The question was out of my mouth before I could stop it.

His grin widened. "That's right, Miss..."

"Moon. Valentina Moon."

"Miss Moon. Nice name. Also, yes. I was a Knight. I graduated from Evergreen a few years before you all stepped through the gates as cute little doe-eyed freshmen." He stood to his full height. "As a result, I know how this works. You nine will sit up front where I can keep an eye on you. Everyone else, up."

We did as ordered and filled up the first two rows while Roundtree shuffled everyone else around. When the class was seated, Roundtree launched into his introduction.

"Like I said, I'm a graduate of the academy. I went on to Ivy League schools and an undergrad and graduate degree like the old man expected. What he didn't expect was for me to take those degrees in economics and become a professor instead of the head of Roundtree Pharmaceuticals. What can I say? I couldn't resist letting Pops down one more time."

The class laughed—me included. There was an air about him that made you want to like him.

"I wanted to come back and give to the school that gave so much to me so I begged on hands and knees for Evergreen to hire me." He threw out his hands. "And here I am. You'll have me for homeroom and economics three times a week. Sound good?"

"That sounds really good," Paisley whispered from the desk behind me. "This guy is yum-my."

"Paisley," I hissed. "He might—"

Roundtree's eyes flew to us.

I sucked in a breath when he winked. He definitely heard.

He continued. "So, this is your senior year so things will be different. If you thought you'd be able to coast after getting into your college, then you don't know this place well. You'll now have one period of study hall where you'll be expected to work on applications, essays, speak to the college counselors, prep for interviews, whatever you need to do.

"Otherwise, you have all advanced classes and a minimum grade average that has gone up to three point six." I stifled my groan, but the rest of the class didn't. "I've been through it so I know how stressful this semester can be. If you need to talk, my door is open. Any questions?"

A murmur of noes went up.

"Great. Then talk among yourselves until they bring the television in for the announcements."

I turned on Paisley the second he took a seat behind his desk. She clapped her hand over her mouth to cover a laugh.

"Sorry. Didn't mean for him to hear me."

I shook my head. "I thought Kai was trouble."

"Hey," he said from my other side. "What did I do?"

A knock sounded on the door while we were laughing at him. The AV club members wheeled in the television and turned it on. I tensed when I saw who was on the screen.

How did I not notice he wasn't here?

Darren Rosewood sat in the seat that used to be Ezra's. Next to him was his co-host, Juliet Cochran. I didn't wonder about how he got the job. He must have given it to himself.

"Good morning, Evergreen." His voice grated on my ears. All I could think about was him grabbing my wrist in a darkened corner of the library. His breath hot on my face as he said he'd make life easier for me if I went for round two and let him finger me against the stacks. "We have a lot of announcements this morning, but first, a message from our headmaster."

The screen went dark for a few seconds, and then Evergreen looked back at us. He was in his natural habitat, sitting behind his desk with his fingers laced in front of him. "Good morning, senior class, and welcome to another year. There has been a policy change and I want to make you aware of it. With regard to only being allowed three weekend passes a semester, this rule will be waived—"

Cheers and whoops filled the room, covering up part of his speech.

"—genuine need. What constitutes a genuine need?"

I strained to hear. I had a feeling he wasn't done.

"If you have a family emergency, a member of your family is ill, or you must attend to a child or children."

"Oh. That is for you, Moon," Natalie taunted. "Mommy has to get home to baby."

I balled my fists, but said nothing. I knew that was for me, but all that mattered was I got my weekend passes back.

Evergreen went on unaware of the heckling. "You may also request a pass for college campus tours and things of that nature. Anything outside of that, we will meet in my office to discuss it. If I determine not to grant the pass, that is it. My decision will be final and I won't be swayed."

That also felt like it was for me, and possibly Ryder.

Translation: Don't sic your mothers on me or it won't end well.

"An updated version of the handbook will be given out by your homeroom teacher. Sign it to show you acknowledge the new rules. Thank you. Goodbye."

Evergreen winked out and Darren's shit-eating grin returned. "Thank you, Headmaster. Those aren't the only changes so let's get into them now. Unlike the old Knights, we care about this school and the students."

I could sense the boys stiffening.

"Our reputation took a hit when *someone* leaked the Evergreen Gone Wild videos to the press. We became jokes in the media, but now it's time to go back to what makes this school great. From now on, the Knights and the Diamonds will be in charge of all events and club activities.

"We will decide the themes, the destination for the class trips, all of that. As for clubs, those that don't add value to the school are over. There will be no anime club, foreign film club, creative writing club, book club, adventure club, art review club, cooking club, or dance club."

I wasn't surprised to hear him say the last one. This is exactly what Isabella wanted.

"The decision is final so don't come to the Knights whining about it. The clubs that are left, besides the academic clubs, are chess club, classical dance club, art club, key club, sports club, and drama club. The previous presidents of those clubs have been replaced by the Knights and the Diamonds. If you want into the club, they have to approve you first.

"We are getting back to our values and rewarding those who uphold them. Evergreen Academy is still the best school in the country. We will make sure the rest of the world knows and stop anyone who tries to bring us down. That is all."

The broadcast cut off seconds after he finished even though his co-host never got to speak a word. In more ways than one, replacing Ezra with that guy had been a terrible idea. At least Ezra had charm.

I looked at my friends as Roundtree passed out the new handbooks. There was nothing charming about the look on Ezra's face now.

"Why would anyone choose them to be Knights?" Paisley asked, not letting her voice carry past my ear. "They can't believe this is better for the school."

It's not about the school anymore. It's about me.

My attention shifted to the phone box. I had never turned it back on after shutting down the conversation with Ace. That was against the "rules" but I didn't care. I was done playing Ace's game.

"What's your schedule, guys?" Kai asked when we left the classroom.

I read out the small slip of paper. "I have Advanced Literature II, study period, Economics, and Calculus on Monday, Wednesday, and Friday. On the other days, I have Advanced Environmental Science, Advanced Psychology, P.E., and Individuals and Societies."

Everyone went around and shared their schedules. No one would be alone—not even Sofia who found she was in the same higher math classes with Ryder. The only problem was me.

"What is Individuals and Societies?" Zane asked. "I don't remember seeing that when we signed up?"

"It's only available for students in Advanced Psychology," I said.

Paisley nodded. "I saw that, but I decided to do Advanced Government because I'm going to double major in Poli-Sci. Val, why didn't you tell me? I would have signed up with you."

I shook my head. "No way. You just said that's going to be your major. I would have felt awful if you changed because of me."

"But you can't be alone, Val." Sofia pushed through the boys to stand in front of me. "Especially not you."

"I didn't have a choice. This is for my major too." I held up my hands when I saw the protests coming. "There is nothing we can do about it, guys. The good news is none of the new Knights are interested in psychology so I doubt they're in the class."

"It's not just them you have to worry about."

Jaxson was right, but I put aside what he said. I wasn't changing my schedule. These were the classes I needed for Somerset and no one was driving me out.

"Let's go. We have to get to lit."

We stepped inside to a new professor and a chill room. Except for Natalie announcing that no one could sit by us and the professor sending us to the back, no one did anything or looked our way.

I couldn't help but feel uneasy. Natalie had the biggest mouth, but it was Isabella who was in charge. She would play this game like she did all the others. She'd play to win.

The group picked up on my mood as we left class. "What's wrong, Val?" Maverick asked.

"It's too quiet. I don't like it."

"She's right," Ezra echoed. "A few disbanded clubs and a room change are nothing. They'll be planning something bigger to get to us."

"And we'll be ready for whatever it is," Kai cut in. He took my hand. "Come on. We have study hall."

The two of us turned to leave. We made it three steps before Kai's hand was taken out of mine. "You trying to lose that, South Africa? Hands to yourself."

Jaxson slid in between us and laced our fingers together. I gave him a look to let him know what I thought of his jealousy, but otherwise, did not stop him.

Study hall was being held in the library. We crossed through the oak doors and stepped into the quiet, softly lit space. A few students were already there and had claimed tables for them and their friends.

"Let's sit at the big one in the back." I pointed over the book carts. "There are enough seats."

We tossed our bags at the feet of the chairs and got comfortable.

"What are your choices?" Sofia asked. "I thought I knew but talking to the reps changed my mind."

"I'd like to go back home," Zane admitted, "but it wouldn't be the same without Sofia and Kai."

"Aww." Kai made big eyes at Zane. "My twin brother loves me."

Zane almost shoved him out of the chair. "Shut up."

I sighed. "I'm only applying to one college. If I don't get in, I'll go to community college and then apply again to Somerset."

"Why would you do that?" Paisley asked. "You could get into so many great schools. Besides, don't you want to get away from home?"

"No, the opposite. I want to be close to Adam."

The atmosphere around the table shifted.

"I'm sorry. That was stupid."

"It's okay, Paisley. I know you guys are still getting used to the idea of me being a mom."

Getting used to it was right. Most of the table got all shifty-eyed like they didn't know where to look.

Sofia came to the rescue. "What about you guys?" She looked between Jaxson, Maverick, Ezra, and Ryder. "Where are you applying?"

"I'll be working for Dad," Jaxson replied.

Maverick shrugged. "Somerset has a great computer engineering program."

"Somerset journalism majors do a semester abroad with actual news crews," said Ezra. "I'd like to do that."

"I'll be doing business at Somerset. Stay close to Mom and Shea Industries."

I opened my mouth, but nothing came out. *They're all staying? My boys are trying to get into Somerset.*

My heart was fluttering wildly in my chest and I pressed my hand over it. The five of us being together was more than I could have hoped for. I hadn't been able to think about losing any one of them.

A laugh broke through my good mood. "You don't fool us." Kai's grin was wicked. "We all know why you're going to Somerset and a top-notch education isn't it. I gotta get me a harem too."

Whack!

"Ouch!" Kai made a face at me as he bent to rub his sore leg. "What was that for?"

"No one would be in your harem, dummy." It dawned on me what I was saying. "And it's not a harem!"

"It's a nonstop booty machine is what it is."

My cheeks were flaming. Beside me, Ezra laughed out loud.

"I like this guy. Why haven't we hung out before?"

I swatted Ezra's arm. "Don't you start."

"I could have a harem," Kai went on. "I'm smart, witty, and devastatingly handsome. I should start taking applications."

Everyone was laughing now. "I thought this wasn't your thing?" I reminded him.

"I've evolved, Val. If half a dozen beautiful women want to love and pleasure me; that's a burden I'll have to bear."

I rolled my eyes so hard I almost hurt myself. The rest of the table was howling. I guess I should be thankful my friends were so cool with me and my four boyfriends. The rest of my classmates thought it confirmed what they had been saying about me since freshman year: I was a massive slut.

"Isn't this cozy."

The good humor dried up like a teardrop in the desert. Our smiles melted away as Isabella, Natalie, Airi, and Darren descended on our table.

"What do you want now, Isabella?" I forced out.

"You're looking at me like I'm not supposed to be here." She tossed the hair she didn't have. It was immensely frustrating that even with a bald head, Isabella was gorgeous. "It's you who is not supposed to be here. New orders from the Knights. The marked and all their little friends are banned from the library."

"What?" Zane lurched to his feet. "You can't do that."

"And yet," Natalie said, "we just did. Pack your shit and get out."

"How do you think you're going to make us leave?" Maverick was next to get up, straightening to his full six feet.

Natalie's smirk widened. "Fair point, quarterback, but you didn't consider this—" She snapped her fingers and the sound of almost thirty chairs being pushed back filled the room.

The rest of the class had filed in while we were joking around and they all stared at us now. A couple of them were just as big as Maverick.

"If you don't leave on your own," Natalie continued, "we'll drag you out. You might be more difficult, Beaumont, but just think about how scratched up your slut girlfriend will get in the struggle."

I bared my teeth. "That pretty face of yours will get scratched up if you put a finger on me, Bard."

My words were tough, but I was doing the math. Nine against thirty wouldn't work in our favor, and by the way the boys were bristling, it would start a fight and someone would get hurt.

"Aw. You think I'm pretty." Natalie gave me what could have passed for a pleasant smile. "That's sweet, but flattery won't get you anywhere. Leave. All of you. Now."

Darren stepped up to me when we didn't move. "You heard, Moon. You're not allowed in here." He put out his hand like he was going to grab my shoulder.

A low growl sounded behind me. "You want that jaw broken again, Rosewood? Don't fucking put your hands on her."

Darren's face twisted into a scowl, but he must have seen something in Ryder's expression because his hand returned to his side.

I bent and picked up my backpack. "Let's go, guys. We don't have time for this."

Silently, we gathered our things and walked out. A flicker of movement made me turn my head and I caught Eric's eyes as we made for the doors. He stood at a table alongside Claire and Ciara. The three of them dropped their gaze when they caught me looking. Shaking my head, I faced forward.

It begins.

"NOW WE KNOW WHAT THEIR game plan is," Zane said as he plopped down on the floor. I wasn't allowed in his room, but we could gather on the first floor and take up the front room. Classes were over and our homework was spread out on the floor now that the library was off-limits. "They are freezing us out."

"He's right," Paisley said. "I've been kicked out of key club. They wouldn't even open the door when I knocked."

"I'm off the football team."

I gaped at Maverick. "They can't do that."

"According to Coach, they can. The Knights told him they would keep the students out of the stands and order the team not to play if I step on the field. He decided it wasn't worth the trouble."

"So their plan to drive us out is—"

"—to take away our reasons to stay," Ryder finished. "I bet it's not going to stop here. Rosewood says they're in charge of events too. Want to bet we won't be allowed at the dances or on the senior trip too?"

"Then all we'll be able to do is go from class to our dorm and back again?" Zane asked in disbelief.

Kai bobbed his head. "They are making this place even more unbearable than it already is."

"What if they ban us from class too?" Paisley's pencil shook in her hand. "That can't happen. I'm trying to get into the Sorbonne."

"They can't do that," I said firmly. "Our parents wouldn't stand for that. I don't think Evergreen would allow it either."

"Does anyone still think... that this is only the beginning?"

Sofia's voice was soft, but it seemed to pierce through us. I clenched my fists at seeing the looks on the faces around me.

This is not the beginning, I thought. *I'm going to end it now.*

It took us a while but, eventually, we got back to our homework. There wasn't a lot of talking except for the occasional question to ask for help. Ryder was the first to finish. He wandered upstairs looking deep in thought.

Twenty minutes later, we were all done. I got to my feet at the same time as Ezra.

"Hey." He slipped his hand into mine. "Do you want to sit on the porch with me again?"

"I'd love that."

We said goodbye to the others and stepped out into the September evening. The sky was awash with blues, oranges, and purples and it brought a smile to my face.

"It's so beautiful here," I said as I sat down. Ezra pulled me into his arms and I rested my head on his chest. "It's sad how ugly the academy is underneath."

"This place can't be all bad. I found you."

"That's true." I tilted my head back and kissed his jaw. "Let's talk about something else. Are you really going to apply to Somerset?"

I felt his nod. "I'm getting in too. Mom is a famous alumnus. There's no way they don't accept me."

"I'd say something about special treatment, but I'm too happy. I'm glad you're not going away."

"I couldn't leave you." Ezra stroked my back in small soothing circles. "I love you."

I froze. *What did he just say?*

"I love you, Valentina," he repeated as though he heard my thought. "All I want is to be with you."

I bit my lip hard. I was brimming with so much happiness, I thought something stupid might come out while my mind was doing flips. When I trusted myself to speak, the words tumbled out, "I love you too, Ezra."

He put his finger under my chin and captured my lips. He kissed me slow and sweet—so unlike the feverish, lip-clashing kisses we usually shared, but I felt his feelings flood through me.

We were panting when we broke apart. It was a while before we caught our breaths, but the whole time, we were grinning at each other like fools. That was until his smile fell away.

"Ezra? What's wrong?"

"Val, there's something that I— There's something that I need to do."

"What is it?" A thread of worry crept up my spine. Ezra's self-assured air had disappeared. "Are you okay?"

"No— I mean, yes. I—" He stopped and took a breath. "We have three weekend passes before we need special permission for more."

I blinked at this topic. "Yes, I know."

"I'm going to use one this weekend to see Mom. After talking to you the other day... I realized that I need to tell her the truth."

My hands moved up to his cheeks. They were cold from the chilly air. "Do you mean you're going to tell her about Scarlett?"

"Yes." His dark eyes were fathomless pools, but I had seen into the abyss and knew the pain and anger that he held there. "You're so strong, Val. It's time I was too."

"Is there anything I can do? Tell me, please. I'll be there for you however you need me."

"You're doing exactly what I need right now. I know it's going to be hard, but it's time."

Smiling, I stroked his cheeks. "You are strong, Ezra. You always were."

He leaned in until our foreheads touched. "I love you."

"And I love it when you say that."

He kissed me again.

"On an unrelated note," Ezra said when we broke apart. "I can't this weekend, but I was hoping next weekend you would use your first pass on me. We have been waiting too long to make love, Val. It's past time we were together."

My heart pounded at the thought. He was right. With everything that had gone on last semester and me having to save my three passes for Adam, we never got to take our relationship to the next level. It was time we did something about that.

"It will be my second pass," I said. "There is somewhere I need to be this weekend too, but next weekend, I'll be with you."

Ezra held me close as the wind whipped and tugged at us, but neither of us thought to go inside. We stayed out on that porch as the sun made its final descent, then we enjoyed the beauty of the stars, like we used to do on the roof where we talked, kissed, and fell in love.

I PRACTICALLY FLOATED up to my room after Ezra and I said good night in front of his door. Stealing pockets of time with the boys was what would get me through this. I held on to that thought as I took my phone out of my bag and turned it on. It vibrated with a message soon after the welcome screen winked on. Then it buzzed again. Then again. Then again.

Ace: Knew what Scarlett was doing? Explain that. What was she doing? How did she betray the Spades?

Ace: Did it have to do with the phone? Was there something on it? Is that why she screamed for you to give it back?

Ace: You don't get to say shit like that and then refuse to explain. You think you've been unfairly targeted, then tell me why.

Ace: I told you about ignoring me. Tell me what Scarlett did.

Ace: Whatever my new Knights have planned will be nothing compared to the fallout from releasing this video. Maybe you will explain yourself to the cops.

I calmly set my phone down on the nightstand and padded to the bathroom. I took a hot, lazy shower, and then stepped out and went through my nighttime routine. It was only when I was comfortable in bed that I picked my phone up again.

Me: Stop banging that drum. If you wanted to release that video, you would have done it a long time ago. I don't want to, but if it came to it, I could explain to the cops why Scarlett died and why we didn't come forward. No jury would convict.

She did things that would make any decent person vomit. You're not a decent person, but I don't think even you would be okay with it. You chose the wrong side, Ace. You have proven that the Spades are nothing more than what everyone has feared. You're a bunch of mindless, bullying thugs taking advantage of people who can't fight back.

I tapped the last period and then shut off my phone once more. It felt insanely good telling Ace off. I was not scared of them and it was time they knew.

I burrowed into the sheets and let my eyes fall shut. I knew as I drifted off to sleep that I would have no nightmares that night.

Chapter Three

"You've got a funny look on your face."

I glanced up from packing my bag and met Sofia's narrowed eyes. She was reclining against my bed like we didn't have to be in class in ten minutes.

"I don't have a funny look. This is just my face."

"I've known that face for four years. That is your I'm-planning-something face."

"You're mixing it up with my we're-going-to-be-late-for-class face. Which we will if we don't leave now."

"Spill it, Valentina Blythe Moon."

"Hey," I hissed. "Don't go tossing my full name around. Anyone could hear."

"I want to know what you're planning. We're a team, remember. Tell me so I can back you up."

Sighing, I dropped my head. "You can't back me up this time. This I have to do myself."

"But—"

"What I really need my best friend to do... is trust me."

Sofia studied me for a long time—long enough that we missed our chance to be on time for class. Finally, she said, "Okay. I trust you."

"Thank you."

She picked herself up off the bed and got her things. Together we booked it to the fourth floor and burst in to Roundtree's tsk.

"Ladies," he began as he rose from his seat. "Late on the second day. I'm afraid that means you'll spend the afternoon in class with me—helping me organize the back room."

"I'll take that punishment," Paisley whispered when I sat down. "I'll take *all* his punishments."

Sometimes I forgot how X-rated Paisley could be, but she was always quick to remind me.

We got through class with no more punishments being handed out. The nine of us broke apart outside the door and headed for our lockers. Ryder fell in step beside me. I waited until we stopped in front of 999 to speak.

"Ryder, I wanted to let you know I'm going off campus this weekend."

"Okay. Why?"

"I'm going to see Caroline."

Ryder went rigid. He froze with his hand half out of his locker. "Excuse me?"

"I'm going to see your mother."

"Why are you doing that?" His voice was tightly controlled. "You're not going to ask her to step in even though—"

"No." I put my hand on his arm and made him face me. "I'm giving the money back."

His anger was chased away by confusion. "The money?"

"All the money she gave me after I found out about Adam. I appreciate what she's done for me. I wouldn't be where I am now without her, but I think if we're going to have a future, I need to have a normal relationship with your mother."

Ryder's eyes traced my face, looking for what I did not know. "So... you're doing this for us?"

Heat rushed my cheeks, but I pushed through. "Yes, I am. I don't know what's involved. It's a large sum of money so I want to meet with her and handle the details. It would also be nice to sit and talk with her for a bit. I think she would like that too."

"She would. Mom genuinely likes you. She asks me all the time how you are. I tell her you're still the same pain in the ass."

I folded my arms. "You're going the right way for a kick up the backside. How's that for pain in your ass?"

Laughing, Ryder gently flicked my nose. "Just kidding, Moon. I only have good things to say about you. You're amazing."

I didn't have time to reply before he grabbed my folded arms and tugged. I flew into his chest and he wrapped his arms around me, holding me close. "Thank you," he whispered into my hair. "I want you and Mom to have a real relationship too." He kissed my head as I drowned in his spicy scent. "I'll get a pass for this weekend as well."

That dragged me out of my fog. "Why? To spend time with me or to make sure your mom doesn't bust out the baby pictures?"

"Both. Definitely both."

I giggled. Ryder could make moody people seem like a bundle of laughs, but I couldn't deny that I felt comfortable with him. We had fun together when his guard was down and he was free to be himself. Plus, he was amazing with Adam. Spending a weekend away with him was something I'd wanted for a long time.

Clearing my throat, I stepped out of his embrace. "We should go. I don't want to be late for another class."

Ryder bumped into me as he walked me to environmental science. The back of our hands brushed in a spark of electricity. The next time he bumped me, he hooked his pinky through mine. I turned my palm out and threaded our fingers together. Nothing felt more right at that moment.

"YOU ARE SENIORS AND this is an advanced class. I expect nothing but hard work and no excuses," said Professor Patchett. She was a short, fussy woman with hair the same length as mine. "This year, we'll be studying geosciences, atmospheric sciences, ecology, and environmental chemistry. Our work will even take us outside and on an end-of-semester field trip.

"Today, I'll give you an overview of the class and where this field will take you for those that plan to further their studies in higher education. Now, take out your textbooks and turn to chapter one."

"Are you planning to take your studies to higher education?" Darren's voice slithered into my ear. My stomach writhed with disgust. I knew when he sat down behind me that he wouldn't resist running his mouth. "Don't you have a violent little kid to think about?"

"My son isn't violent. He just doesn't like assholes any more than I do."

"He gets that from you, does he? What does he get from his dad?"

I tensed. "We're not chatting, Darren. Leave me alone."

Darren went on like I hadn't spoken. "Who is his dad? We know you had him in middle school. Isabella cornered Claire and got out of her that you disappeared from school because of a bad case of mono, but she couldn't think of anyone you had been with at the time."

My nails dug half-moons into my palm. "Did you hear what I said? Leave me alone."

"I only want to know who his dad is. Or... do you not know?" He clicked his tongue. "Like mother, like daughter. Your mom doesn't know who your dad is either, isn't that right? Got knocked up on some spring break cock cruise? No, wait— Ryder found the guy in freshman year. How did the reunion go?"

"You think because Ryder is sitting across the room that you won't get your face bashed in? You're going to find out how wrong you are if you keep talking about my family."

"I—"

"You two," Patchett bellowed. "Quiet and open your textbooks."

Darren thankfully closed his mouth and did as she said.

I got through my morning classes and left psychology with Paisley. We met up with Sofia outside of her math class.

"I'm actually looking forward to lunch," she said. "I missed breakfast and my stomach is eating itself right now."

"I missed it too," I said. "I know the chef never does the same dish twice, but I'm hoping he pulls something out with salmon. He does magic with that fish."

"You have to stop blatantly loving the food here, Val, or Evergreen will never ease up on the diet."

Paisley laughed. "If anything, us loving it might get him to change. He loves taking away things we enjoy."

I joined in on the laughter to cover my swirling emotions. *It's time. It's almost time.*

"I think the new Knights get the credit for taking away what we love," Sofia replied. "Science club hasn't started, but I have a feeling Cade would close the door in my face."

"Maybe not," Paisley said. "The academic clubs are run by the professors. They can't have turned something like that over to a student."

"This entire school is run by students."

Paisley couldn't argue with that. The conversation came to a halt as we approached Sofia's locker. She grabbed the lock, but then hesitated like she didn't know the combination, but of course she did.

Seeing her standing there pulled the memory out of my mind.

"Darren got off easy." Sofia walked next to me, radiating anger. "Ryder should have broken more than his jaw."

I faced ahead and ignored the looks being thrown our way. "He said he'd get the mark lifted if I gave him what he wanted. He was always disgusting, but he's gotten even worse since Ace made him a Knight."

"A real Knight taught him a lesson he won't forget for the next six weeks." Sofia paused in front of her locker and spun the combination. "He'll spend his summer vacation with his filthy mouth wired shut."

"I can't wait until the nurse explains it to his par—"

Sofia threw open her locker. Everything happened faster than I could see. One second we were talking and then the next second Sofia's scream ripped through the hall.

She turned to me, eyes huge, as blue dye dripped down her face. Laughter rang through the hall, loud enough to cover her when she started screaming.

I shook away the sight. We knew that the Spades could get in and out of our lockers as they wished, but that was the first time we had opened one to find more than a joker card. The dye got in and stung her eyes. I rushed her to the nurse amid their laughter, but her eyes were red for days—almost as long as it took the dye to fade.

She stepped off to the side and opened the locker. Nothing happened. She relaxed as she put away her books. "I can't wait until we graduate," she mumbled. "I'm sick of this place."

We continued to the lunchroom when she was done. Along the way, we picked up more of the group. Zane put his arm around Sofia and whispered something in her ear that replaced her frown with a smile.

I'm glad Zane is staying after we graduate, I thought as they kissed. *I want my best friend to be happy even if we're far apart.*

A tinge of sadness laced the thought. We might not be in the same place next year. It was hard to think about that after all that we had gone through. A year was still a long way off, though. I still needed to get through senior year. I needed to get through today.

Paisley, Zane, Sofia, Kai, and I pushed through into the cafeteria. The four seated on the dais took note of us when we stepped inside. They stood.

"Shit," Kai said under his breath. "I bet they're about to start something. Can't we just eat in peace?"

"Hey, you!" Natalie leveled a finger at us. "Out."

Kai raised his voice. "Relax. We're just getting our lunch."

"Not in here, you're not," Airi cut in. "You're banned from the lunchroom too."

The four of them climbed off and planted themselves in front of us.

"What the hell are you talking about?" asked Paisley.

"You're not allowed in here," Isabella confirmed. "You eat in Roundtree's class now. The staff has been told to bring your meals there."

"So we'd better not see you in here again," Darren finished. "Get out."

The Knights stepped forward as rage blotted my vision. *That is enough of this. I'm doing it now.*

Natalie put out her hands like she was getting ready to shove me. I darted around her.

"Hey!"

I ignored her as I stormed up the dais. "We're doing this again," I cried into the room. "More bullying, more insults, more freezing me out. Another stupid card shows up in my locker and you turn on me—"

"Valentina!" Airi shouted.

"—but have any of you asked why?" I climbed on the dais and kept climbing until I was on top of the table. The new Knights rushed me and I was reminded of the last time I stood up here. "Do you know why I was marked? Do you know why you've been torturing me and the people who have tried to help me?"

"Get *down*!" Natalie seized my leg. Her nails dug into my skin hard enough to make me cry out. Without thinking, I doubled over and brought my hand up.

Smack!

Natalie let out a scream as her head snapped to the side. Her friends grabbed her as she stumbled back from the force of my slap and I took my chance.

"I know exactly who marked me in freshman year—"

"Valentina!" This shout drew my attention. Maverick, Ryder, Ezra, and Jaxson had entered the lunchroom. Ryder was the first one to run at me.

No, I have to do this.

Every eye was on me as the secret I had been keeping for years fell from my lips. "It was Scarlett LeBlanc. She was an art professor, a Spade, and... a pedophile. She marked me when I found out the truth."

The final word was barely out of my mouth before Ryder took hold of me. The room blurred as I flew off the table and into his arms. Ryder spun and raced toward the door, trying to get me out as quickly as he could, but there was one more thing I needed to say.

"You've been attacking me on the orders of a child-molesting predator!" I shrieked. "So what are you going to do now?!"

Mayhem descended the moment the doors swung shut. The shouting and screaming echoed through the halls and was only ended by the stairwell door. There was no Knight room to take me to so Ryder burst onto the main floor. I yelled at him to put me down the whole way to our dorm, but he didn't listen.

It was only when the door was locked and bolted behind us that he let me scramble out of his arms.

Our chests heaved as we gazed at each other across the front room.

"Valentina." Ryder's eyes were glittering silver pools. "What did you do?"

"I did what I said I would do last year. If I had, none of this would have happened. Ace wouldn't have come for me. The class wouldn't have followed the mark."

"People are going to investigate her now—her disappearance. They'll interrogate you!"

I tossed my head. "You don't have to be worried. I won't tell anyone what Scarlett did to you or—"

"You think I'm worried about me?!" The bellow blew me back. "We don't know what Ace is going to do now! You've outed one of them as a pedophile. If there is an investigation and you start tossing the word Spades around to the police; they'll have to dig deeper. They have hidden themselves for decades. They won't be brought out of hiding now. What if they decide to shut you up permanently?"

Everything Ryder said I had considered a hundred times. I knew what I could be setting off, but I also knew a war with the Spades was inevitable. It was either going to be me who started it or Ace, because a thousand marks wouldn't get me out of this school.

I held his gaze without wavering. "I had to take that risk. I'll do what it takes to protect all of you."

Ryder opened his mouth to say what I would never know, because, at that second, the door flew open and the others ran in. Seven voices pelted me at once and Ryder was pushed to the side as Sofia grabbed me in a tearful hug.

We ended up missing our classes. I only managed to get out when the final bell rang because I reminded them my phone was still in the box. I said I would go alone, but got a resounding no from the entire room.

I could feel Ryder's eyes on me as we crossed the courtyard. His gaze was as penetrating as Jaxson's, Maverick's, and Ezra's. We desperately needed to talk alone.

Roundtree looked up when we entered the classroom. "I thought you forgot."

"Forgot what?" Sofia asked.

"You're spending the afternoon with me."

I had forgotten. Ryder looked for a moment like he was going to argue, but I placed a hand on his arm.

"What do you need us to do, Professor Roundtree?"

He shook his head. "Not you, Miss Moon. The headmaster wants to see you in his office an hour ago. You should go now."

"Okay." I turned to leave, but it was Maverick's turn to take my arm.

"Val, wait. We have to talk first. What are you going to tell him?"

"I'll tell him what I can," I said softly.

Ezra stepped to my side. "I'll go with you." There was a determined set to his jaw. "I'll—"

I smiled to let him know what that meant to me. "Not this time. I don't know what I'm walking into. Let me speak to him first."

"Miss Moon," Roundtree interrupted. "Get going."

I slipped out of Maverick's hold and made for the door. Jaxson stepped into my path as I reached for the knob. He didn't speak. Instead, he cupped my cheek and kissed me, banishing any doubt that I was doing the right thing. They had protected me. Now I had to protect them.

Jaxson stepped to the side and let me go. The halls were quiet as I walked to the headmaster's office but my mind was anything but. Mrs. Khan looked up when I entered. There was no smile on her face.

"You can go in, Valentina. They are waiting for you."

They?

I went inside and found out exactly who they were. Headmaster Evergreen sat at his desk. Behind him stood Gus and Mrs. Stanton, the school nurse.

Mrs. Stanton came around the desk as soon as I lowered myself into a seat. She sat down in the one next to me and put a hand on my shoulder.

"Miss Moon. Do you know why you're here?"

I studied Evergreen. His emotions were usually written across his face. I could tell when he was angry, fed up, or disappointed. This time, I could see nothing.

"Yes, I do, Headmaster."

"You made an allegation against a former professor," he continued. "I have gotten many reports, but I would like to hear this from you. What happened between you and Mrs. LeBlanc?"

I did not speak right away. The head of security was here, and it seemed like Mrs. Stanton had been asked to come and support me. Maybe a part of me had feared Evergreen wouldn't believe me—sweep it under the rug for the precious reputation of the school.

This is really happening. It's time for it all to come out.

I took a steadying breath and let it out slowly. "It all started in freshman year on the night of the masquerade ball. I heard shouting in the woods and ran to help. I discovered a student arguing with someone who later turned out to be LeBlanc."

Gus broke in. "Later turned out to be? You did not know it was her?"

"No. It was pitch black and they were wearing masks. All I could make out were raised voices. They were shouting about an awful thing LeBlanc had done and the student threatened to tell the truth."

"The student?" It was Evergreen who interrupted this time. "Who is this student?"

I lifted my chin. "I can't say. They aren't ready to come forward."

"Miss Moon, you understand that we cannot act on hearsay. If this student is the victim; they must report it themselves."

"This is not about what happened to them; it's about what happened to me."

I expected more argument, but to my surprise, Evergreen inclined his head. "I understand. Please continue."

"Thank you. Like I said, they were fighting and LeBlanc threatened them and said they would regret it if they told anyone. I got worried that it would escalate so I called out. That's how she found out I was there.

"They both ran before I could see who the student was fighting with. When I opened my locker the Monday after, I discovered I was marked."

Gus reached into his pants pocket and pulled out a notepad. "So you naturally assumed that these events were linked," he stated as he scribbled on the pad.

"It was the only explanation. I didn't understand it at the time, but I had witnessed something horrible enough that some— that a Spade wanted me out. I was sure of it as things got worse and there were multiple attempts on my life. It was a secret worth killing an innocent person for so I tried to put it together. I had to find out what truly happened that night."

Mrs. Stanton reached for a box of tissues. I was hardly on the edge of tears but I appreciated that she took her job of comforting me seriously.

"In the end, I found the student Scarlett threatened in the woods. They told me everything. LeBlanc had molested them when they were younger and they had never been able to come forward, but when they heard she would be working with children again they had to do something. After that, I confronted Scarlett."

Evergreen's stoic mask cracked as a flicker of surprise crossed his features. "Confronted her?"

"Yes. I knew it was her. It was her who hurt the student and her who tried to kill me to keep me quiet. The problem was I didn't have proof. The only way to end it was to get LeBlanc to confess."

"You could have come to me," Gus said. "That would have been safer than confronting a person you suspected of trying to kill you."

I looked him directly in the eyes. "After everything I've gone through, I had no reason to think anyone would step in to help me. I had to do it myself."

Gus pressed his lips together in a thin line. I knew he didn't like my reply, but he couldn't deny it.

"What happened when you spoke to Mrs. LeBlanc?" Evergreen asked when the silence stretched longer than was comfortable.

"She denied it at first. She played the sweet and innocent act until I hit her with everything I knew. Every detail the student had given me. Then she changed her tune."

"Did she admit what she had done?" asked Gus.

"She admitted to trying to drop a planter on my head. LeBlanc even said she should have tried again and 'made damn sure.'"

Gus and Evergreen shared a look I couldn't read.

"What about her actions against the student?" Gus went on after a beat. His eyes flicked from me to the notepad as he wrote. "Did she confess to that as well?"

"She was deluded. LeBlanc refused to call it what it was—molestation. But she did say that she *loved* them and was there for them when no one else was. She said they *needed* her." My stomach writhed thinking of that twisted snarl and the even more twisted mind behind it. "Anyway, I left after I got the truth out of her."

"She just let you go?" Gus questioned.

"I had my bodyguard waiting outside packing a gun. She didn't have a choice." His response was to nod and write some more. "I got out of there but I wasn't sure what to do next. I finally knew the truth, but I couldn't force the student to come forward and I didn't think LeBlanc would skip down to the police station with me and confess... and I was right. The next day, there was a resignation letter on her desk and she was gone."

As I uttered the final word, I slumped back in my seat. I had fudged the truth toward the end, but they knew everything they needed to know.

"What happens now?"

Evergreen jerked at my question as though he had been lost in thought. "Now, I ask you if there is anything else you need to tell us. Anything you're holding back."

My brows snapped together. *What was he trying to say? Does he know something?*

RUBY VINCENT

The headmaster rose from his seat. "You might feel more comfortable speaking to Mrs. Stanton alone."

Just like that, it hit me what he was trying to say. "No," I said quickly. "Scarlett did not touch me in that way." He slowly lowered himself down. "But if you want my advice, you should speak to the students. You should also contact any school she has worked at. Make it clear that the truth is out and you'll provide a safe space for anyone who wants to come forward." My hand curled into a fist beneath Stanton's. "There's a chance the student wasn't the only one she molested."

"That is a good suggestion, Miss Moon. Thank you." Evergreen looked at Gus once more. "First, we'll contact the police and see how they want us to proceed."

"The police?" I couldn't help the surprise that laced my voice. "But you've never gotten the police involved before."

"This is not a situation that we are equipped to handle on our own, or one that we should. The police need to lead the investigation... and I need to apologize to you."

"To me?" I repeated, not quite registering what I heard. I had seen a lot of emotions on Evergreen's face, but this one was new. It looked like... remorse.

"I have failed you, Miss Moon, and this student who for years has suffered in silence rather than come to me and report what was done to them. I will never forgive myself if you are right and... there are more."

I tried to fight it, but a niggle of pity wormed its way in. "You can't blame yourself for Scarlett or what she did, but... you can blame yourself for allowing the Spades to create such a culture of fear and intimidation." The words were out of my mouth and falling too fast for me to stop. "The Knights don't run this school. The Spades don't run this school. *You* do. You're our headmaster, and even though you didn't admit it then and you still haven't to this day, you knew I was marked and you did nothing to stop it. If you want to apologize, apologize for that."

A deep silence followed my speech. Neither Stanton nor Gus said anything. I'm not sure they were breathing. They didn't move as Evergreen and I locked eyes.

The wall clock ticked as he gazed at me. It counted out sixty seconds before he finally got to his feet. "You are correct, Miss Moon."

I held still, waiting for more.

"You may leave. We need to contact the police." Evergreen held out his hand toward the door.

Without argument, I stood and walked out. I threw open the door to the main hall...

...and slammed right into a warm body.

"Val." I jerked my head up and looked into Ryder's face. "We have to talk."

He set off, a firm grip on my hand, and I saw we weren't alone. Jaxson, Maverick, and Ezra fell in behind us.

"Where are we going to go?" I asked Ryder. "We're running out of places to talk privately."

"Fountain. Front lawn."

That was all I could get out of him until we were across the courtyard and out on the lawn. The sun was setting on Evergreen and a fierce wind made the blades of grass dance. I pulled my blazer tighter around me. There was something in the air, and it wasn't just the chill.

Ryder sat me down on the lip of the fountain and Maverick and Jaxson immediately took up my other sides. They pressed into me, chasing away the cold.

"How did it go?" Ezra asked.

"I told him. I didn't mention any names or the cliffs, but I told him that Scarlett tried to kill me."

"Did he believe you?"

"He did. I wasn't sure that he would, but he truly seemed to. He's going to call the police."

"They'll want to talk to you," Maverick said.

"I'll tell them exactly what I told Evergreen."

Ryder began to pace. "They're going to investigate. They'll look into everywhere she has taught. They'll ask people who know anything to come forward."

"They will," I agreed.

"What will Ace do?" He stopped and spun on me. "Have they texted you? What did they say?"

I was shaking my head before he finished. "No messages. Not one." I took my phone out of my pocket and handed it over so he could see himself. "But there is one thing. I'm sure Ace didn't know about Scarlett. They were losing their minds over me knowing a truth about her that they didn't."

Ryder was quiet while he read the evidence of that for himself.

"What about the rest of the school? The mark? The seniors? The Spades?" Ezra rattled off.

"They have a decision to make," I said. "The seniors, the Knights, and the Spades if there are more of them. They have to decide if they'll keep trying to drive us out now that they know about Scarlett, or if they will finally do the right thing."

Jaxson leaned in and pressed his head against my temple. "How are you so calm about this?"

"I've been thinking about this for months."

"Months?" Ezra's eyes grew wide. "Why didn't you tell us?"

"You would have stopped me, but that would have meant all of this would keep going on. Ace and the Knights would have fought harder until, one way or the other, they got what they wanted. I had to force an end to it."

"But that's—"

"She's right." That one sentence stopped Ezra in his tracks. "You know she is right, man," Maverick repeated. "For the first time since this started, we have a real chance to end it. Ace didn't know what Scarlett was before, but they do now. They might take the marks back themselves."

"We don't know that," said Ezra.

"We don't know anything. So there is no point in arguing about it." He pointed at my phone. "When they reply, then we'll know what comes next. Then we'll make a plan. Until then, we should get something to eat." He rubbed a finger along my cheek. "You must be starving."

"I am now that you mention it." I smiled up at him. "It would be nice to sit and eat with you guys. Laugh and talk like we used to do before everything went to shit. Thirty minutes of normal—that's what I want."

The boys looked at each other. A silent communication passed between them in a language I still hadn't learned. That was okay. I liked that they were so close.

"Okay." Ryder handed back my phone. "Thirty minutes of normal."

That was what they gave me. The boys walked me to the dorm and then went back inside for our dinner. When they returned, I had laid out a blanket and pillows in the front room. We began the night with just the five of us, but our noise brought the others out of their rooms. They saw what we were up to, ran to get their own food, and joined us.

Thirty minutes stretched into five hours. No text came from Ace, but I barely remembered the phone in my pocket. This was one of the best nights I ever had at Evergreen. My friends and the boys I loved together and being what we never got to be—a couple of regular teenagers.

Jaxson walked me upstairs when the night winded down. "I'm going to do it one of these days."

I looked at him across the stairs. "Do what?"

"I'm going to break the cameras, get you in your room, and have my way with you."

Peals of laughter burst out of me.

"I'm serious. While he's scrambling, we'll have plenty of time to get a little freaky."

We stepped onto the landing and stopped in front of my dorm. I faced him with a smile. "I'd love it if you pulled that off, but getting a weekend pass might be safer." I trailed my hand down his chest. "Then we wouldn't have to rush."

He growled low in his throat. "Good point. You doing anything this weekend?"

"Yes." I hooked my finger through the part in his buttons and pulled him closer.

"What about next weekend?"

"Busy then too." Rising up, I gave him a scorching kiss that pulled another growl out of him. I smirked at him when I stepped back. "I'll just have to pencil you in, playboy."

One last wink and I let myself into my room.

"I'm definitely breaking those cameras," I heard him mumble as I shut the door.

Chapter Four

I woke the next day to an empty inbox. There had been no messages from Ace. I kicked off the covers and started my routine in a sort of trance. My body went through the motions while my mind was elsewhere.

Why haven't they said anything? They must know. Even if they weren't in the cafeteria at the time, the news would have spread. Everyone in that school must be aware that I've accused Scarlett LeBlanc of being a predator and a Spade. There will have to be some kind of response.

A knock broke through my thoughts. "Val? Are you up?"

I went to the door and let Sofia in. She got me in a hug milliseconds after she came inside.

"How are you? I wanted to talk to you last night, but we were having so much fun and I figured we both needed it."

"We did." I squeezed her back. "It was nice to have a break from the craziness for a while."

"Do you want to talk about what happened with *her*?"

"Yes." I stepped back and met her concerned gaze. "I've been wanting to tell you about it for a long time."

We sat on the edge of my mattress. I told her the same thing I said to Evergreen. I wished I could be completely honest with her, but if she was ever questioned, I didn't want to put her in the

86

position of saying things she knew were lies. There was also the fact that some of these secrets weren't mine to tell.

"That is so much to deal with by yourself." Sofia put her head on my shoulder. "I wish you had told me sooner, but at least I know now."

"I wonder what is going to happen next," I mused aloud. "Evergreen said he is going to bring in the police and then there's Ace."

"Evergreen didn't call the police when someone— when Scarlett tried to set you on fire. This is serious."

I sighed. "It is serious. It's also time to face it. We should go."

Sofia nodded against my arm. She went to get her things while I finished packing up. The rest of the group were waiting for us at the bottom of the stairs. It was the opposite of the night before. No laughing or joking as we made for the main building.

I had told myself that the whole school would know by morning and it was confirmed when we set foot inside. Freshmen students stared openly at me while I passed by. Closing the door on them was a relief.

"It will be okay, Val," Kai said softly. "Whatever happens, we're here."

My heart filled with a rush of gratitude when they all echoed him. "I know you are."

I held on to the feeling as Jaxson held open the doors for the fourth floor. There was a group of girls idling in front of their lockers. They snapped their mouths shut when they saw me. Penelope snagged one of her friends and pulled her away. The group escaped down the hall, moving faster than they did in gym class.

I let out a breath. "I guess that answers the question of if I'm still being freezed out. I underestimated how afraid people are of the Spades. They won't go against the mark."

"This changes nothing," Ryder announced. "If Ace wants a war; they've got one. We're not backing down." Ryder took my hand. "Let's go. We don't want to be late for class."

We split up. I didn't speak as we walked toward our lockers, but I saw Ryder looking at me from the corner of my eye.

"Are you upset?"

"No. Yes." I tossed my head. "I don't know. I just can't believe news like this isn't enough to shake the hold of the Spades. I'm starting to think that nothing will."

"We will. The problem is that we've been fighting people we can't see. If we knew who they were, we'd know how to end it. We've spent too much time trying to get ahead of Ace when we don't know if they are in front or behind. We have to step up our attempts to find them." He pulled up and I realized we were in front of his locker. "We have the list of suspects. We had no way to narrow it down before, but tonight we should look at it again—the five of us. Something might jump out."

A smile spread across my lips as he spoke. He noticed it when I didn't reply. "What? Why are you smiling?"

My answer was to slip my arms around his waist and rest my head on his chest. That was what I liked about him. He always had a plan. No matter how awful things appeared to be; he was thinking of a way out.

"That's a good idea. We'll do it tonight."

Eventually, I let him go and we dumped our things for home-room. I began the walk to the classroom without a problem, but as I neared the door, I got slower. I was lagging a foot behind Ryder when Roundtree's room came into view.

He peered at me over his shoulder. "You up for this? We could skip class again."

I shook my head. "Putting it off won't make it easier. Besides, it's not me who should hide." Saying that infused my spine with steel. I picked up the pace and grabbed the knob before he could reach it.

I threw open the door and walked into a class that was already quiet, but the silence became absolute as everyone turned to me. I moved into the middle of the room and paused, meeting their eyes. No one spoke as I traveled up and down the rows of faces looking for what I expected to see.

I frowned. *Wait—*

Natalie moved her backpack out of her lap and got to her feet. I braced myself for the vileness that was going to pour out of her mouth. "Professor Roundtree. Can you give us ten minutes?" There was no expression on her face to give her away. "Knight business."

I heard a sigh from behind me. "I know how this works. You've got ten minutes and no more." Roundtree crossed in front of my vision and walked out, leaving me alone with my class.

Isabella, Airi, and Darren got to their feet with Natalie. They faced me down while the class held so still, they might have been frozen.

My friends and the other boys had made it to class before me. They were all seated apart from Ryder who came to my side.

I swept over the four of them. "Well? Say something, *Knights*."

Isabella opened her mouth.

"Is it true?"

I twisted my head around as one of the guys shot out of his seat. Eric Eden looked back at me. The artificial lights shone on the sweat collected on his brow and the button he missed when getting dressed. I could see from where I stood that his balled fists shook.

"Is it true, Val? About Professor LeBlanc. About why you were marked? Was what you said really why this happened?"

I looked at the guy whose friendship I had gained and lost twice with the appearance of a card. "Yes."

A hush spread through the space.

Penelope shot to her feet. "But that can't be true!"

That broke the spell.

"How can you say it's not true?!" Genesis Smith yelled at her. "Why would she lie?"

Penelope snapped back and then the whole class was off—yelling back and forth in an unintelligible mess that I couldn't make out. I didn't know who believed me and who didn't. The noise reached dangerous levels until I got fed up.

"Stop it!" I bellowed. "All of you! Be quiet!"

This was the one time the new Knights and I were on the same page because they were shouting the same.

"It's different now," Eric's voice could be heard when the room started to settle down. "Valentina was innocent. She didn't do anything that would deserve her getting thrown out of Evergreen."

Juliet Cochran, Darren's co-host, pushed herself up on legs that wobbled. "My older sister was s-sexually assaulted. I don't care what they do. I'm done listening to the Spades."

Penelope leveled her finger at me. "We only have her side of the story. She's probably lying to get the mark lifted again. She'd do anything."

"She wouldn't lie about that!" The person who spoke in my defense was none other than Lola, Penelope's best friend. "You heard her! She found out that woman was a pedophile and LeBlanc marked her."

"We didn't hear anything." Isabella's tone was measured as she moved from her desk and put a hand on Penelope. She pushed her back into her seat. "We don't know the full story, so tell us, Valentina. We're listening."

I glanced at Ryder. She sounded sincere. I figured I would have to tell my story many times. I would share it now if it would bring this to an end.

"Okay." I shifted to face the class. "It started the night of the freshman masquerade dance..."

No one interrupted or so much as coughed while I told them what I said to Evergreen. When I finished, I got the opposite of silence. I was pelted with questions.

"Who is the student?"

"Do you have proof?"

"What is Evergreen going to do? He let a fucking pedophile teach us. What if she assaulted other students?"

"What about the mark? You can't just mark people because they find out you're a twisted sicko." This came from one of Darren's crew. "Juliet is right. I'm not following that mark."

"Do the Spades know?"

"The Spades?" A sickly pallor was cast on Claire's face. She looked like she would throw up. "Is this what the Spades are really about? Are they a group of horrible people like Scarlett and the ones they've marked over the years were those that found out the truth about them?"

"Hold on." Ciara grasped Claire's forearm. "We don't know that. I'm sure that's not—"

"You're sure?!" She ripped her arm away. "How?! It's not like they haven't hurt innocent people before. They killed Walter McMillian and he did nothing wrong. Everyone *knows* he did nothing wrong! This is what the Spades really are and I-I hurt one of my friends to protect a pedophile!" Then she clapped her hand over her mouth. Claire raced to the front of the room and heaved into a wastebasket. Her boyfriend ran to her side, bending over her as he rubbed her back.

It was at that moment that Roundtree came back inside. He surveyed the chaos and said, "Damn. Whatever has been going on, it's time to give it a rest."

There was no continuing after that. Roundtree made us take our seats and pull out our homework. I tried to read my psychology textbook but the words swam on the page. It was hard to concentrate with Claire sobbing a few desks down.

What would happen now?

Kai repeated the question on my mind when homeroom ended. "People believe you, Val. You heard Claire, Lola, Brian, and Eric. Maybe the Spades believe you too."

I looked toward the phone box while I threw the psych book in my bag. "All we have are maybes. We'll see if anything really changes."

THE REST OF THE FIRST week of school passed quickly, but not quietly. The new Knights kicked Roundtree out of class three more times and there were more shouting matches that went nowhere. I was hit with questions on all sides while my boys looked like they were barely restraining themselves from stepping in.

I knew it was killing them seeing what I was going through, but I didn't want them being put through this inquisition. This wasn't how someone who had dealt with assault and violence should be treated, but decency was thrown out of the window under the shadow of the Spades.

Who were they? What was this secret society truly about? Protecting the legacy of Evergreen Academy? Or hiding its dark shameful secrets? Lines were being drawn and I honestly did not know which way it would go. The entire school was breaking apart at the seams.

I stepped out of Evergreen's office that Friday evening never more relieved that it was the weekend. The Shea family car was idling outside the gates and I was happy to hop inside and drive far away from this place. There was only one more thing I needed to do.

"Thank you for speaking with me, Valentina." Officer Plymouth followed me out into reception and shook my hand. Evergreen had warned me the police were going to drop in and interview me so it wasn't a surprise when I found him and Officer Plymouth waiting outside my final class of the day.

Officer Plymouth was kind and patient as I told my story. She listened without interrupting and only asked a few questions to clarify. I could sense she wanted to help me.

If only her suspect wasn't lying at the bottom of a cliff.

"I appreciate how hard it must have been to come forward. I want you to know the search for Scarlett LeBlanc has already begun. We've put the word out to former employees. We've also contacted friends. Finding her is our top priority."

I halted with my feet pointed toward the door. "What happens if you can't find her?"

Plymouth's phone trilled in her pants. She took it out and answered me with one eye on it. "Hmm. Oh. We will. I have no doubt she will be located and charged. Justice will be done." Plymouth looked up from the screen. "I'm afraid I have to go, but you'll be kept informed. Goodbye, Miss Moon."

She blew out of the door before I could get another word in. I let her go. There was no point pressing her about it. As long as a certain video never surfaced, no one would find Scarlett LeBlanc.

Time to go, I thought as I grabbed my overnight bag off the chair. The list of Ace suspects was tucked away in my pocket where it had been since the five of us stayed up going through it. We had not been able to cross anyone off, but I had been keeping it with me and scribbling things in the margins.

Ryder honked when I stepped out of the gates. I slid into the passenger seat and tossed my bag in the back. "I'm glad we're doing this. I needed a break."

"My house will be chill. Mom's been in a good mood and she's excited we're coming. She has the chef cooking us a feast every night and she's brought out all her favorite old movies for us to watch together."

"That sounds perfect." My first smile of the day appeared on my lips. "So what will you and I do together?"

"I've got plans." He left it there and wouldn't say more even under my pestering.

The ride to Shea Manor was short. Twenty minutes later, we were pulling into his driveway. One of his staff came out to meet us and took the keys off his hands while he opened my door. His car sped off in a spray of gravel as Ryder led me inside.

"You and Mom are going to the bank tomorrow morning, but tonight, she thought we would start the movie marathon. She has the *Maltese Falcon* queued up in the theater."

"Ooh. *Maltese Falcon*. Caroline has great taste."

He laughed. Ryder was loosening up before my eyes. The stiffness to his jaw eased and the taut line of his shoulders went away. He had been looking forward to this too.

"Are you hungry? Chef can serve dinner whenever you're ready."

I shook my head. "I'm not hungry yet, but let's eat before the movie so I won't stuff myself on popcorn."

"Cool." He grabbed my hand. "Let me show you to your room."

"My room?" I let Ryder tug me along after him. "I thought that we would—"

Ryder peered at me over his shoulder and raised his brow. "You thought we would be sleeping in the same bed?"

"Yes," I replied, even though my cheeks were hot.

"I'm all for it, but my mom is right down the hall." He winked. "Don't worry. We'll have time to ourselves. I told you I have something planned."

"Okay. Guess I'll have to trust you," I teased.

Ryder gave me a mini-tour of my room. It was a few doors down from him and could fit my entire house inside. It was a gorgeous space with plush carpet that swallowed my toes and a massive bed that sadly wouldn't have him in it. I didn't come on this trip for *that* but I did want our relationship to move forward.

Ryder left me to clean up before dinner and I sunk into my bath with him running through my mind.

A relationship with Ryder was never going to be easy. There was too much history there. But I chose him. I need him to know that he's worth that choice.

The soaker tub tried to claim me for its own, but eventually, I forced myself out. I changed into a comfy pair of jeans and a loose top and went in search of Ryder and Caroline. My feet remembered the way, and I found them in the dining room without a problem.

Caroline's smile could have lit the space. "There you are, dear. How do you like your room? If it's too small, we can move you."

"It's perfect." I stopped at the head of the table and kissed her cheek. Ryder sat on her left and the staff held out the chair for me on her right. "Thank you for letting me stay."

"You are welcome here anytime. I'm sure Ryder will be glad of your company too." She gave him a knowing look that made my brows shoot up.

"Is that right, Ryder Shea? Do you want me around?"

"He most certainly does. He talks about you all the time. I heard your name all summer."

Ryder looked between me and Caroline as I stifled a giggle. "I'm seeing now that this is going to be very bad for me."

Caroline and I laughed out loud and soon Ryder joined in. My visit had just started and already I was enjoying myself. This was exactly what I wanted and more.

We kept up the playful teasing and chatter for the whole of dinner. A dinner that was equal parts delicious and surprising. I expected twelve courses and food I couldn't pronounce, but instead the chef served up baked macaroni and lemon chicken. It reminded me of the simple meals I cooked at home for Adam while he watched me in his high chair.

"I hope you like classic movies, Valentina." Caroline held Jacob's hand as he escorted her to the theater. "I told my son there is nothing else worth watching."

"And I told Mom that once she gives in to high-definition and special effects; she'll leave those over-acted classics in the past."

Caroline gasped. "Over-acted? How dare you. Those are the greatest entertainers in our history. I can assure you none of those exploding, car-chase headaches will be celebrated in film history classes."

Their banter went on while I hung back and watched. Ryder slid into Jacob's place halfway to the theater and he ended up escorting her. They were a cute pair. I felt lucky to see them both happy and relaxed.

"Valentina?" Caroline called. "Where did you go?"

"Coming."

Their home theater wasn't so much big as it was cozy. Eight leather recliner chairs took up one side of the room and before them was a screen that covered the whole front wall. Ryder sat between me and his mom while Jacob was a silent figure in the back row.

The staff wheeled in a tray with six flavors of popcorn and at random times during the movie Ryder would twist his head around with his mouth open so I could throw some in. Our chuckles made Caroline shush us but we were both having so much fun.

Caroline went to bed early after the movie finished, but Ryder and I stayed to watch some more. He dug out a few that had been made in this century and we snuggled in to watch. His hand on the armrest between us drew my eyes away from the screen every few minutes. Now that it was just the two of us, I could think about nothing but his fingers laced through mine.

"Val? Val?"

I snapped back to reality, dragging my eyes away from his hand. "Huh? What is it?"

"I asked if you wanted more popcorn."

"Sure. Chocolate, please."

He stood and filled our bowl with more goodies from the cart. When he reclaimed his seat, he set the bowl in his lap.

"It's so good." I reached for another handful. "I can't get—"

I was stopped by Ryder. His fingers curled over mine and pulled them away from the chocolatey kernels.

"Let me," he whispered.

I swallowed hard. My pulse quickened under his touch.

Ryder took one kernel and pressed it to my lips. I slowly parted them and let him place the popcorn on my tongue. My lips wrapped around his fingers as our eyes connected in the darkened room. He lingered as he pulled out, caressing my lips with his thumb.

My heart was thumping so loudly in my ears it drowned out the movie. Feeding me popcorn seemed tame, but this was one of the most intimate moments of my life.

My tongue darted out and licked the tip of his finger before he could pull back. A thrill surged through me when he sucked in a breath. "Are you sure about the separate rooms?" I asked.

"A lot less sure than I was an hour ago."

Ryder twisted to face the screen. I would have been more disappointed if he wasn't still holding my hand.

We made it through one more flick before my eyes started to droop. After the movie, Ryder walked me up to my room and said good night at the door.

The next morning, I woke early but stayed in bed. My phone was in one hand, and in the other, was the list of suspects. I had taken to pulling it out and going over it in the mornings and this morning was no different.

<u>The List</u>

Penelope Madlow

Darren Rosewood

Lola McConnell

Emma Brinker

Eric Eden

Ciara O'Brien

Claire Montgomery

Cade Trevelyan

Axel Leon

Genesis Smith

Professor Markham

Professor Felton

Professor Coleman

I went through them all over again. The professors did not have to put their phones in the box, but these three had gone on the winter trip and I knew Ace was there. I had the ski-induced lump on my head to prove it. I didn't want to think they were involved, but Scarlett had taught me not to rule anyone out.

My eyes moved to the top of the list and Penelope Madlow. Penelope was not my friend before I was marked, but after she was only too happy to take me down.

Not to mention she's accusing me of lying about Scarlett and why I was marked. Why is she so determined not to believe me?

I wrote that down next to her name and underlined it.

Then there was Darren. A sleazy, shady dude if there ever was one. He wasn't only awful to me when I was marked, but he kept it up after the mark was lifted. Darren did not like me and that most likely had to do with the Evergreen Gone Wild video.

Maybe he followed me into the woods to get revenge. I had a secret phone stashed away. He might have had one too for the purpose of getting something he could use.

I was quick to write that down. That made a lot of sense.

The next two names had nothing beside them. I didn't know Lola and Emma well, except that they started the bullying about me having an eating disorder. All I knew for sure about them is that their phones were missing from the box when I got that text.

I paused over the three names under Emma. I made myself write them down when we made this list all those months ago, but I did not want to believe it. Ace seemed to harbor real hatred of me. It came through loud and clear when they made me cut my hair, kiss Kai, and tried to force me to strip. Eric, Claire, and Ciara would have had to be phenomenal actors to hide that hatred all the times they were around me.

Eric does hold the traditions of the school very highly, a voice countered. *His whole family does. He dropped me not once, but twice.*

But he also stood up for me when I came out about Scarlett, I thought. *Maybe he's not so entrenched in the traditions after all.*

Thinking of that morning reminded me of Claire's tears. Would Ace have gotten sick and cried for me? Could I even suspect a girl who came from the same side of the tracks that I did of being Ace?

Groaning, I tossed the list aside. I wasn't narrowing it down. I was just going around and around in circles until it made me dizzy. The truth is the way people are acting now that the knowledge of Scarlett is out doesn't help me. Someone patting me on the back and saying they're on my side could still be Ace. They could have had a change of heart after finding out they blackmailed me over defending myself from a pedophile.

If Ace even cares about that. I don't know what they feel because my phone hasn't buzzed with a single message. I don't know what any of this means.

A knock on the door saved me before I could go down the rabbit hole again.

"Come in."

Ryder let himself inside. "Morning. Mom sent me to see if you were ready for breakfast. She wants to leave for the bank in..." Ryder trailed off when he saw the list lying on the carpet. He picked it up but didn't put it in my hand when I reached out.

"Ryder," I said when he put it in his pocket. "I need that."

"We both know you have it memorized. Can I ask you for something?" My hand was still outstretched. He took it and helped me out of bed. "This weekend... can we do normal again?"

I opened my mouth to refuse. There was no normal anymore. Police, secret societies, murders, and blackmail had seen to it that we couldn't have normal again for a long time.

"Okay." I blinked when that word tumbled out. "Normal would be nice."

"Thank you." Ryder's smile transformed his already perfect face into a work of art. My breath caught as those silver pools drowned me.

"It's not fair how beautiful you are," I whispered. He pressed his finger to my lips and memories of the night before flooded in.

"What's not fair is how much I want to kiss you right now."

"Then why don't you?"

He stepped back and the finger was gone. "Now isn't the right time. Mom is waiting."

I sighed. "Maybe if you told me what the right time is. What are you waiting for, Ryder? I thought you had gotten past the belief that you didn't deserve me."

"I *don't* deserve you. I never will."

My throat tightened at hearing him say that. It hurt more that he sounded like he believed it.

Stepping up to him, I folded my arms. "You want normal? Then how about this: this weekend we are a normal couple with a boring past. You never tried to drown me or throw me off a roof. I never outed a dark family secret and tried to destroy your life. We're totally different people. You're Lincoln Mandelbaum from the local high school. I'm Marie Freebush. You saw me across the lunchroom, asked me out, and tonight we are having our first date. Deal?"

"Lincoln Mandelbaum and Marie Freebush? Where the hell did you come up with those names?"

I jabbed his chest. "Do we have a deal, Lincoln?"

He laughed. "Only if you never call me that again." Ryder backed away toward the door. "Get dressed, Marie. After you come back, we have normal couple shit to do."

I did as he asked and then went down for breakfast. Caroline was up and dressed in her best when I came down. A chic, wrap-around dress covered her from collarbone to ankle and thick shades perched on her nose. They matched nicely with the floppy hat that obscured part of her face.

We ate quickly and then headed out. The trip to the bank was quick and painless. After we wrapped up the details, I called Mom the moment we stepped outside.

"I did it, Mom. We're middle class once again."

She chuckled. "Not so middle class when you're hoarding enough diamond earrings and gold necklaces to feed a small country. You have expensive taste, kid."

"Oh no. I don't have to give those back too, do I?" I asked, half-joking.

She laughed at me again, but quickly sobered. "This is good for us, baby. We're going to start over on the right foot."

I smiled. "Lincoln and Marie."

"What?"

"Nothing. Can you put Adam on?"

"Sure."

My cheerful baby came on the phone and I cooed at him while we rode back to the manor. We said goodbye when the driver passed through their gates.

"Valentina?" Caroline said when I hung up.

"Yes?"

"It's such a nice day. Will you sit with me by the pool?"

The car came to a halt. Jacob walked around the vehicle and was there to take Caroline's hand when she opened the door.

"I'd love to."

"Wonderful," she said over her shoulder. "Give me an hour to rest and then I'll meet you out there."

I searched for Ryder in the meantime and found him in the kitchen—one of the kitchens. An assortment of colorful foods were spread out in front of him. I watched him for a minute while he chopped carrots.

"So Lincoln can cook."

Ryder twisted around and found me leaning against the countertop. "Hey. I didn't hear you come in."

"What are you making?"

"Corned beef and cabbage." He went back to chopping as I drew closer. "My grandmother used to make it for Mom when she was little. I taught myself how to cook it."

"That's sweet." I picked up a potato and began cleaning it under cool water. If I was going to be here, I might as well help. "You're going to put your chef out of a job at this rate."

"Mom won't always eat his cooking, but she feels bad when she doesn't finish what I make for her."

My hands still beneath the water. "Does she often... not finish meals?"

Ryder didn't look up from his task. "She doesn't always have an appetite."

I let it drop. "Can I help you? Show me what to do."

"Will you chop the cabbage while I peel the potatoes?"

We switched places and got to work. There was an easy atmosphere while we cooked. We talked and laughed over the bubbling pot.

"Your mother's family is from Ireland," I repeated. "Have you ever been there?"

"A few times when I was little. We haven't visited much since my grandparents passed away."

"I'm sorry." I didn't know her parents were gone. I was realizing now how much more I needed to learn about Ryder and Caroline. "Your mom must love that you give her a piece of her childhood back by making the foods she loves." I bumped his hip. "If you're not careful, I'm going to start thinking you have a soft, gooey center."

He bumped me back. "Does that mean I'm not irritating as fuck anymore?"

"Nope. You're definitely still irritating. You can be both."

He turned on me with a smirk. "What was it you said the other day? Something about going the right way for a spanked bottom?"

Ryder advanced on me as my eyes widened. "I definitely did not say anything about spanking."

"That's what I remember." Ryder stalked me, eyes darkening as my heart rate doubled.

"Don't you dare, Ryder Shea." I backed into the countertop and hurriedly slid along the rounded edge.

"But isn't that what a normal boyfriend would do?"

"No!" I forced out. I couldn't breathe, I was laughing so hard. "You stay back, Lincoln."

"That's it." He leaped forward, grabbing for me, and I darted away. I made it two steps before his strong arms encircled me and lifted me up.

His laughter rumbled against my back as he held me. It echoed mine. This was everything to me. I wanted us to laugh and grow closer.

"You can't spank me." I leaned my head back and peered at him through my lashes. "But you can do a few other things with me. Things that a boyfriend would definitely do. Want me to go into detail?"

His grip tightened. "Fuck, Val," he hissed. "You're not going to make this easy for me, are you?"

"Not at all."

"I should have known that. Making things hard is what you do." He put his mouth to my ear and his hot breath sent shivers up my spine. "Making me hard is what you do."

The words passed through me and went straight to my core. "Let's go upstairs. Now."

"W-we can't." To be fair, it sounded like it physically hurt him to say that. "Mom is waiting for you and I have to make sure she eats."

He was right. This tiny peek into their lives was opening my eyes to how much Ryder did to care for his mother. I didn't want to get in the way no matter how much I wanted to be with him.

"Can we spend time together afterward?" I asked.

"I was planning on it." He set me on my feet. "I'm way behind on my 'labors.' One of the things I wanted to do this weekend was make up for that."

"Really?" The boys had done so many wonderful things for me to show how sorry they were. The day Ryder and I spent with Adam in Santa's village was one of the best Christmas memories I had—despite Adam beating up Santa. "I can't wait."

We gazed into each other's eyes, smiling, and then Ryder bent his head. My eyes fluttered shut in anticipation of the kiss I had been waiting for. They snapped open when Ryder pressed that kiss to my forehead.

"You should go. Don't want to keep Mom waiting."

"Okay." I wasn't sure if he picked up on my disappointment. I stepped away and made for the pool. Ryder was back at the stove before I left the room.

I noticed Caroline had changed clothes when I walked out onto the terrace. The dress was gone in favor of a sweater and pants, but they seemed more comfortable. That wasn't the only addition. A bundle of fur occupied her lap, purring loud enough for me to hear as Caroline stroked her.

"There you are," she said.

"Sorry to keep you waiting. I was helping Ryder make corned beef and cabbage." I sat in the patio chair beside her and reached for the cat. "Hello, Cara. I still like your old name better."

Caroline laughed. "Is he cooking for me again? I want him to relax when he's home, but Ryder insists on fussing over me. He has such a good heart." Her eyes grew unfocused as she gazed across the pool. "I'm glad I did one thing right in my life."

That sounded so close to what Mom said to me in the courtyard that it prompted me to reply. "He's not the only thing. You've done a lot of good."

"Thank you for saying so." She placed her hand on top of mine. "But I must admit, this is not the life I saw for myself."

"What kind of life did you want?"

"I thought I would write, paint, travel the world, and fill a home with children. All of that seemed possible when I was at Evergreen."

"It's still possible. You can do anything you want now."

That Benjamin is gone.

I let that thought hang in the air between us.

"No... I can't."

The mood had shifted. I wasn't sure how or why it had happened so fast, but Caroline's smile was dimming and the cat's purring stopped as her hand stilled. I cast about for a subject change as the silence stretched. In the end, it was Ryder who broke it.

"I made your favorite, Mom," he said as he came out onto the veranda. "Valentina helped."

Her smile briefly returned. "I'm not very hungry, love, but I'll have a little as you both worked so hard."

Ryder lowered the tray and I saw two plates were on it. He gave one to his mom and the other to me. I took one bite and moaned. "That is incredible. How can a dish this simple taste so good?"

"Of course, it's good. It's my mother's recipe." Caroline took a hearty bite. "She was a magician in the kitchen. She could make thirty-four different meals with a bag of potatoes."

"You're putting us on, Mom." Ryder pulled up a chair, grinning.

"I am not. Thirty-four. I swear."

"So then you should be able to name them."

Clicking her tongue, she swatted his arm. "Don't you trust your mother?"

"I'll never doubt a thing she says... after she lists the thirty-four dishes you can make with a potato."

Caroline tossed her head back laughing. I may not have known how to lift her mood, but Ryder did. "You get that smart mouth from her too, but you'll regret doubting me. It's fries, mashed potatoes, potato soup, hash browns..."

She actually went through the whole list. I was deeply impressed but there was no stopping Ryder's smart mouth.

"Number twelve and nineteen don't count. Those are just two different kinds of potato salad. Potato salad counts as one."

"If I say it counts, it counts." Caroline made to get up and Jacob was at her side in seconds. He helped her to her feet and then she bent and kissed her son. "I'm going to rest for a while, my love. When I wake up, we can watch *Casablanca*."

"We've seen *that* thirty-four times."

"Here's to thirty-five." Caroline patted my cheek on her way out. "You two have fun."

I turned to Ryder when she was gone. "The corned beef and cabbage was really good. I'll have to make it for Mom and Adam." I leaned back in the chair but Ryder stood.

He held a hand out for me. "Come on. It's time."

"Time for what?"

"Labor number two."

I let him pull me to my feet and lead me inside. Ryder was quiet as we walked through the cavernous halls of the mansion. Our bare feet were soundless on the hardwood floors.

It's so quiet here. This place was meant to be filled with warmth and laughter.

I shook away my thoughts before they could turn morose. My heart would always twinge thinking of what I had seen within these walls. Benjamin snapping and tearing apart a young Ryder for the smallest things. Caroline a figure only heard about and not seen while he worked to crush her spirit. The man was rotted through to his soul. Maybe the pain these walls had seen would always cling.

I just said I wouldn't get sad. No more thinking of Benjamin Shea. He's dead and gone, and Ryder and I are moving on. I peered at the back of his head. *We're going to have everything he tried to take from us.*

"Are we going out?" I piped up. "Do I need to get changed?"

"No. We're not leaving the house." We rounded the corner and came out in front of the grand staircase. Ryder held me securely as he took me up.

"Can I get a hint?"

He laughed. "A hint? You'll find out in two minutes."

I kept up the questioning anyway. "Will I like it?"

"It wouldn't be much of an apology if I didn't think you'd like it."

"I can never be too sure with you."

He gave me a look over his shoulder. "You trying to talk yourself into losing it? 'Cause you're doing a good job."

I made a show of zipping my lip and tossing away the key. The act caused him to smile which made my heart do a little flutter. I swear a cardiologist would be very concerned if they found out how much my heart acted up around these guys.

We topped the landing and Ryder turned left. It was the opposite direction of my room, but the right direction for his. I didn't hold back my grin when we stopped in front of his door.

"Oh. It's *that* kind of labor." I glided in front of him, slid my hands up his chest, and then draped them around his neck. Ryder's eyes went round as I pressed myself against him. "Am I allowed to say that those are my favorite kind?" He grunted as I hopped up and wrapped my legs around his waist. "I am going to put you to work."

"We— I— That's not—" His breaths came in hot pants. "Fuck, woman! Will you behave yourself? We're not going in there to have sex."

I pouted. "Why not?"

"I can't fucking remember now." He tossed his head back and sucked in a couple shuddering breaths. He seemed to be trying to summon his resolve and I couldn't let that happen. I bent my head and dropped kisses on his jaw as his breaths grew more ragged. "Because there's... something I want to do with you... to show... how I feel. It's important to me."

I hummed. "Well, if it's important to you, then it's important to me." I slid off of him but held on to his hand. "I'm ready."

"Okay." It took another minute for the fog to clear behind his eyes. I was the one who opened his door and pulled him inside. I looked around as we stepped through. His room was the same as always. I didn't see anything different or out of place except for one thing.

"Your piano is back." The black masterpiece sat in a place of honor beneath a bay window. The light shone through the curtains, making the polished wood gleam.

"It was removed from the Knight room when the others took over." To my surprise, he walked me over to it. "When we were little, I remember you'd hide in the doorway and watch me play."

My cheeks warmed. "I didn't *hide* in the doorway. I just— just listened."

He grinned. "I'd catch you listening a lot." Ryder let go of my hand and trailed a finger along the ivory keys. "Once, you snuck in here to play my piano and I acted like an awful shit when I found you."

"We don't have to think about that," I said softly.

"We do," Ryder replied, "because I want to do what I should have done back then. I'm going to teach you how to play."

"You are? I—" The words stuck in my throat. I had always wanted to learn to play an instrument—to make beautiful music like a young Ryder could tease from his keys. Lessons were expensive though, and after entering the academy and becoming a mom, there was no time for anything like that.

I don't know how he does it, but Ryder keeps seeing inside to what I truly want.

"I would love that."

I sat down and our lesson began. I wasn't going to become a master pianist in an afternoon, but Ryder taught me the different notes and where to place my hands. He was patient as he showed me how to play a simple tune.

"Just like that. C, C, D, E."

I struck the wrong note and the discordant sound told me right away. "Oops. That's wrong."

"It's okay. Let me help." Ryder put his hand on top of mine, lining up our fingers as he gently pressed them down to the right notes. I felt the heat from his body and it made goose bumps erupt on my skin. I could smell the lingering scent of pine soap and a musk that was all Ryder.

I looked up at him as he made my fingers dance. "Will you play something for me?"

"Of course." Ryder removed his hand. I missed his touch, but anticipation tempered the loss. I could not wait to hear him play.

In moments, the room was filled with a melody I didn't know. The difference between my banging and Ryder's playing was night and day. His fingers glided over the keys in a way that was enchanting to watch and to hear. The song was hauntingly beautiful. For reasons I didn't understand, tears were prickling at the back of my eyes by the time he played the last note.

"Ryder, that was amazing."

"I've played that one so many times I've lost count. It's one of Mom's favorites."

"It's my favorite now too." I leaned my head against his arm. "Thank you for this. I loved it."

"It doesn't have to stop. I can teach you to play. If you want to learn."

"I do." I tilted my head back to let him see my smile. "It would mean a lot to me."

"Perfect." Ryder closed the lid over the keys. "Is there something else you would like to do? Mom will probably rest for a few more hours so we can bowl, play pool, watch a movie, anything you like."

"What doesn't this house have?"

"Nothing. We have everything."

I laughed, but it faded as I drifted back to what he said. "Caroline has to rest often. Is it okay if I ask...?"

"What's wrong with her," he finished.

"I wasn't going to put it like that. It's just today I seemed to upset her talking about the future. I want to be sensitive to what she needs. I don't want to bring her down again."

"It wasn't you, Valentina." Ryder addressed me, but he spoke to the piano. His eyes were fixed on the shiny surface. "Mom is going through a lot. She doesn't like me to talk about it, but she gets down often. She sleeps most of the day and doesn't get out of bed some mornings.

"This wasn't how it always was. She used to be so happy and alive. When I was small, she'd take me out every day and we'd go to the park, the beach, and on picnics—just the two of us. Benjamin was never a good father, but he was hardly around when I was little so I didn't notice. Mom and I were happy on our own... until things changed. Looking back, that must have been when he found out I wasn't his son, because he did everything he could to make us miserable."

I curled my fingers around his arm but did not speak. I let him get it out.

"The things he put us through... they leave a mark. They don't just go away even though he has. Mom isn't the same person, but she's still my mom, and she's always been there for me in every way she could."

"I understand."

"I know you do." My hand fell off his arm as he raised it and put it around me. "You're the only one who understands me. It's a good thing I'm stuck with you." His tone turned teasing. "There really isn't anyone else like you who would put up with me."

"That's very true. You are astoundingly lucky."

"No arguments here."

I burrowed into his side. "Will you play another song for me?"

"Yes, but before I do, there's something I need to tell you."

There was something in his tone that made me pull away. "What? What happened?"

Ryder took his eyes off the piano now. He twisted around until he faced me. "It's the guys. They wanted to tell you, but they didn't know how you would take it, so I said I would tell you."

"Tell me what?"

"You know why Ezra went home this weekend. He decided to tell his mom the truth."

I nodded.

"Well, Maverick and Jaxson got weekend passes too. They're going to do it. They are telling their parents what Scarlett did to us while we were in prep school." He gripped my shoulders. "We can't stand watching you deal with the fallout to protect the unknown 'student.' They wanted their folks to be the first to know, but next we're going into Evergreen's office and revealing what she did."

My mouth fell open, jaw working but no sounds coming out. "Talking to their parents is a big step," I said when I found my voice. "But I don't need to be the reason. You don't have to do this for me. You should do it for you." I clambered to my feet. "I have to call the guys. I have to tell them—"

"They already did it, Val."

That halted me in my tracks. Slowly, I turned to him, tears collecting in my eyes. "I want to b-be there for them—for you. I have to."

"You are here for us, and when they're ready, they will come to you." He put out his hands and they drew me back to him.

"What about you?" I whispered as he pulled me to his chest. "Should I go so you can talk to Caroline?"

"No." His hand was warm as he rubbed my back. "It's different for us. Mom would never forgive herself. She'd take the blame and spend days in bed crying because she thought she wasn't there for me when I needed her. Scarlett's done enough. I'm not letting what she did hurt Mom too."

I hesitated. Ryder did not always respond well to me telling him what to do in regard to his mom. "Ryder, it's going to hurt, of course it will, but Caroline would want to be there for you. You've been taking care of her for so long, but you're her son. She wants to take care of you too."

The silence stretched between us and I feared that I went too far.

"You're probably right," he said so softly I almost did not hear him. "I've wanted to tell her so many times over the years, but nothing would come out. I don't know how to do it, Val. I don't know if I'll ever be able to."

I hugged him tighter. "You will. When you're ready, you'll find the strength... and Caroline will find the strength to be there for you."

I don't know how long we stayed like that, holding each other before the piano, but we didn't move until one of the staff came to tell us Caroline was ready for the movie.

My stay at Ryder's home was so perfect, I did not want to leave when Sunday afternoon came around. Somehow, we were able to overcome the pain that followed our talk about Scarlett and enjoy the rest of our time together. We cooked, joked, watched about a dozen old movies, and Ryder and I snuck in another piano lesson. For one weekend, I had what I wanted—a fun, normal time with the boy I cared about, but now I had to return to the academy.

"Visit as often as you can." Caroline pressed featherlight kisses to both of my cheeks. "I haven't had that much fun in ages."

"I will. We'll pick up our discussion on *Citizen Kane*."

She raised a brow. "That wasn't a discussion; it was an argument. One that I will win. *Citizen Kane* is the best movie of our time."

"I still say it's *Psycho*. Hitchcock revolutionized the slasher film genre."

She waved that away. "He scared a few people out of their panties. *Citizen Kane* inspired a generation."

A snicker to my right told me Ryder was laughing at us.

"Oh, yeah. We're definitely picking up this argument next time," I warned. "We're also doing a Hitchcock movie marathon."

"Oh, no." She pressed a hand to her chest. "I think I'll have to rest that weekend."

We laughed as she pulled me in for a hug. Underneath everything, Caroline had a sense of humor as sharp as her son's.

I waved goodbye to her on the porch and then hopped in Ryder's car. We soon made it back to the academy and passed through the gates. The smile faded from my face with every step that brought me closer to the dorm. Most of the group was gathered in the front room when we entered. Unease took hold of me as I looked around. I noticed immediately that Ezra and Maverick were not there. The next thing I saw were their expressions.

"What's wrong?"

They shared a look that only made me worry more. It was Jaxson who answered me. "We're not sure."

"What do you mean?"

"We went to grab food from our *new* lunchroom, but there were no trays. We were forced to go to the cafeteria and the Knights were there."

Ryder stepped forward. "Did they do something?"

"No," Kai replied. "But Isabella asked for Valentina. She looked annoyed when we said you weren't here. Although that's how she usually looks so who can tell the difference."

Sofia got to her feet. "Val, she said that a decision had been made."

I tensed. "A decision? What decision?"

"She wouldn't explain. The last thing she said before the four of them walked out was that it was time to end this."

"Time to end this?" My bag slipped off my shoulder as I collapsed next to Kai. "How the fuck do we take that? She must be talking about the mark, right?"

Jaxson shook his head. "If it came from Natalie, I'd say it was definitely bad for us, but she just stood there. Isabella has been strangely silent while everyone else has been raging about the Spades and Scarlett. She stops the arguments from getting out of hand, but she hasn't given an opinion either way."

"Maybe because she was waiting on someone else's opinion." I looked down at my bag where my phone was concealed in the pocket.

Ace has not been talking to me, but they could be talking to her.

"We can't sit here panicking," I continued. "We'll find out tomorrow what she means. We'll end this."

I SAID WE SHOULDN'T panic but still we spent half the night going back and forth on what the next day would bring. Were the marks going to be lifted for good this time and the Spades brought to their knees, or would we find ourselves worse off than we were before?

I did not have an answer to that, but I did have a question when the group broke apart for the night.

"Jaxson?" He stood at the window, staring unseeingly out into the pitch-black night. All night I had wanted to pull him aside and talk. "Hey."

It didn't seem like he heard me. I slipped my arm through his and he jumped.

"Oh, Val. Sorry. Did you say something?"

I shook my head. "I haven't seen Ezra or Maverick. They haven't texted me back either."

"That's because they never came back to school."

"What?" I breathed. "Why?"

"Their folks called Evergreen and pulled them out of school for a few days." Jaxson didn't look at me. "He didn't fight them under the circumstances."

"Are they okay?"

"Ezra and Rick are, but their parents not so much. Amelia hasn't stopped crying since Ezra told her. Maverick's parents have gone between crying, raging, and talking to the police."

"They went to the police," I repeated.

"Marcus wouldn't hear about doing anything else. He even threatened to sue the school for hiring her in the first place. That forced Rick to tell him the cops were already looking into her. Amelia and Marcus are going in with them when they give their statements."

I rose on tiptoe and kissed his cheek. "What about you? Did you talk to your father?"

He nodded.

"Do you want to tell me about it?"

He nodded again.

I waited. The silence pressed in on us as Jaxson gazed into the night, but I didn't rush him. I promised I would be there for him and that's what I would do.

When he spoke, his voice sounded strange. "I've only seen my dad cry once before this weekend," he whispered. "That was when Mom died. He wouldn't stop, Val. I didn't know how to make him stop."

"Jaxson," was all I got out before I was crying too.

Jaxson didn't cry, but that night we fell asleep on the floor beneath the window. I couldn't bring him into my room, but neither of us could be parted from each other. I fell asleep feeling warm and safe in his arms. I hoped he felt the same in mine.

Chapter Five

Weariness clung to me as we climbed the four flights to the senior floor, and it wasn't only because I went to bed late.

Walking into Roundtree's class felt like stepping onto a battlefield, but as we put our phones away and found our seats, I saw there was no war coming.

The class worked quietly on their homework, and whenever someone made a sound, Roundtree shushed them. There would be no screaming matches today.

I tried to do my individuals and societies homework, but every minute or two, I lifted my head to search the faces around me. Was Ace in this room? Were they the ones who made the decision we were waiting to hear?

The bell jarred me out of my thoughts. I put away my half-finished homework and followed my friends to lit class.

"Good morning, everyone," said our professor. "Next class, you will be choosing your book for your midterm assignment, but today, we're going over the elements of a great college essay. We'll go over examples, and then you'll craft your own using sample topics. Any questions?"

No one had questions so class got underway. I copied the notes even though I had done and redone my essay a dozen times. Somerset applications had opened a week before school started, though they weren't due until October. The essay topic chosen for the upcoming freshman class was almost fate.

What is the greatest hardship you've faced? How did you overcome it?

Where did I begin? Being raped, ending a life, becoming a teenage mother, entering the academy, finding that card in my locker, endless taunting, hounding, and bullying. I could have written them a book.

Deciding what to talk about hadn't been easy. I went back and forth until I had an essay I was pleased with, but depending on today, there could be more hardships to add.

I spoke about moving forward in my essay. I hoped that today we would do so.

I sensed the same feeling buzzing through the group. Kicked out of the library, we spent our study period in the dorm. After, we went back to the main building for lunch. Jaxson leaned into me when we reached the fourth floor.

"Val." He bumped my shoulder. "With everything that's going on... I needed last night. Can it just be you and me again tonight?"

"I'd like that." I was desperate to know what was going on with Ezra and Maverick, but I respected that they needed their space. They would call me when they were ready.

Jaxson and I walked into Roundtree's classroom holding hands.

The professor waved his half-eaten apple at us. "No food in here. You'll have to hit the lunchroom."

That was no surprise. I pulled ahead of them, leading the way to the cafeteria, but Ryder and Jaxson were right on my heels. We stepped into the lunchroom and a ripple went through the room. One by one, people fell quiet under the effect my presence seemed to have.

I looked toward the dais and found the new Knights where I expected them to be. Isabella cut a piece of lasagna, brought it to her lips, and chewed delicately. After she swallowed, she dabbed the corner of her mouth with a napkin.

Anxiety twisted my gut into a tight knot as I waited.

Finally, she dropped her napkin down and pushed away from the table.

I thought she would address me. Isabella didn't look my way while she walked to the edge of the dais. "I know you all have questions—"

"Is the mark lifted?" Lola demanded.

"It has to be over," Juliet said. "Valentina didn't do anything wrong."

"Valentina Moon told us that she was marked because she discovered the former art teacher was a pedophile." Isabella swept the room until she landed on me. She looked me in the eyes and said, "She lied."

"What?! I did not lie!" I shouted, but I was not the only one.

"Why would you say that?" Claire cried. "How do you know it's a lie?"

"Of course it's a lie," said Isabella. It bothered me how calm she was. She spoke as though she was reciting an English paper. "If she was innocent from the beginning, she could have said so. There was no reason for her to keep quiet, especially after LeBlanc left the school." Behind her, Natalie and Darren got to their feet. "Valentina wasn't marked to hide someone else's secret; she was marked because the Spades discovered her own."

I reeled back. *What the hell is she talking about?*

"Rather than leave, she fought us, attacked us, turned the old Knights on the school, and then made up a story about a teacher who wasn't here to defend themselves to get the mark lifted."

Anger boiled my blood. "That is a load of flaming horseshit, Isabella! LeBlanc is who I say she is."

"Is she?" She lifted one perfectly plucked eyebrow, remaining the picture of calm. "Well, that load of horseshit came to me... from the Spades themselves."

Gasps went up around the room. The name "Spades" was on every mouth as they looked at Isabella in shock.

"I don't care what they told you," I announced. "They're wrong."

"If they're wrong, why hasn't this unknown victim of Scarlett LeBlanc materialized? They could prove your story, but no one has because they don't exist."

"They do exist, dumbass." I stalked toward her until I was a foot from the dais. "They've already gone to the police and told them everything."

Isabella's calm cracked. Surprise flickered across her face as her lips parted. "They have—"

"Gone to the police," I said again. "They have also told Evergreen the truth. So what do your precious Spades think about that? Who is lying now?"

Her mouth opened and closed but nothing came out.

"What are they going to say, Isabella?" Claire pressed. "The victim has gone to the cops *and* the headmaster. Everything Valentina is saying lines up."

"It sounds like they're the fucking liars," said Brian, one of Darren's friends. "What the hell are they trying to do? Why are they protecting her? You spoke to them. You know them. Tell us who they are so we can ask ourselves!"

"Yeah!"

The cry echoed in the space as Isabella's head whipped this way and that. "I-I don't know them."

"You're lying!" Genesis Smith roared. "She's protecting them too!"

She lurched to her feet and most of the class did too. I took the tiniest step back. I could sense something brewing in the air and it was turning nasty.

Isabella backed up too until she ran into the table. "I'm not protecting them. I don't know who they are. They— They sent me texts anonymously."

"You believe some anonymous person over Valentina?" Claire asked.

"We believe them"—Natalie shot forward and stood next to her friend—"because they told us the real reason Valentina was marked. She's the one who lied. She is doing all of this to hide the truth."

"What truth?" I snapped. "What are you talking about?"

Natalie leveled her poisonous gaze on me. "Why won't you give the innocent act a rest? It's all out now so why keep lying?"

I threw up my hands. "You're still batshit stupid. I don't know what you're talking about!"

"Fine. If you won't spill it; I will." She spun to face the room. "Valentina was marked in freshman year because the Spades found out her secret. They discovered she was hiding a kid that was fathered by..."

Every fiber of my being went still as those words came from her mouth. *No. They can't know. They can't—*

"...her middle school teacher."

I was far away when the end of her sentence reached me, or at least, that was what it felt like. The roaring in my ears was drowning everything out as my brain tried to make sense of it.

Fathered by... who?

"That's not true!" Ryder's shout broke me from my fog. "They're the ones making shit up!"

"Really?" Natalie challenged. "Then why has Valentina been hiding her kid for all these years?"

I didn't need Ryder to defend this one. "Because he's none of your fucking business."

Her smirk widened. "Just like you'll say the father is none of our business, but why is that? Why won't you tell anyone?"

I swallowed hard. My body shook as I glared at her.

"Go on. Tell us who your kid's dad is." The chaos had finally settled. No one was yelling or arguing as Natalie faced me down. "Ace said that you wouldn't—that you *couldn't*. You're the one who has been protecting a pedophile. You seduced Mr. Garret, got knocked up, and hid it so he wouldn't end up in jail."

My chest heaved from the force of my ragged breaths. My middle school teacher's name had been Mr. Garret. He was kind, thirty years old, and moved out of the country before I graduated. He was long gone and there was no way he could be used to disprove their story. Ace had certainly done their homework.

"Mr. Garret is not the father of my son," I forced through gritted teeth. "He was a nice person who never laid a finger on me and you and your Spade buddies should be ashamed for dragging an innocent man into this, but this is what they do. They aren't above disgusting things like this to get what they want."

"If that's true, tell us who the father is."

"He's none of your—"

"I'm the father."

My head snapped around. Ryder moved to my side, silver eyes locked on to Natalie. "Adam is my son."

Natalie's confidence took a hit for the briefest moment as she lost her grin. "What? You?"

"That's right. I've known Valentina since before the academy. She got pregnant and gave birth to my son. We didn't tell anyone because we don't have to. Our kid isn't your business."

I gazed at Ryder as he took my hand. *I can't believe he's doing this for me—for us.*

Natalie looked unsure for a moment, but then the snarl slammed back into place. "If you're the father, you'll be on the birth certificate, or better yet, a quick paternity test will prove it." She scoffed. "You think I buy your boyfriend's little confession? The kid doesn't even look like him. He's making it up. Just like whoever you've got singing to the police is making it up."

"You'll believe what you want to believe." I turned from her and addressed my class, looking over the confused, angry, and sickly faces. "This is the truth. Scarlett LeBlanc was a horrible person who used her authority to hurt children. When I found out, she used her power as a Spade to hurt me. I don't know why the Spades would defend someone like that—"

"They're not!" Natalie cried. "The Spades are about one thing and one thing only: protecting the academy. We're the best school in the country, and we stay that way because Evergreen only allows the best. The Spades didn't want a slutty, old-cock-loving afternoon special ruining our reputation."

I gave her a hard look. "Are you finished?"

She scowled, but didn't reply.

"As I was saying," I continued as I turned back around. "The Spades have decided to protect their own, but the problem is they are using *you* to do it. They speak through the Knights like puppets. They ask you to drive the marked out while they hide in the shadows with their motives. You decide who you will believe. You decide how you're going to act, but I'll tell you this: I'm not going anywhere. I won't be driven out because those fuckers have gone too far."

My eyes passed over the crowd. "You shouldn't have brought my son into this, Ace. You've made it my mission to hunt you down, expose you, and beat your ass. The truth will come out and you'll remember this moment as your biggest fucking mistake."

Hot with rage, I turned my back and stalked to the door. Sofia had just put her arm around me when a noise from behind stopped us dead. The sounds didn't make sense to me, and when I peered over my shoulder, the sight didn't either.

Half of the class had gotten to their feet and they were following me out. Across the room, Airi Tanaka finally rose from the table. She looked at Darren and her friends, then without a word, she climbed off the dais and fell in behind Juliet.

The door swung shut on Natalie's and Isabella's shocked faces.

"IT WAS INTENSE. THE whole thing was unreal. Half of the students showed their support for me." I blew out a breath. "I still can't believe it."

"I can't believe that they *all* didn't walk out," Ezra countered.

Walking back to the dorm and discovering Ezra had texted lifted my mood. I called him right away. It was great to hear his voice after everything that happened.

I leaned back onto my pillows and curled my legs under me. "It sucks, but Eric, Claire, and Ciara did. Even Lola and Brian and they acted like beasts when I was marked. I guess there was good hiding behind their fear of the Spades. They've finally been pushed too far."

"Val, that's good but... you know it's not over, don't you? Ace has come back and hit you hard. I can't imagine what they'll do now that half the class has been turned against them."

My mood was sinking faster than an exploded blimp. I knew he was right, but today had been a victory. If this was war; I needed more allies. "They'll strike back, but I'll be ready for it. The list is getting shorter, Ezra. No matter what happens, I'm going to find them and end the Spades for good. No one will suffer under their hands again."

"I've learned never to doubt you, Valentina Moon. If anyone is going to do it; it's going to be you."

The smile returned to my lips. "Let's stop talking about Ace. Tell me about you. How is your mom?"

"She's doing better—coming to terms with it. She wanted me to stay home for another week, but I'll be back at school on Monday."

"Jaxson told me you've gone to the police."

"She insisted, and if it gets people to believe you, then I'll do anything. Even though we both know their investigation will lead nowhere."

"I don't know..." A thought detached itself from my subconscious. Something someone said had been nagging away at the back of my mind. "Their investigation won't go anywhere... but ours might."

"What does that mean? Do you know something?"

"Nothing for sure." I shook my head. "Hey, we said we were going to give this a rest for a few minutes. About this weekend. Are we still—"

"Yes," he answered. "We are still on for this weekend. I've been waiting too long to be with you. We're not putting this off for another second."

A smile played at my lips. "I'm glad to hear that. I miss you."

"I miss you too. I've got the whole weekend planned. I promise you'll love it."

"I know I will."

"Ezra?" Amelia's voice came through the phone. "Sweetie, are you almost done? I need to talk to you."

"I should go," said Ezra. "I love you."

"I love you too."

I hung up and placed my phone on the nightstand. It had been a long day, but sleep was way off. I padded out of my room and down to the first floor. Jaxson's door was open. I stepped in front of the entrance and found him on his bed, talking on the phone like I was.

I drank him in. Jaxson Van Zandt was truly gorgeous. His pants were low on his waist, allowing the band of his silk boxers to peek through. He wore no shirt which let my eyes travel over the bumps and ridges of his torso. I thought he was cute when he was fully shaved, but the style he sported now was perfect on him. His blond locks fell into his eyes and begged me to brush them away.

It was hard to steal time with the boys with everything that was going on, but it was worth it to have even five minutes with them.

"I know, Dad," he said. Jaxson glanced up and waved when he saw me. "No, I want to be here. She's gone. Right. Okay. I'll talk to Evergreen. Good idea. Alright. Love you too. Bye."

Jaxson sighed as he hit end. "He's been talking to Marcus and Amelia. He thinks he should have pulled me out of school too."

"Do you want to stay home? Get away from the craziness for a bit while you sort stuff out?"

"Getting away from the craziness means getting away from you. I definitely don't want that." Jaxson heaved himself off the bed and snagged his shirt from the floor. "They've also been talking about hiring private investigators. They don't trust the police to track her down themselves."

I stepped in as far as the ever-watching cameras would allow me. "We don't want her to be tracked down."

Jaxson crossed the room and took my hands. They dangled between us as he leaned in until our noses brushed. "We started something that can't be stopped. If we try, it will look suspicious. There's no reason to think any investigation will lead to the cliffs."

"Unless Ace releases that video."

"I've been thinking about that." Jaxson reached back and flicked off the light. "Come on. Let's talk outside."

We slipped through the front door into the evening. The sun was beginning to set but there was still enough light out for us to paint the sky. Jaxson picked up where he left off when the dorm was at our backs.

"Ace could have released that video at any time, but they haven't. I don't know what they want, but getting us in trouble with the police doesn't seem to be it. Plus, it was an accident. None of us pushed her and if it came out now, people would see a predator screaming and threatening her victims. It would only support that LeBlanc isn't innocent."

I nodded. What he was saying was making sense. "Ace has chosen to paint me as a liar and LeBlanc as the random person I accused. A video of her ripping my hair out and dragging me toward the edge of a cliff wouldn't support that theory."

"Yes." He moved in front of me, stopping me in my tracks. "We may not have to worry about the video, but we're not in the clear. There is plenty more the Spades can do."

"I know." I shook my head. "I can't believe they would pull that crap with Mr. Garret. At least I know why Ace went silent on me. They were working overtime on how they would discredit me."

"Whoever is leading the Spades is twisted like I've never seen. You'd think it would be easy to spot someone like that."

I grasped his forearms. "We're getting close, Jaxson. I can feel it. Somehow all of this fits together. I just need to make the connection." I looked over my shoulder at the castle-like structure that was Evergreen Academy. "I'm going to expose the darkness that has been hiding beneath this school."

"I'M GLAD FOR A BREAK." Sofia folded a pair of jeans and placed them in her bag. "It's great we have more people on our side now, but it's been feeling like a powder keg that is moments away from exploding."

"Can't disagree with you there," I muttered.

The ban had continued for the marked and those on their side. We were barred from the cafeteria, library, and everywhere the remaining Knights—and the Spades who acted through them—could control. The difference now was that it was friend against friend, teammate against teammate, or even family against family. The sides had been chosen and anger and bitterness were brewing against those they felt had chosen wrong.

"You heard Airi today," Sofia continued. "Saying that she was a Knight too and she's not going to stand for being kicked out of the cafeteria."

"I heard all the people agreeing with her too, but if we roll in there demanding a place, I doubt the other side will sit by quietly."

"They say this is what Walter did." Her hands stilled in the middle of folding a blouse. "He turned people against the Spades. What if they try to hurt us? We can't go everywhere as a group all the time."

"Yes, we can." I crawled across her bed until she was looking me in the eye. "We'll always watch out for each other. We're a team."

She smiled. It was a tiny one and gone as quickly as it came, but it was there. "You're right."

"Of course I'm right. So you focus on your weekend with Zane. I think pretty much everyone got a pass. We're all taking a break from this place."

"Zane and I are going to have my house to ourselves. There is a problem with one of the overseas deals and Mom went to meet Dad." Sofia lowered her voice. "But that's not the interesting part. Tomorrow night, Zane and I are going to double-date with Kai... and Paisley."

"Are you serious? He asked her out?"

"Yep. About time, am I right? They don't want anyone to make a big deal of it while they're figuring it out so we've been sworn to secrecy." She shrugged. "But I tell you everything so now you know."

I laughed. "You do tell me everything. You gave me graphic details about that thing Zane did on the night of your anniversary. I couldn't look at him for a week without blushing."

"*I* couldn't look at him for a week without tearing his clothes off. Hopefully there will be more of that tonight." She winked. "For you too."

I flopped back onto the sheets. "I can't wait to see Ezra. It's weird being at school without him."

"What about Maverick? How is he doing?"

"We've talked every night since Tuesday. He's sure he'll be back next week, but doesn't know what day."

"It's crazy they both got food poisoning."

"Yeah," I replied, averting my eyes. "Crazy."

Sofia packed up the rest of her things and we went down to the front room. Sofia wasn't lying about everyone getting away. Bags littered the floor and people were running around getting last-minute things and pulling on their jackets.

"Zane!" Kai shouted down the hall. "Get your ass out there. The car's waiting in front of the gates."

"So is mine." Paisley gave Sofia and me a hug. "Have a good weekend, Val." She let go and dashed for the door. I saw her throw Kai a secret smile on the way.

A hand snaked around my waist as Jaxson kissed my temple. "Dad wants me home so I'm heading out too. I'll call you."

I twisted around to give him a proper kiss on the lips. He left after we broke apart and I spotted Ryder coming down the hall.

"You're going home too?"

He nodded. Ryder walked up to me and pressed his mouth to my ear. "I've been thinking I need to have a talk with Mom."

"You mean...?"

He didn't go on. He just brushed his lips against my cheek. He was gone before the tingling sensation went away.

"Let's go, Val," said Sofia. "I'm more than ready to get out of here."

I didn't need to be told twice. The last ones out, I locked the door behind us and we headed down the hill to the wrought-iron gates. Sofia and I split up at the sidewalk, waving goodbye as she made for her driver and I went up to Ezra.

I broke into a run when that grin crossed his handsome face. I jumped into his arms and he caught me and swung me around.

"I guess you missed me."

"So much." I squeezed him tight. "I can't wait to start our weekend."

"It starts now."

I squealed when he suddenly snagged me under the legs. Bridal-style, he carried me to the car and placed me on the seat. The driver took off the second he closed the door.

"What are we going to do?" I asked as I snuggled into his side.

"I owe you two more labors."

"What?" I drew back and looked him in the face. "Ezra, I love that you guys wanted to do that for me, but trust me, I know you're sorry and you know that I've forgiven you. You don't have to do them anymore."

He bent and pecked me on the lips. "Yes, I do."

I sighed. "I had to choose the most stubborn men on the planet."

"You chose men who would do anything to show how much they care about you." He grabbed my chin and held me fast. "Damn, you're lucky."

"Am I?" My tongue darted out and tasted his finger. I had been away from him for too long and my body was feeling the loss. The combination of his touch, sweet scent, and those dark eyes drinking me in was undoing me. "Show me how lucky I am."

"Oh, I will." He glanced to the side. "When we're alone."

Get yourself under control, Moon. You're not jumping his bones in the back of a car, but just in case...

I scooted away and put some distance between us. He was too tempting. "Can I know what you have planned?"

"We're not staying at the house."

"We're not?"

"No. Things with Mom are still— Well, I figured it would be better if we had time to ourselves." I couldn't resist reaching across to take his hand. "We'll be staying in a hotel in Chesterfield."

"Chesterfield? Why there?"

Chesterfield was a town about an hour east of Evergreen. I had never been there, but it was where a couple of my classmates grew up.

"Because it's where I found it."

"Found what?"

"My second gift to you."

"I'm intrigued. Am I going to get this gift today?"

"Yep." He raised his arm to look at his watch. "We're going to make it just in time. You'll get that gift and then tonight"—a wicked grin curled his lips—"you'll get a few more."

"You're so naughty, Ezra Lennox."

"You have no idea."

Oh, but I did. The sexual encounters we've had have been *hot*. I could imagine what tonight would be like and my imaginings were driving me wild.

We started the ride on opposite ends of the car, but as we drove through the forest-lined streets, we drifted closer. Soon, I was back where I belonged, resting my head on his shoulder while he threaded his fingers through my hair. I was so content, I ended up jerking awake when the car came to a stop.

"Oops," I said as I stretched. "I fell asleep."

"That's alright. It's better you do that now, because you're not sleeping tonight."

Laughing, I nudged his shoulder. "So are we here?"

He nodded. A pleased grin took over his face as he pointed out the tinted windows. "We're here. I've been looking for months and finally found it."

Excitement building, I grinned too as I threw open the car door and rushed out to see...

...a movie theater.

I tried to hold on to the grin while Ezra climbed out behind me. It must not have worked because he burst out laughing when he saw my face. "You look disappointed."

"No, I'm not. I'm happy to be anywhere with you, but... you've been looking for months for a movie theater? You know there's one in Evergreen Promenade, right?"

He laughed again. He was enjoying himself too much and I was starting to think I missed something. "I wasn't looking for just any movie theater. It had to have something in particular."

"Reclining seats?"

Grinning, Ezra put his arm around my waist and walked us up to the ticket booth. "Two for Dawn's Majesty, please."

I was brimming with confusion, but I swallowed my questions. Whatever it is, I would find out soon enough.

"Are you hungry?" he asked as we stepped inside. "I have dinner reservations but we could get some popcorn or nachos."

"Nachos would be great."

He held me securely against his side as we stepped up to the concession stand. A few people lingering in the lobby glanced our way. Appreciative eyes looked Ezra up and down, taking in those piercing dark eyes, tousled hair, fit body, and the fine, expensive clothes that covered that body up. I didn't see myself as a possessive person, but at that moment, I was glad that he was all mine.

"Large nachos and two large sodas, please."

"Coming right up."

"I've been wanting to see this movie," I said as we moved to the side to await our food. "How did you know?"

"A movie about a strong, but dangerous woman plotting to retake the throne from the monarchs who unseated her family." He gave me a look. "That was all you, baby."

I swatted his shoulder even while I laughed. "What's that supposed to mean?"

"It means I love and fear you."

A pleasant thrill flooded me at hearing that he loved me. It was stronger than my eye roll. "You're so ridiculous."

"Here you are." The worker returned and set the nachos and two empty cups in front of us. Then he walked off.

"Wait," I called. "You haven't poured our drinks."

"It's okay, Val. We get them ourselves here."

"Oh. Okay."

I grabbed one cup while Ezra picked up the other and the nachos. We headed for the theaters. "I read the reviews the other day," I said, picking up our conversation. "They said it was great. There's supposed to be an incredible plot twist."

"I heard that too."

"If there's a sequel we have to... come back... and..." Words deserted me as Ezra stopped in front of the machine. With one look, I knew why we were here.

Suddenly, he appeared nervous. He rocked from foot to foot as he looked from me to the machine. "I've been looking for months," he whispered. "I've called a dozen theaters and even phoned the manufacturers until I found out only one theater in our area had these. My next step would have been to fly you out of the state."

I chuckled, eyes filling with tears as I looked at the customize-your-soda machine. It was the same model as those that used to take up the Evergreen halls.

"Why did you go through all of that trouble? I would have been happy seeing any movie with you while we drank plain sodas."

"Because." Ezra slipped his hand into mine and drew me in. "I fell for you over a cup of strawberry root beer. You blew into that library and faced me down without caring that I was a Knight or who my mom was.

"You never cared about any of that stuff. You've always just seen me. Even when I didn't want you to see what was underneath, you've opened me up, called me on my crap, and pushed me to be a better man.

"When I looked at you over that cup of soda, blushing even while you were annoyed with me, I saw that future. I saw *our* future. You were going to be the person who undid the perfect mask I was trying to create. I know that I don't deserve you. You've given me everything I hoped while I've let you down, but we're here now. We've made it to us, so it's right that we go back to where it started."

The tears were falling now—running hot down my cheeks as my heart filled with so much love, I thought it would burst. A thousand replies sprang to my lips. I wanted to tell him that he did deserve me. I wanted to say that he had given me so much over the years too. I wanted to say as beautifully as he did the future I saw for us. There were a thousand things I wanted to say, but I could only think of one that could say it all. "Ezra, I love you too."

Ezra captured my lips in a kiss that wasn't the wild battle of tongues, but sweet and slow like the night he first told me he loved me. I poured everything else I needed him to know in that kiss, and as he kissed me back, I knew he understood me.

"So," he began when we broke apart. I loved that he struggled to catch his breath. "What flavor you in the mood for? Orange Sprite? Vanilla Coke? Crème brûlée Pepsi?" He stepped back. "I think I'll try the—"

"No." I grabbed his arm, pulling him up short. A strong feeling had overtaken me and I wasn't pushing it aside any longer. "We need to go now."

He blinked. "Now? But what about the movie?"

"Fuck the movie." I spun and tugged him after me. "Is the driver still here? He needs to bring the car around."

"But— But— I got us dinner reservations."

"Your hotel better have room service."

We escaped out onto the sidewalk. I immediately swung my head around looking for the car. I thought I spotted it when Ezra stepped in my view.

"Val." He took my face in his hands. "Trust me, we want the same thing right now, but I want to do this right. I planned the whole night—the entire apology. The restaurant we're going to has peanut butter brownies and a courtyard where we can eat and look at the stars. I also—"

I gently placed a finger on his lips. "Ezra, that is so sweet and romantic. It means a lot to me that you've done all of this to show me how you feel, but I need you to listen. You don't have to apologize anymore, because I *know* how you feel. You love me and you don't have to prove it to me anymore. You've shown me in every way except one." I moved my hand and cupped his cheek. "So tonight, let's be together like we've been waiting so long for. What do you say?"

He let out a breathy laugh as he gripped my hand. "I say the hotel better have room service."

We found the car and the driver idling in a parking space and Ezra practically yelled "Chesterfield Grand Hotel" at him.

We made out furiously in the back seat as he hurried to the hotel. Our clothes stayed on and our hands above the waist, but the windows were nicely fogged up when the driver dropped us off in front of the sliding doors.

I thought I would burst out of my skin as Ezra checked us in. Months of waiting and now all that stood in our way was a chatty receptionist.

"Dinner is being served in the dining room now," she said. "You can also have room service delivered up to eleven o'clock."

"That's great," Ezra replied. He bounced on his heels as we tracked her movements. She was in no hurry as she made our key.

"Breakfast is from six a.m. to ten. May I suggest you enjoy it on the terrace tomorrow morning? If you wake up early enough you can enjoy the sunrise."

"Yep."

Beaming away, she set the key down in front of her instead of handing it over. I almost screamed while she typed something into the computer. "Do you have bags that need to be brought up?"

"We've got them." His hand inched toward the key. "What's our room number?"

"You are in room 254," she said brightly. "You're all checked in. I hope you have a pleasant stay at the—"

"Thank you." Ezra snagged the key and we ran for the elevator, not caring how it looked to people watching.

We attacked each other before the doors closed. Our hands were everywhere—pulling, tugging, and caressing. I had his shirt half off when he put his mouth to my ear.

"The things I'm going to do to you tonight..."

I moaned as my core pulsed with heat. "Please, finish that sentence. Tell me what you're going to do."

He laughed and I shivered as his breath skated over me. "I'd rather show you."

We fell out of the elevator when the doors opened and hurried to our room. Ezra got the door open. I shot past him, racing toward the bed, but he caught me in the living room.

I shrieked as he spun me around and grabbed the hem of my dress. He had it over my head and on the floor in seconds and the rest of our clothes soon followed.

Ezra lifted me up. His hands cupped my ass as he carried me to the bed.

I couldn't stop myself from getting one last tease in. "You do have a condom this time, don't you?"

"You're very funny, Moon. I've got a box of condoms in that bag and no reason to leave this room. We're finishing what we started in that sauna."

I yelped when I suddenly found myself flying. Ezra threw me on the bed, and then jumped on top of me before I could recover. He kissed me mid-laugh. I was brimming with happiness. I loved him. I would finally show him how much.

We smiled at each other when he pulled back. "I promised the first time we did this that I would go slow and take my time. I don't know if I'll be able to keep my promise."

"That's okay." I draped my arms around his neck. "We can count the last year as going slow."

Ezra bent and kissed me again. His mouth remained on mine as he nudged my legs apart. I knew what he was going to do as I slid my hand down between us. Ezra swallowed my gasp when he slipped his fingers into my core. Then I swallowed his.

I wrapped my hand around his length and stroked, matching his pace as he probed the spot he knew drove me crazy. He picked up speed and my back arched off the bed until I couldn't maintain our kiss. I moaned as I tugged and stroked him, enticing the most delicious sounds from Ezra. I wanted to make him feel as good as he was making me.

The sensations tantalizing my body were reaching a fever pitch. He crooked his finger and black spots danced in front of my vision. I knew it was coming and I went faster. I wanted us to go over the edge together.

"Fuck, Val," he hissed. "You have no idea the things you do to me."

I might have said something in reply, but Ezra hit that spot again and the black spots exploded into bursts of light. A breath after me, I heard him groan and I stroked his length as he rode the wave down.

"Damn."

I laughed breathlessly. "My thoughts exactly."

Ezra didn't have time to recover before I grabbed his shoulders and shoved. He let out a small shout as I flipped him over and straddled him. His hair wasn't perfect anymore. I pushed back the strands that fell across his face and bit my lip hard when I looked into his eyes. A dark promise of passion and all-consuming lust were held in those obsidian pools.

Our eyes were locked as he put his hands on my thighs. "Don't move," he whispered.

"I won't."

He didn't break eye contact as he moved down the bed and positioned himself between my thighs. It was me who closed my eyes as he licked my core. A moan ripped from my throat as my eyes fluttered shut. Ezra's tongue tasted and probed me until another orgasm rocked my body.

I slipped off of him and fell boneless at his side. My chest heaved as I struggled to catch my breath. "C-condom," I got out. "Now."

He chuckled. "I kinda like a lady who is bossy in bed."

He moved quick but I landed a whack on his arm as he dove for the bag at the bottom of the bed. We were grinning at each other like fools when he came back to me and pressed his body on top of mine. Being with him was what sex should be. I felt safe and comfortable with him. I had fun with him. It was everything I once thought it couldn't be.

"I love you, Valentina."

"I love you too."

Ezra pushed inside of me as I uttered the final word and I lost the capability to speak. We devolved into moans, cries, and pants as he moved. My cries reached their peak as he thrust hard, and soon, I was brought to a screaming orgasm. My nails dug into his back as he followed me.

Ezra peppered kisses along my jaw as the room came into focus. He settled next to me and pulled me to him until we were gazing at each other across the pillows, noses brushing.

"I knew it was going to be good," he said, "but that was incredible."

Giggling, I gave him a peck on the lips. "How big is that box of condoms? 'Cause I'm pretty sure we're going to need more."

"HEY, THAT'S MINE."

I smirked at him as I popped his fry in my mouth. "I've let you do unspeakable things to me for the last two hours. You can share your fries with me."

We were snuggled up in bed, naked as the day we were born, and indulging from the trays of rooms service laid out before us.

He laughed. "I guess that's fair. Want to steal my salmon too?"

"Yes, please."

Ezra cut off a piece of the flaky, buttery fish and fed it to me. I sighed as I snuggled into his side. "This is perfect. I don't want to leave."

"I wish we didn't have to. It's nice to get away and do something that's..."

"Normal."

"Yeah." Ezra turned his head toward his bag. "Normal."

My smile dimmed. "Your bag has been buzzing all night. Is it your mom?"

"Most likely. I told her I would be gone for the weekend, but I didn't give her details. I know she wants a decision."

"About what?"

He sighed. "About us going to counseling."

I raised my head off his shoulder to look him in the eyes. "Counseling?"

"She's been having a hard time. She thinks that if she hadn't worked or traveled so often, she would have been there to see what was going on. She's trying to make up for it now, but I think the counseling is mostly for her."

I pressed a kiss to his cheek. "Do you want to go?"

Ezra held still for a while, but after a minute, he nodded. "I do, and I'll call her and tell her that I will, but right now"—his lips curled into a grin as he looked at me—"is all about you."

Smiling, I slipped my hand under his arm, reaching for his tray. "Can I at least finish your dinner before you have your way with me?"

"Nope."

The room service spilled to the floor as we went down laughing.

"I'M GOING TO DROP YOU off at school. Then I'll go back home to get my things and talk to Mom."

"Sounds good."

The car pulled up to the gates of the academy. I kissed Ezra goodbye and hopped out. Evergreen Academy expected students out on a weekend pass to return to school by noon on Sundays. Ezra got me back five minutes before the deadline. Stepping onto the pavement, I saw that I wasn't the only one cutting it close.

Sofia and Zane strolled across the pavement, laughing at a private joke. She lit up when she saw me. "Hey, Val. Did you have fun with Ezra?"

"It was amazing. What about you guys?" I wagged my eyebrows at her. "Did you have *fun*?"

She grinned unrepentantly. "We definitely did. The double date went well too. We went back to my place after, but Paisley and Kai stayed in the Promenade and ended up at the park. She said they stayed up all night talking."

"I'm happy for them. I know Kai was having a hard time after leaving his ex-girlfriend back home."

Zane threw his other arm around me. The three of us headed up to school arm in arm. "It's good my brother is moving on, but they both want to keep this quiet. This place is getting insane, and they want to have something that the new Knights, the Spades, and their minions can't touch."

"I get that," I replied. "Maverick and Ezra are coming back this week. I'm glad we're all going to be together, but I have a feeling things will only get more complicated."

"No doubt you're right."

"Hey, Thomas."

The three of us pulled up short. I turned around and found Jaxson on our heels.

"I already have to fight your twin to keep him off my girl. You gonna be a problem too?"

Zane threw his hands up in surrender. "I don't want any trouble."

Jaxson cut off my laugh with his kiss. Sofia and Zane walked off throwing catcalls over their shoulders as we deepened it.

I rested my forehead against his when we broke apart. "How are you? Is everything okay?"

He nodded. "I'm fine, but I don't know about Maverick."

"What?" I pulled back. "What do you mean?"

"He sent me a text. He said something is going down at the dorm."

"At the dorm? Did he say what?"

Jaxson held up his phone. "He just texted me. I didn't get a chance to ask."

"Then let's go." I grabbed his hand and spun in the direction of the dorm. I could see my friends converging on the lone building steps away from the fountain. Sofia and Zane reached the door and walked in while Kai and Paisley strolled a few feet ahead of us. Worry quickened my steps until Jaxson was running to keep up with me.

"Baby, I'm sure everything's okay. He would have said if it wasn't."

Kai glanced over his shoulder when he reached the porch and caught us on his tail. "Hey, you two. What's—"

I sidestepped him and ran up the steps. I threw open the door and skidded to a stop behind Sofia. My mouth fell open as I took in the sight that brought my best friend and her boyfriend to a halt.

"Listen up!" Gus bellowed. "Boys are on the second floor and girls on the first and third. No fighting over rooms. They have been assigned. All dorm rules apply..."

I took my eyes off him as Maverick stepped out of his room loaded down with a duffel bag. He walked over to us when he saw me.

"What is going on?" I asked as I slipped through Zane and Sofia.

Maverick's reply was to hook his finger through the lining of my jeans and draw me in. "Mav—"

He captured my lips in a searing kiss that blew away my anxiety. It suddenly hit me hard how much I had missed him.

"Can we go outside and talk?" he whispered against my lips.

I nodded without speaking.

Together we walked out of the chaos and onto the porch. Maverick led me off to the side as people came in and out of the door.

"It's exactly what it looks like," he began. "The guys have been telling me what's going on and it seems everyone that stood by you has been kicked out of the dorm. They live here now."

I gaped at him. "Everyone? But that's half the senior class. There aren't enough rooms."

"You're right." Maverick folded his arms as he leaned against the wall. "That's why most of us are going to have to double up."

"This is— This is insane! They can't do this."

"They *are* doing it, and it's not just the seniors. Gus has been shouting at us to hurry up because he has to supervise the junior, sophomore, and freshman moves."

"You mean the underclassmen—"

"The school is split down the middle."

I twisted around at the third voice. Eric stood on the steps with a suitcase at his feet. He walked up to us, his face unreadable. "Those who will follow the Spades and those who won't."

Stiffly, I faced him. "You've chosen to be one who won't. Why?"

"This is getting out of hand, Val. I don't know what to think, but I'm not willing to be on the wrong side of this one."

My hands curled into fists. Maverick reached out and grasped my shoulder, most likely sensing the effect those words hand on me. "All I ever wanted was to go to school, make friends, and get my diploma. I didn't want to get involved with the Spades. *They* got involved with me."

His expression didn't change. "I see that now. It's why I'm here."

"I did not want it to come to this." I stepped closer until there were only inches between us. "But now that it has... I'm not backing down. Scarlett hurt innocent kids. She attacked me. She used her position as a Spade to turn the school on me. I can believe the Spades didn't know what she was, but now they do and they have chosen to stand against me. I'm not backing down." My eyes pierced into him. "And I don't have time for anyone who doesn't have my back."

"I get why you don't trust me—"

"I have no reason to trust you. You've abandoned me *twice*."

"That wasn't about you."

My eyes popped. "Excuse me? How is it not about me?!"

The muscles in his jaw tightened. He broke eye contact, glancing away as his gaze grew unfocused. I thought for a while that he wouldn't answer, but slowly his reply came. "You know that Edens have been at Evergreen since the start. Since I was little, all I've ever heard about was my legacy. My grandmother drove home that the Edens were a part of making Evergreen what it is today, and *I* would be a part of its future. In my house, there's no question of if you should obey the Knights. You do. There's no wondering if the mark system is right. It is. There is no doubting whether you should fear the Spades. You should."

He shifted to look me in the eyes. "Choosing to back you meant going against my family and... you've met my grandmother."

I tried to fight it, but a niggle of understanding was working its way in. What he did was wrong. He was the worst friend imaginable, but at the end of the day, I always knew I had my family's support no matter what I did. I guess Eric didn't feel the same.

He must have seen that understanding in my eyes because he changed. Eric's expression softened until the veil pulled back far enough for me to see the internal battle raging in him.

"I did what I thought I had to do then," he continued, "and now I have to do this. Can that be enough?"

We stared at each other for a long time, neither one of us moving. I was holding his gaze when I said, "No."

He blinked. "No? What do you mean no? No, it's not enough?"

"That's right."

"Val." Maverick's voice was soft, but I heard the question in that one word.

"It's not enough that you walked out of that cafeteria," I plowed on. "You walk away all the time."

He winced. "So you want me to leave."

"No, I want you to help." His face crumpled in confusion. "I told you I'm not backing down. I'm going after Ace and I'm going to find them and expose that psycho and any other Spades hiding in the shadows. It's not enough for you to sit by. The only way I'll know for sure you're on my side is if you take them down with me."

He threw up his hands. "What do you expect me to do?"

"To start with... I want to go back to your house. Or you can go home and bring it back to me."

"Bring what?"

"Your dad's senior yearbook." I peered over my shoulder at Maverick as he came over to join us. "It's something that Evergreen and the police kept saying about Scarlett LeBlanc—something I never heard or thought of before."

Maverick's eyes sharpened. "What did they say?"

"They called her Mrs. LeBlanc."

"Mrs." Eric spoke before Maverick could find a response. "She's married?"

"She must be," I replied. "Or she used to be. I didn't consider that someone like her could be a 'Mrs.' but it explains why I didn't find her father in the yearbook. She has a different last name."

"So you want my dad's yearbook so you can try to find her father? What's the point?"

"I didn't get a chance to look at the entire senior class last time because I was interrupted by your grandmother. Even if I can't be sure who it is, I can narrow it down."

Maverick spoke up. "How does that help us?"

"I didn't get to look through the yearbook but I did learn something. I asked Eric's grandma why she was chosen to be a Knight and she said it was pretty much set in stone because of her last name." I gestured at Eric. "When I first met you, you were pissed that you weren't chosen. You thought your family made you a lock. Well, what if LeBlanc's family had to do with her being chosen as a Spade? What if her dad was one too? If we could find him, maybe he would talk to us—tell us what he knows."

Maverick reached for my hand. "Even if he is still around and we could track him down, why would he admit to being a Spade? Why would he talk to us at all? We're accusing his daughter of being a child molester and attempted murderer."

"We don't have anything else to go on. I've gone over the list of Ace suspects a million times, but I'm no closer to figuring out who they are. Now that they've stopped talking to me, I need another angle. We need to know more about the Spades because they know everything about us." I spun on Eric, making him jump. "Bring me the yearbook."

"Fine. I'll get a pass for next weekend."

"Thank you. Also, I need you to tell me everything you know about Evergreen, its history, and about your dad."

"My dad?"

"He was a Knight when everything went down with Nora Wheatly, Walter McMillian, and the Spades. He has to know more about what pushed the Spades to do what they did, or why your grandmother called Nora a common slut. He must have told you. What did he say?"

"My father doesn't tell me as much as you think." He began backing away. "Look, I need to finish unpacking, but I'll do what you want. I'll get the book, talk to my dad, and tell you what I can find out." Eric bent and gathered the straps of his bag. "There's no going back after this. Helping you is my only option."

"Glad we're on the same side for once."

Eric didn't reply. He just took himself inside and shut the door softly behind him. Maverick was waiting with his arms out when I turned around and I fell into them.

"I missed you, Beaumont. I didn't want to call too much because I figured you needed space."

"Thanks for that. I missed you too, but it's been intense. Mom and Dad haven't had as much time to deal with it as I've had."

"Did they—"

"Hey, can we talk about something else?" he cut in gently. "It's been too long since I've held you. That's all I want to do right now."

"Okay." I burrowed into his chest, breathing in a scent that was distinctly Maverick. "That sounds good to me."

Chapter Six

"You don't have to do this." I clamped down on his hand. It was too hard if his hiss was anything to go by. "The police and Evergreen know. That's enough."

"That's not enough. They are using our silence to paint you as a liar," Ryder replied. He freed himself from my grasp, but touched the back of his hand to mine, keeping contact. The five of us were standing in the courtyard before the main building. That was as far as I got before I made them stop, sending everyone else ahead.

"We have to do this, Val," Jaxson agreed. "The hard part was telling our folks. We can handle whatever is next."

"But they still might not believe you," I argued. "They could think you're saying it because we're together."

"Maybe," Maverick said, "but it will still be harder to dismiss all five of us."

Gentle pressure against my back moved me forward. "Come on, Val," Ezra said. "It'll be okay. Trust us."

It was hard to argue with Ezra, let alone all five of them. I knew nothing I could say would change their mind, especially when they saw themselves as protecting me.

I snagged Ryder's hand again when we entered the stairwell. As the boys drifted further ahead of us, I whispered to him.

"We didn't get a chance to talk yesterday. Did you speak with your mom?"

He kept his eyes straight ahead as he nodded.

I squeezed his hand. "How is she doing? How are *you* doing?"

"She is... taking it harder than I thought."

"Ryder, I'm sure she—"

"Val." He wasn't loud or harsh, but something in his tone made the words die in my throat. "I don't want to talk about this right now."

"Yeah," I croaked after a minute. "Of course."

"Thanks."

Ryder didn't look at me the whole time we spoke, and he kept his face forward as we left the stairs and walked onto the fourth floor. The bell was minutes away from ringing so there were no students to gawk and whisper at us. We took that for the win it was and hurriedly got our things from our lockers before meeting back up in front of Roundtree's classroom.

"Go in first, Val," said Maverick. "We'll be right behind you."

"But—"

"Please."

I forced my feet to move. Even while I could understand that this was something they needed to do themselves, everything in me wanted to be there for them. I pushed through into the classroom and got the reaction I was expecting. The room quickly fell silent. I looked around and stopped dead in front of Roundtree.

This I was not expecting.

The expression "battle lines were drawn" was ringing clear in my head as I took in the two distinct groups glaring at each other across the room. Natalie and her crowd had taken up residence near the window while the group that included my friends were on the other side. There was a space between them big enough that you could drive a car through.

It wasn't a conscious thought that made me turn on Roundtree. The guy was tapping away at his computer. The easy smile hung on his lips and that handsome face looked everything but concerned. He didn't notice I was standing there until I spoke.

"Aren't you going to do something about this?" His fingers stilled. "How can you just sit there when you know what's going on?"

Slowly, he raised his head. The smile hadn't dimmed. "You should sit down, Miss Moon."

Rage flared up in me fierce and burning. "You should do your damn job! The whole school is being torn apart and you're either sitting on your ass or standing out in the hall. What is the fucking point of you?"

The silence in the room became even more absolute. It was as though no one was breathing as Roundtree and I locked eyes. Slowly, he rose to his feet.

"You're right, Miss Moon. So how is this for doing my job: you have detention with me every day for the rest of the semester."

"But you can't—"

"Want to go for next semester too?"

I closed my mouth with a snap. I glared at him hot enough to burn a lesser man to cinders, but he just smiled at me.

"Put your phone away and take your seat. Now."

Rigidly, I did as ordered. Sofia grasped my arm in support when I took the seat in front of her. It was everything I could do not to fling a textbook at his pretty face when he went back to his computer. What got me to take my mind off of him was the door opening and the boys entering the room. Just like that, I didn't give a flip about Roundtree.

The four of them spread themselves out before the class and looked out over everyone with their heads held high. My breaths came shorter until they stopped altogether, bound in a clenched throat.

"Listen up," Ezra began. "We've got something to say."

A scoff to my left made me stiffen. "Sit down," Natalie spat. "You're not Knights anymore. We don't have to—"

Ryder pierced her with a look as cold as the silver in his eyes. "Shut the fuck up, Bard."

She turned bright red, but wisely didn't continue.

"Like I was saying," Ezra went on, "the whole school is spinning out because of Valentina coming forward and sharing the truth about Scarlett LeBlanc and why she was marked."

Penelope lurched to her feet. "She can't prove—"

"We're the proof." Maverick cut her off at the knees. "It happened while we attended the prep school with LeBlanc as our after-school art club teacher."

"She molested us," Ezra finished. "All four of us."

I thought I knew silence after telling off Roundtree. It was nothing compared to the hush that followed their speech.

Then Natalie shot up. "How do we know you're not just saying that to back up your girlfriend's story?!"

The spell broke and everyone was on their feet—shouting, yelling, threatening, and fighting. Through the havoc, I looked across at the guys. I gave them a smile that, one by one, they returned.

CLASSES WERE A STEP below unbearable that day. Arguments broke out wherever the boys and I went until professors demanded we work in total and complete silence for the rest of the lessons. They were so fried that Patchett kicked Juliet out of class when she made the mistake of asking the boy in front of her for an eraser.

It was almost a relief when I stepped into Roundtree's class. There was no one else in the room but the two of us. I could get the peace and quiet I had been sorely missing.

"Afternoon, Moon."

I don't know when we dropped the formal titles and went with last names, but I decided to follow suit. "Roundtree."

He patted a chair I hadn't noticed was sitting next to him. "Sit here. You'll be helping me grade assignments."

"Am I allowed to do that?"

"There isn't a rule against it. Semester grades are posted for the whole school to see after all."

That was a solid point so I walked around the desk and took my seat. Roundtree separated the stack of papers and placed half in front of me. "This is the answer sheet." He put another piece of paper dripping with red ink on top of my stack. "Get to work."

I got started without a word. For a while the only sound in the room was the faint scratching of pens and the occasional cough or sneeze. Roundtree went on with his work like I wasn't there, but now and then, my eyes would drift to the left, openly studying him. After about twenty minutes, I couldn't take it anymore.

I threw down the pen. "Can I ask you something?"

Roundtree replied without looking up from the worksheets. "No."

I scowled. "Well, I'm going to ask anyway."

To my surprise, he barked a laugh. "You just don't learn, do you? I can see you're a tough one."

"I am." I twisted around in my seat until my knees pressed against his leg. "I've dealt with bullying, murder attempts, assault, and cruel rich kids. Another semester sitting in a room grading papers is nothing."

He raised a brow. "It seems I need to upgrade my punishments."

"Or you could just talk to me."

Sighing, Roundtree twisted around in his chair until our knees knocked together. He decided to forgo the gel that morning so his brown hair fell into his eyes and over thick brows that were drawn together in slight irritation. "Don't let it be said I didn't encourage a bright, inquisitive pupil. What do you want to know?"

If he was willing to talk, I wasn't going to beat around the bush. "You said you used to be a Knight. Did you ever deal with the Spades?"

Roundtree scoffed. "Are you kidding? You can't really believe I'll have this discussion with you."

I folded my arms. "Of course you will. You're all about encouraging bright minds, right?"

He cracked a wry smile, but otherwise made no attempt to speak.

"Come on," I pressed when the silence got uncomfortable. "What could it hurt to tell me about your time at school." I gave him a mirthless smile of my own. "Unless... you're still afraid of them."

The corner of his eye twitched. "I wasn't afraid of them in the first place—let alone now."

"So what went on when you were a Knight? Did you have to deal with them? Did Ace talk to you?"

Roundtree studied me. Although his face gave nothing away, I could guess at what he was turning over in his mind. "The Spades were a creepy ghost story and Ace was nothing but a legend when I was a Knight," he finally said. "They did not speak to me or the other three."

"So you didn't believe they were around?"

He shrugged. "I believe someone put a card in my locker and made me shave my head. Why?"

I peered over my shoulder at the phone box. "Because Ace speaks to me—or at least they did. I pissed them off enough that they revealed themselves. Kind of like Walter McMillian forced them to act. But you know what I can't believe? That in all these years since his death, no one has tried to figure out who the Spades are. Someone must have searched. They must have seen something, heard something, or been in the right place at the right time. Someone has to know something that can lead me to them."

Roundtree cocked his head. "Possibly, but if all that has been said about the Spades is true, that someone is better off keeping their mouth shut."

"Do you know anything?" I challenged.

"Just told you I didn't."

"Would you tell me if you did?"

He laughed. "If there is some big conspiracy here, Moon, I can assure you I'm not a part of it. Nothing went down the four years I was a Knight. Everyone stayed in line, no one was marked, and the Spades had no reason to act." He reached out and tapped my forehead. "Nothing to stir an investigative mind."

"The fact that they're around at all should stir everyone's mind. I've been learning about the history of Evergreen and it still amazes me that they were ever allowed to form. Why did the headmasters and headmistresses let the Spades exist under their noses? They already had the Knights to keep people in line."

Shaking his head, Roundtree clicked his tongue. For some reason, he was frowning at me. "Come on, Moon. To have made it this far, you'd have to be as smart as you are tough. Why do you think no one in charge has ever stopped the Spades?"

"Because this school is full of crazy people."

I jumped when he suddenly leaned forward. My breath stuck in my throat when he leaned in close enough that his hair brushed against my forehead.

"Think, Moon." There was an intensity in his gaze that unsettled me. "What does this school value above all?"

My brain was fritzing out having him so close to me. I fought past the fog and tried to think of an answer. What does this school value? What does it—?

You know this, Moon, a voice spoke up. *What's rule number one?*

"Evergreen values its reputation more than anything," I whispered.

The smile returned. "That's right. So how do the Spades help Evergreen keep its shining reputation?"

"I don't know." I shook my head. "I mean, Sofia said once that they removed kids that can't be expelled, but still have to leave."

"Why can't they be expelled?"

"Because— I— They— I don't know!" I burst out. "If you're getting at something, just tell me."

His laugh ghosted over my face. I was locked on to his eyes so I jerked when he grabbed my hands. He pulled back as he held my hands out in front of us, palms up.

He shook my right hand. "Knights." Then he shook my left. "Spades. Since this school was founded, the Knights were formed to keep everyone in line, but they are only four people in one class. What problem do they face?"

"I guess they... can't be everywhere at once," I said as I gazed down at our hands. "They can't know everything that is going on in other grades and other classes. Not to mention people could clam up whenever they are around." I shifted to my left hand. "But the Spades don't have that problem. They can be everywhere and anyone. You could be spilling all of your secrets to a Spade and not know it."

Roundtree inclined his head, a smirk twisting his mouth. "She is smart. So tell me why that fixes the problem? Why do they use marks?"

I sat up straighter as it clicked into place. "Okay, so— So if some kid brags about buying a term paper or sneaking coke in the broom closet and a Spade overhears, there is no big fuss. No one gets hauled into administration. The press doesn't get wind of cheating or drugs at Evergreen. Our reputation isn't put at risk. They wake up one day and find a card in their locker and the problem takes care of themselves because... they would never admit what they did wrong nor would they stick around and be everyone's punching bag. They just go and Evergreen remains the school of perfection."

He nodded without breaking eye contact.

My hands felt slick in his palms. My unease was ratcheting up to a thousand but I didn't pull away. "That means that the Spades are," I whispered, "a bunch of snitches."

A laugh tore from Roundtree's throat. It seemed to surprise him as much as it did me. "If you boil it down, that is exactly what they are, but that's how it works. That's how it has always worked."

Roundtree held up the hand that represented the Knights. "The enforcers." Then he lifted my other hand. "And the informants." He pressed my palms together. "A society can't be kept in line without both. The Spades exist because they serve a function and they do it better than clueless professors and out-of-the-loop headmasters. No one stops them or questions a mark because they figure they must know something we don't want to know."

He gave my hands a little shake. "Knights and Spades are two sides of the same coin. Working together." He peered at me over the tips of my fingers. "Working as one."

A shiver went up my spine. He spoke like this was a friendly chat about the weather, but this was far from a joke. "But that backfired with me," I protested. "I didn't do anything wrong and this time a pedophile used their position as a Spade to handpick Knights that would stay as far away from her as possible and use a mark to silence me when I found out her secret." I pierced him with a look. "Or do you think I'm lying too?"

He didn't flinch. "It doesn't matter if I do. I'm either sitting on my ass or out in the hall, remember? I'm not the one you need to convince."

"You mean Ace," I stated. "But the Ace of Spades has made it clear they don't believe me. The only thing I can do now is find them and expose them for what they have done." I leaned in until my lips hovered above our hands, inches from his.

"I'm going to expose this *entire* rotten system for what it is. I don't care why it started or what dumbass thought it was a good idea. There are more important things than this stupid school's reputation and that is all the innocent kids that have been hurt. Me and the former Knights are just the ones we know about. There could be so much more because everyone was happy to stick their heads in the sand and convince themselves that the Spades knew best." I glared into his eyes and hissed, "That ends now. The Spades will be through for good by the time I'm done."

The effect of Roundtree's grin was twofold. It made goose bumps pop on my skin even while it made my stomach flutter. "I could almost believe that coming from you," he said softly. "Almost. You'd have to find them first, Moon."

"I—"

Bang!

"Val, are you— What the fuck is this?!"

I shot away from Roundtree like we were doing what it *looked* like we were doing. Ryder stood in the entrance, staring at us as Roundtree lazily reclined back in his chair.

"It seems our time is up," he said as my heart rocketed in my chest. "You can finish this tomorrow, Miss Moon."

I sprang up before he finished the sentence. Ryder's eyes burned into me as I yanked open the phone box and reached in. I made to face him when the phone buzzed in my hand.

I froze. My head was half in the box as I lifted my cell and pressed my thumb to the scanner. I don't know why I wasn't surprised when I saw Ace on the screen.

Ace: I'm impressed that you got your little boyfriends to lie for you. I don't know many guys who would announce to the world they have been molested just to please a girl. They must really love you.

As I say, I am impressed, but it is still a lie. Scarlett LeBlanc was a lot of things, but she would never do that. I want to apologize to you, Val. I did not take you seriously before. I did not realize what a cold, ruthless bitch you are or how willing you are to do whatever it takes to get what you want.

You are a true match for me. To show my respect, I will not underestimate you again. I am ready for your next move, Val. I hope you're ready for mine.

"Miss Moon?"

Roundtree's voice drew my attention in the middle of reading the text for the third time. I turned to face him and met that familiar grin, shining at me over the phone in his hand. "Goodbye."

"B-bye," I rasped.

I grabbed my backpack and raced out of the room. I made it three steps out of the door when Ryder grabbed my arm.

"Val, what the hell was going on in there?"

I didn't get a word out before Ryder pressed me against the lockers and placed his hands on either side of my head. "Did he try to kiss you?"

That snapped me out of my daze. "What? Are you insane? Of course he didn't."

"Then what was that?" he growled. "Why were you all snuggled up behind his desk?"

"No one was snuggled up." I put my hands on his chest and pushed him back. "We were just talking. He... helped me realize something."

Ryder's frown hadn't gone anywhere. "He needed to be in your face to help you *realize* something?"

I sighed. "Ryder, come on. Don't be like this. I know he's five-alarm hot—"

"Who said that?!"

"—but he can't help it. Men like that ooze sex appeal like an open wound spurts blood."

Ryder goggled at me. "Val, what the hell are we talking about?"

"I'm saying that people probably assume he's flirting with them if he even breathes in their direction, but he didn't say or do anything inappropriate with me. He was actually kind of an asshole."

He scoffed. "More reason for me to be suspicious. Everyone knows you love assholes."

I swatted his shoulder before he could duck me. "I'm about to shake one asshole loose if he doesn't behave himself."

"I'll tell Jaxson he needs to be worried then."

A giggle escaped me despite myself. I didn't know what I was going to do with this guy. "Seriously, Ryder, our professor isn't the problem, but he helped me understand what is." My phone was still in my hand. I held it out to him. "There's also this. Ace texted me."

In the next second, Ryder had my phone and was reading the message. His face twisted with every word he read.

"Get ready for their next move," he said. "Fucking hell. They're planning something else? Why won't they give it a rest? What more do they want?"

"Me." I raised my head and looked into his eyes. "This doesn't end until they've gotten rid of me."

"That's not going to happen."

"I know," I replied, inclining my head. "Which means I'd better be ready for whatever is coming next."

"*We* had better be ready."

That reply brought my first smile of the day to my lips. "Speaking of my we, we need to get the other guys and talk. I told you Roundtree helped me figure something out. Text them and tell them to meet us by the fountain."

Ryder didn't waste time asking for details. We sent out the alerts to the boys and twenty minutes later they were sitting on the rim of the fountain while I filled them in on what happened in Roundtree's class.

"Snitches?" Maverick repeated.

"Yes." I stood so the four of them could see me at once. "Don't you see what this means?" I got four blank looks. Heaving a sigh, I explained. "Roundtree has pretty much confirmed that there are more Spades—probably a lot more. If the Spades are supposed to be snitches, then there can't just be one. We know that Ace is close to us, but what about the other grades?

Who is keeping watch to make sure they stay in line? Who is down there while the Knights are up here with us?"

I could see instantly when it hit them over the head. "Shit, Val," Jaxson cried. "You're right. There has to be more. They'll be all over the damn school."

I held up my hands. "Enforcers and informants—working as one to make sure there is never a blemish on the sparkling façade of Evergreen." I gazed at one hand as an even harder truth washed over me. "And if the point of the Spades is to be informants, then we can be sure of one thing, they will be watching us. They are most likely—"

"Among the people who have said they're on our side," Ezra finished. "They might even be tucked up in our new dorm."

I wanted to deny it, but that was the only thing that made sense. "Yes."

There was a lull as that sunk in. The fountain bubbled happily behind us as the enormity of what we were facing became real.

"We can't trust anyone," I said. "Even those who cried and begged for forgiveness. Whatever our next move is, we don't let anyone outside of the five of us know."

"What about Sofia, Zane, Kai, and Paisley?" Maverick asked.

It hurt me to have to shake my head. "I trust Sofia absolutely and I know our South African transfers have nothing to do with the stuff that has been happening here, but I don't want to put Sofia in a position of having to lie to Zane. I don't want Zane to have to keep things from his brother, and I don't want to tell Kai we don't know if we can trust his girlfriend."

Ezra piped up. "Wait. Thomas is dating Paisley?"

I nodded as I forced myself to say the rest. "Paisley and I have gotten close again and I don't want to believe she could be a Spade, but after Scarlett, I know I can't afford to take chances. It's just us five. Okay?"

Ryder stood and took my hand. "It's always been just us five."

A smile found its way to my lips. "I've got the list. We should look at it again, go over what we know, and make a plan. Ace is going to hit hard. We need to hit back harder."

"That works for me."

Chapter Seven

In the weeks that followed, Evergreen Academy became a different place. The boys revealing the truth had the effect I anticipated even though it disgusted me. People accused them of lying to cover for me and that caused the people on the side of the Spades to dig in even deeper. But on the other side, those who supported us backed us even harder. Where we didn't have the numbers to fight back before, we did now—all the way down to the freshman class. We didn't know who among them we could trust, but even if people were faking it, they were doing a good job.

The new Knights kept up their campaign to keep us out of the lunchroom, library, clubs, and school events, but when we showed up en masse to the Halloween dance and a fight broke out, Evergreen stepped in and officially split the classes. We now had separate meal times, separate study periods, separate dorms, and separate homeroom teachers.

"I can't believe we have Markham again," Jaxson complained. He set my breakfast tray down in front of me and kissed my forehead before taking his own seat. "We'll never get free of that woman."

"I heard she asked to teach us after our English lit teacher quit," Eric added. "Evergreen jumped on it since she's had the most experience dealing with this class and our shit."

171

I snorted. "Tell me about it."

Maverick wrapped his arms around me and pulled me in closer. I was sitting in his lap while the rest of our group was spread out through the cafeteria. We were allowed back in by headmaster decree, but we had an early morning window of six a.m. to six thirty. We could take our breakfast back to the dorm but it wasn't the peaceful haven it used to be now that there are eighteen students crammed in a building only meant to hold twelve. The last few weeks had been tough, but through it all, Ace had not sent me another text. That worried me as much as it should.

I put my head in the crook of Maverick's neck and let the tension ease from my body. *At least the boys and I have never been closer. Even the mercurial Ryder has been opening up to me.*

I peeked across the table at him and caught his eye. He winked at me like we shared a secret.

"I suspect she's going to be dealing with a lot of shit on the end-of-semester environmental science trip," Kai piped up. "I heard the *other* class tried to get us kicked off, but it's for a grade so Professor Patchett shut them down. Still, Patchett is having Markham come to back her up and keep us all apart."

"This school has enough money to send us on separate trips," said Paisley. "It would be a good idea if they did."

"I think the Knights tried to get Evergreen on board with that after kicking us out failed," Kai said. "He didn't go for that idea either."

Paisley groaned. "Is anyone else not looking forward to this?"

We didn't have to answer. Of course we weren't looking forward to being forced together with the *other* class.

I scarfed down a couple bites of omelet until the bell rang warning us that we had five minutes to eat and get out before the other class came into the cafeteria. I pulled Eric aside as our group walked up to return our trays.

"Eric, what is going on with the yearbook?" I asked under my breath. "It's been weeks."

"It's not my fault." He took my tray, returned it, and then walked with me out of the room. "My mom has turned down all my requests for a weekend pass. She says I need to be at school focusing on studying and applying to college and telling her I want to go home and get Dad's yearbook isn't coming across as a good reason."

"Tell her it's for a school project or something."

"My mom is no dummy; she'll want receipts. Just trust me," he said out of the corner of his mouth while we neared Markham's new class. "I'll get it."

"Fine."

I let it drop as we entered the classroom. Markham nodded at us on the way to our seats. She stood in front of her desk, arms clasped in front of her as she waited patiently for us all to arrive. Ezra was the last to walk in. He sat down in the seat behind me and I put my hand out under the desk until I felt his fingers thread through mine. Things had been crazy but I was committed to spending time with my boys. Especially my littlest boy.

Thanks to Evergreen's new rule, I was allowed out on the weekends to be with Adam. I surprised him with a trip to the beach and bought him a bunch of clothes that he would grow out of in a week. Ezra was out last weekend too for therapy so he picked me up from home and we stopped at a hotel before continuing to school.

I blushed just thinking of the day before. Ezra had propped me against the hotel window and screwed me until I saw stars. There was no chance of anyone seeing my bare backside through the drapes, but at the time, I'm not sure I would have noticed if they were open or not.

"Attention, class." Markham pulled me out of my heated memories. "As you know, this weekend is the end-of-semester science trip. I want to ensure a few things are clear before we set foot off this campus.

"There will be no fighting or altercations on this trip. For the first time in the history of this school, we have lost a professor because they could not handle the stress of dealing with the senior class. From now on, and certainly on this trip, you will be on your best behavior. Is that understood?"

"Yes, ma'am," we chorused.

"Good." Markham took another minute to level us with her stern gaze before continuing. "As you know, your field trip will be to the Rayonner Bayou. You will put what you've learned this semester to the test by collecting water samples to examine for quality and organisms. In afternoon breakout sessions, you will discuss what you've learned about the water cycle, the life cycle of the animals that live in the bayou, and how we depend on swamps and river systems to survive. On the last day of the trip, you will have a free day where you will combine all you have learned in a two-page paper." She scanned the room. "Are there any questions?"

Sofia raised her hand. "Can we work in groups?"

Markham shook her head. "Except for group discussions, you will complete your assignments on your own. Professor Patchett is assessing your individual proficiency. The work you do on this trip will count toward fifty percent of your final grade so I hope you will keep that in mind.

"In regard to sleeping arrangements, we will be staying at a small hotel near the bayou. There are two to a room and you may choose your roommates. It goes without saying that opposite genders are not allowed in each other's rooms..."

Markham went on to say more, but I tuned her out. I had heard much the same from Professor Patchett and then again on the morning announcements from Headmaster Evergreen. We were leaving on the trip the next day and would be away for four days. We would get back on Friday and our parents would be waiting to take us home for winter break. The administration was determined that it not be a disaster. I wish I had as much faith in their rules and scolding.

We would all be crammed together in a little swamp and I couldn't help but think that it would be the perfect time for Ace to strike when we were miles away from campus with no Gus, no security cameras, and only two chaperones. If it crossed my mind, it must have crossed theirs too.

No, I was not looking forward to this trip.

"VAL, I'M TAKING YOUR Cucumber Splash conditioner. I ran out of mine."

"What's mine is yours, Richards."

Sofia stuck her head out of the bathroom. "We are sharing a room, right?"

I gave her a look. "Like that's a question. No one else is going to put up with your snoring."

"I don't snore!"

I laughed as she stomped back into the bathroom and continued raiding my medicine cabinet. "Zane will back me up on this," I called.

"Not if he knows what's good for him."

I laughed again. My mood was high even though in thirty minutes we would be hopping on the bus that would drive us five hours to the bayou. The sun had yet to dawn on this early Tuesday morning, but the dorm was a riot of noise. People shouted up and down the stairs, and through the open door, I could see people passing as they carried their things down to the front hall.

"I feel bad for leaving Paisley on her own," I heard her say. "Maybe Markham and Patchett will let us sleep three in a room."

"She can always bunk with Claire or Ciara." I put the last sweater in my bag and zipped it up. I was ready to go. Sofia still had her things scattered all over my bed. We had managed to keep our own rooms when the new guys moved in, but we often ended up spending the night with each other anyway. "Do you think there is any chance this trip will be as fun as our junior winter trip?"

"You mean when someone brained you with a ski?"

"Before that."

"No chance, Val." Sofia walked out of the bathroom loaded down with my hair products and tossed them in her suitcase. "I heard from the seniors before us that we're slogging in the swamp from sun up to lunch, then the rest of the time we're discussing life cycles and organisms until we pass out from boredom. This trip is all about the grade, not about the fun."

"But we'll still have fun, right, babe?"

I looked up to find Zane leaning against my doorframe. Kai stuck his head around his brother's body.

"Yes, baby," Kai moaned. "Tell me we're going to *muah muah*." He swirled his tongue around his lips, licking and smacking as I howled.

"I think I'm going to pass on that," Sofia said in between giggling. "But why don't you take that to your girlfriend?"

"Oooh. Good idea." Kai took off, leaving his brother shaking his head in his wake.

"You can't prove we're related," Zane mumbled. "Do you guys need me to bring anything down?"

"No, but they're handing out breakfast burritos in the cafeteria. Can you pick us up a couple?" I gestured at the mess that claimed my bed. "Sofia clearly needs more time."

"No problem."

By the time Sofia finished packing and we stepped outside with our things, the bus was idling in front of the gates.

"Only one bus," I said. "Why are they doing this to us?"

"It's too early. I hope the other class doesn't start something."

"We'll all get in trouble if they do." I picked up both our bags and set off for the gates, shuffling behind the rest of my dormmates. "The way things are going, the professors are getting fed up with us."

"They are welcome to get off their asses and intervene."

Sofia and I shared a look. The truth in that statement was so real I didn't need to comment on it. Professors have been quitting, moving, and doling out punishments, but no one has touched what we're really fighting about. They weren't going to enter this war.

As we slipped through the wrought-iron gates, I spotted Markham standing before the entrance to the bus holding her clipboard.

My eyes narrowed. *Except for you. I'm not letting you stay on the sidelines any longer.*

"I'm hoping everyone is too tired to start something," I said aloud, eyes still fixed on Markham. "I plan on going back to sleep."

"I'm with you."

I dumped our stuff under the bus and let Markham check us off her list. The bus was mostly full with the kids from our dorm. They took up the back rows so we headed back there to join them. Sofia slid in next to Zane, cuddled into his arms, and closed her eyes. I took the empty seat next to them and that afforded me a look of the rest of the class boarding.

Our eyes met through the glass. Natalie, Isabella, and Darren led the way for the rest of the class. Natalie's mouth twisted when she saw me while Isabella remained neutral. Darren blew me a kiss.

His reward was my middle finger. *If any good has come out of the classes being torn apart it's that I don't have to be around that asshole.*

"Morning." The seat sank as I put down my finger. Maverick pressed a kiss to my cheek that instantly lifted my mood. "I'm glad to get away from the academy for a bit."

I took his arm and put it around my shoulder. "I'd be excited too if I wasn't anticipating serious drama."

His arm around me tightened. "Nothing is going to happen to you, Val."

I didn't ask why that was where his mind went. Of course he realized this was a good time for Ace to deliver the retribution they promised. "I know I'm not alone—whatever happens."

"You're not. I'll be close by for this whole trip. Very, very"—he put his lips to my ear—"*very* close."

I bit down on my lip to hold back a grin. "Maverick, we will either be tramping around in the muck or sitting in group discussion. There's no way we'll be able to find a minute alone to mess around."

"Mess around?" Maverick pulled back and gave me a funny look. "Who said anything about messing around? I was just talking about keeping you safe." He tsked. "You've got a one-track mind, baby."

I shoved his shoulder although my grin was now on full display. "We both know we're on the same track, Beaumont." I draped my hand on his neck and pulled him closer. "You're going to come and see me over winter break, right?"

He nodded against my forehead. "My parents decided to stay home this year. If you don't have plans, I'd love it if you, your mom, and Adam came to my place for Christmas dinner."

Happiness unfurled inside me and spread through my bones. The boys had been so great about Adam. As much as I loved them, there was no future for us if they couldn't accept that I was a mom first. That they were inviting both of us into their lives made me sure that we were building something that would last. "We'd love that too."

We shared a small kiss. "Great. Knowing that we're going to spend Christmas together will keep me from getting depressed when I get my rejection letter from Somerset."

"Hey, don't put that in the universe. I'm on edge waiting for December fifteenth. I *should* be on edge. You shouldn't. You're not getting rejected. You have a 3.9 and you're a computer genius."

"A computer genius that might as well have sent in used toilet paper as my essay. With everything that was going on, my head was wrecked when I wrote it and I know it wasn't any good."

"I bet it was better than you think." I rose up and gently nipped his nose. "There's no way you'd miss seeing me as a wide-eyed coed. That dorm you will be able to sneak into."

While we talked, the rest of the class had gotten on the bus. We bounced as it rumbled to life and pulled away from the curb. As expected, everyone was too tired from the four a.m. wake-up to do much more than lean their heads against the window and fall asleep.

"Are you going to stay in the dorms?" Maverick asked.

"Well, no. I guess not. I'll be home with Adam and commute to school."

"About that..."

Something in his voice made me furrow my brow. He looked nervous all of a sudden. "What is it?"

"I was thinking that... you shouldn't commute to Somerset."

"But I have to. I'm not leaving Adam."

"I know. What I meant is instead of driving back and forth, you could get an apartment near campus." Maverick put his finger under my chin. "*We* could get an apartment near campus."

"We?" I whispered.

"Yeah." A hopeful smile played at his lips. "There is a great preschool minutes away from campus. You wouldn't have to drive an hour back and forth every day. Adam could have his own room, and we could be together all the time."

"You want to move in with us." The idea was sticking in my mind as feelings I couldn't name swirled within me.

"I do—even if I don't get in."

"You will." There was no doubt in my mind about that. "I just... can't believe you looked into preschools and apartments and—"

Maverick brushed a finger over my lips. "You can't believe I would think about our future? Val, that's all I'm thinking about. I love you."

I wonder if you could actually burst from happiness. My heart was so full, I was sure I would find out. I curled my fingers around the hand under my chin.

"What do you think?" he asked. "Would you like to—"

"Yes," I breathed. "Yes, of course."

I surged forward and captured his lips. I poured everything into that kiss—all that I felt for him and the life I wanted us to have together. Kissing Maverick is what I imagined it was like to kiss the sun. My body burned with heat as he nipped at my lips, enticing gasps that allowed him to slip past and tangle with my tongue.

My emotions were on a roller coaster that was veering from warm and fuzzy to tantalizing desire. How I wished we weren't on a bus full of people.

Maverick broke away, panting. "Wait. I have something for us."

Confused, I held myself back from jumping him as he bent down and riffled through his bag. What could he possibly need in the middle of a kiss like this?

Maverick pulled and yanked out a blanket. He draped it over us, covering us up to our chins. "Now, where were we?"

I happily picked up where we left off, losing myself in the sensation as the hand on my hip slid beneath the hem of my shirt.

Lazily his thumb glided over my skin, setting my nerve endings ablaze. I was so highly aware of that hand that I gasped when it slipped under the lining of my jeans.

"Maverick," I whispered as my top button came undone. "We could get caught."

"Everyone is sleeping," he said against my lips. "No one will notice."

His wink sent blood rushing to my cheeks. If you had asked who would try to get some with me under a blanket on a bus, I would have gone with Ezra. Underneath that perfect exterior was something else entirely. But my Maverick was the opposite. He was soft sheets, candles, and music, so that he was the one initiating this somehow made it even more exciting.

I stifled a giggle as I spread my legs to give him better access. "Don't let me get too loud."

"I like it when you're loud."

"Mav— *Oh.*"

I bit my lip hard as his fingers found their destination. His chuckle filled my ears and I knew he was enjoying this—watching me fight to keep control.

Two can play at this game.

I fumbled at his jeans as he played with me, lightly probing my core. A hiss escaped his mouth when I wrapped around him. In the next breath, his lips crashed on mine and we kissed in a feverish battle as our hands did what they wanted.

No one stirred or peeked over the seats as Maverick and I enjoyed our five-hour bus ride to the bayou.

"OKAY, EVERYONE," PATCHETT called. She stood on a mound of grass before the bus as it emptied out. The seniors formed a semicircle in front of her and Markham. Behind them, our hotel sat amid a charming flower garden and a raised porch. It was cuter than I was anticipating for a hotel out in the swamp—bigger too.

"We are stopping here to empty the bus, put our things away, and grab a quick meal before we start the day," Patchett said. "You have two hours and then I want you all back here so we can head out to the bayou. Today we'll take a tour, go over safety tips, and get acquainted with the area we'll be working in." She lowered her glasses to pin us with a stern look. "I expect you all to listen closely and be on your best behavior. They tend to stay out of the area we'll be in, but there are alligators in this bayou so do not get it into your head to wander around or think you can ignore the safety instructions."

"Umm, excuse me." I didn't need to look to know who was speaking. You couldn't mistake that tone of superiority. "Did you say there were alligators in that swamp?" Isabella demanded. "You can't expect us to go in there. My mother won't—"

"I have taken students on this trip every year for eight years and we have not once seen an alligator in our designated areas. You have nothing to worry about, Miss Bruno, as long as you follow instructions."

"But—"

Patchett clapped. "You have two hours, people. Get your things and go inside."

The group broke apart, but I spotted Isabella stomping up to Patchett to complain some more. Shaking my head, I went over to the bus to get my bag. Everyone was crowded around, diving for their things so they could hurry inside. I stuck my head under the bus and reached for my pack when a hand crossed in front of my vision.

"I've got them, Val."

I froze. Eric came in closer and grabbed a brown duffel bag.

"Right here. I've got the yearbooks."

"Really? That's perfect. Let me—"

"No." He pulled it back when I reached for it. "It'll look weird if you walk off with my bag," he whispered. "This is what we do. When the trip is over and we get back to school, you'll take this off the bus and into your car. Everyone else will be too caught up to notice."

I frowned. "What? Why go through all of that? It's just a yearbook."

"Do you want to see them or not?" There was an edge to his voice that surprised me. I didn't know why he was acting like this, but this may be my only chance to find out more about the one person I knew for sure was a Spade. I wanted that yearbook.

"Okay, Eric. I'll wait until we get back to school."

He nodded and then grabbed the duffel and another blue backpack. He backed out and walked off. I snagged my pack and wandered out of the fray. I hitched it onto my shoulder when a hard shove knocked me off-balance and sent it crashing to the ground.

I spun on Natalie with a snarl as she burst out laughing. "Oops. Sorry, Moon. Didn't see you there."

I surged forward, ready to knock her on her ass, when over her shoulder I saw Markham turn in our direction, eyes peeled on us.

Swallowing my anger, I stepped back.

"Careful, Natalie." Darren slinked to her side. "You don't want to touch her or she'll go around telling the school you're a rapist."

"I don't want to touch her, period." She smirked at me as they walked off. "Be careful in the swamp, Moon. We'd hate to see something take a bite out of your ass."

They went off laughing as Sofia came over to me. She picked my bag off the ground. "I wonder if they're dating. They're the perfect match made in hell."

I shivered. "Can you imagine the children they would spawn?"

"I don't want to imagine that."

We got the rest of our things and found our group. Together, we headed inside the hotel. I whistled. It was even more charming in here. The Rayonner Hotel had the look of a manor house and the interior kept with the old-world feel. A grand staircase led up to the top and creaky wooden floors lay beneath our feet.

A woman stepped out from behind the counter when we entered. "Good morning, Evergreen students. Welcome to the Rayonner Hotel."

A few of us greeted her in return.

"After your school activities are complete, I hope you will make the most of your stay by enjoying the pool, having fun in the game room, or attending the movie screenings we hold every night in the main living room. I know you've had a long journey so grab your roommates, take a room key, and then come back down for tea, scones, and fresh fruit in the dining room."

We didn't need to be told twice. I hooked an arm through Sofia's and ran up to get our key.

"Boys on the first floor and girls on the second," Markham called after us.

I heeded her orders and claimed key 278. The two of us climbed the stairs and found our door at the end of a long hallway. The room we stepped into was cozy. Twin beds took up the back wall, but there was a nice sitting area with a small couch, coffee table, and a television.

"This is cute," I said as we dumped our bags on the bed. "What do you think?"

Sofia stuck her head into the bathroom. "It'll do."

I rolled my eyes. There was just no pleasing my high-life-living best friend.

She came out and threw herself on her bed. "Val, I wanted to talk to you about winter break."

"Please say you're staying over." I walked around my bed and climbed in next to her. "I have plans with Maverick on Christmas, but still, I want you to come. It wasn't the same without you last year."

"I can, but not until after Christmas. Mom is planning an event to launch our newest line and she wants me there with a smile plastered on my face. Then on Christmas we'll be having the Thomases over." She flipped over until we were face-to-face. "I think they're finally accepting that Zane and I are for real. It was Dad's idea to invite them."

"Is he in the country now?"

"Dad flies back the day we return to school. He's going to pick me up."

"Okay. I'm glad you guys are going to spend time together. I'll content myself with getting you after Christmas."

She laughed. "You and your mom totally have split custody of me. Don't tell my parents, but I'd go with you in the divorce." She pecked my cheek before popping up. "Alright, let's go. I heard scones."

We finished putting our stuff away and then went down to the dining room. Zane claimed Sofia as soon as we walked in. I put two chocolate scones on my plate when Ryder loped over.

"I got a table in the back, Moon. Join me?"

"Since you asked so nicely."

I picked up a carton of milk and followed him to a two-seater in the corner next to the fireplace. It was the perfect spot. The table rested next to the bay window and the morning light cast its glow over us. It was also far enough away from the rest that we could talk without being overheard.

"We aren't supposed to have partners, but stick close, Val," he said under his breath as we took a seat. "I don't like the looks on Darren and Natalie's faces."

I peeked at them through my lashes. It was true. The two of them looked way too happy about something, and I doubted it was for the days of mucking through the swamp.

"I wish I could get Ace to talk to me," I replied. "I've tried to provoke them into giving something away, but they refuse to answer."

"Provoking them isn't the best plan. That's how you ended up with a knot on your head."

My hand shook as I buttered the scone. I felt tight with frustration. "Waiting and wondering isn't any better. Especially when you think of the fact that we could be surrounded by Spades who are pretending to be on our side."

Ryder laid his hand over my arm, stilling me. "Nothing is going to happen to you, Val. I promise."

Despite my tumultuous thoughts, the barest smile came to my lips. "I believe that coming from you."

"Good, because it's true."

Ryder moved up my arm until he slipped the knife out and replaced it with his hand. Ryder and I were on a different level than the other boys. I was intimate with them in every way, but with Ryder, it was slower. I guess I knew it would have to be different with him, but while it got to me in the beginning, now I cherished every time he held my hand, touched me because he could, or shared a secret smile with me. Sex came easy for Ryder, but opening his heart to someone didn't.

"Let's change the subject," I offered. "Will I get to see you over the break?"

He nodded. "Mom isn't interested in traveling. Her friend is going to come over with her daughters on Christmas Eve, but otherwise we've got no plans."

I was trying to listen to him but his thumb was stroking the inside of my palm in a way that was incredibly distracting.

"So I was thinking of dropping by your place over the break and whisking you away for my final labor."

I blinked. "You were? So you were just going to show up on my doorstep again."

"Yep," he replied, grinning. "The last time I did, I surprised you in a towel so it works for me."

I leaned in, lowering my voice. "You don't have to go through all of that to see me in a towel."

"I'll keep that in mind."

Our flirting got more outrageous from there. I know I made up my mind to go at Ryder's pace, but by the time we finished eating and tromped outside, it took everything in me not to drag him into a closet and have my way with him.

"Alright, everyone," Patchett said. "Are you ready for a day of learning and adventure?"

She got a few mumbles in reply but it didn't diminish her mood. It was like she had a complete personality flip from the woman who looked like she wanted to hop on the bus and ride away from this insane class, to the woman who stood before us in massive rubber overalls. She looked completely ridiculous, and when I looked down at the bins at her feet, I realized I'd be her twin.

"The overalls only come in three sizes so pick whichever fits comfortably. The water will come up to your knees and thighs, but the algae makes it slippery so you should still be covered if you trip."

Kai raised his hand.

"Yes, Mr. Thomas?"

"Is not going into the muck-filled alligator trap an option?"

Patchett's laughter rang out over the assembled students. There was a healthy pink to her cheeks that told me she was loving this too much to let anything get to her. "Come on, Mr. Thomas. Where is your sense of fun? This is life and science the way it's meant to be experienced. Out of the classroom! No textbooks! Hands-on!"

She clapped, bouncing a little on her heels. "Come, everyone. Get your waders on. Mr. Clancy will be here in five minutes to start the tour of the bayou."

We stepped forward and picked our overalls with much less enthusiasm than her. I went to the bin labeled small, but when I pulled the overalls on, I saw it was anything but. I was swimming in the thing. There was a gap big enough between my chest and the rubber overall that I bent my head and saw right down to my knees

"Baby." I glanced up at Jaxson's voice. He strutted over to me, decked out in blue rubber. "How do I look?"

"Jaxson, I once thought there was nothing that didn't look sexy on you. Now, I know I'm wrong."

"What was that?" He shot forward.

I squealed—and squeaked—as I tried to get away, but he caught me and pulled me to his chest. "I'll make you take that back."

"Oooh. Do it then."

Grinning, we leaned in for a kiss.

"Slut." The hiss made me freeze. "Even if the mark was fake, we were right about her being a whore. No wonder she ended up pregnant at like twelve."

Jaxson's eyes flashed. "What the fuck did you say?"

Penelope planted herself in front of us, hands on rubber hips. "You heard me, Van Zandt. What kind of slut sleeps around with four guys and broadcasts it? And don't get me started on you and your boys. Do you share *everything*?"

I held Jaxson tighter as rage lit in his eyes. Markham and Patchett were waiting for one of us to give them a reason, I wouldn't let Penelope provoke one.

Instead, I gave her a smile that made her smirk twitch. "Penelope, grow the hell up. You need to spend less time worrying about my relationships and more time sorting out your pathetic life."

Her mouth fell open. "You— I—"

I grabbed Jaxson's hand and marched off before the insults started. Professor Patchett was a bit away talking to an elderly man with a weathered face and matching overalls. We walked up to join them and Ryder, Maverick, and Ezra fell in beside us.

"Hello, all. My name is Fin Clancy. You can call me Clancy." Clancy gestured behind him. "Soon as everyone is ready, we'll head out. We'll start the tour by exploring the area where you'll be working. Afterward, we'll come back, rid ourselves of the rubbers, and then take a drive to the wildlife center to learn more about the animals that call the bayou home and see the alligators. Any questions?"

No one raised their hands so he turned and led us out. The hotel was in the perfect spot. Thick, ropey trees made up its backyard, and we passed through them to a well-worn path. Clancy kept up a steady stream of chatter as we made the mile-long journey down the path. The deeper we went, the more patches of water we saw through the branches, and the thicker the cloying moist air became. Soon I could barely hear him over the noise of hundreds of buzzing insects.

The path narrowed until we were walking two by two, and a few minutes later, we stopped.

"This is it," Patchett said. She pointed through the trees at a bank of grass that sloped off and became all swamp. "No time to waste. Everyone, follow me."

The class stomped out on her heels, but I hung back. Everyone kept talking about alligators and I couldn't help but notice how impossible it was to see through that water. If one was in

there, how the hell were we supposed to know before we trod on
its head?

The class was ahead of me when I realized there was someone
at my side. I glanced at Ryder. "You scared too?"

He chuckled. "No, but you looked like you were." He held
out his hand. "Let's go in together."

"If we do see a gator," I asked as I took his hand, "will you
throw yourself on it for me?"

"I'll sacrifice myself to its jaws. It will be very heroic. They'll
write songs about me and everything."

That got a giggle out of me that propelled me forward. Together, we walked off the bank and stepped into the murky water.
The overalls did a great job at keeping me dry, but it couldn't
keep out the curious heat of the swamp.

Patchett was a few feet ahead of us so we waded closer.

"...safe here. You'll collect your samples and identify what
you find. Remember that this is an independent assignment and
I will be grading you. If I suspect cheating, you will receive a zero."

A flicker of movement drew my eye away. Turning, I lit upon
a dragonfly as it zipped past my nose and landed on a gnarled
root sticking up from the water.

Wow.

Delicate, see-through wings fluttered over a blue iridescent
body. The critter was prettier than I thought. I slipped my hand
out of Ryder's and drifted closer for a better look. It turned as
though it knew it was time to pose, and I took in its massive eyes
and bulbous head.

I wish I had my camera, I thought as I edged closer. The dragonfly was holding still, and I took my chance to move in while it was interested in my attention.

Slowly, I crouched over until I was level with the root. "Hey, little guy. You are a pretty thing, aren't—" I took a step and brought my foot down on something hard and slippery. I barely had time to let out a scream as my foot went shooting away and I pitched forward.

The last thing I saw before the brown-green water welcomed me was the dragonfly take off. The world blotted out as I sank beneath the surface. The swamp rushed into my overalls, soaking me through as I flailed.

Quickly, I got my hands under me and flipped over, popping out of the water in time to hear, "Valentina!" Through the water droplets obscuring my vision, I saw Ryder dart toward me.

"Wait!"

Time seemed to slow down as Ryder tripped over the same root as me. Our eyes widened as he came down with no way for me to escape.

Splash!

The swamp claimed me again, but this time I had a hulking mass of boy pinning me down. I was under for a few seconds before strong hands yanked me sputtering out of the water.

Chest heaving, we stared at each other in disbelief. I looked down at us, both soaked with mucky water, and said the first thing that popped out of my mouth.

"So much for a heroic rescue."

Ryder pressed his lips together, face tightening as he tried to hold back a laugh. I didn't bother. Seconds later, I was howling and immediately he did the same.

We laughed until our salty tears mixed with the water on our faces.

"Y-you don't think they'll write songs about this?" he asked.

"Not o-ones that we'd like."

Then we fell out again, almost slipping back under the water as our bodies wracked with mirth. It took a minute for my chuckles to slow, but my grin remained as I looked up at Ryder. He was so beautiful when he laughed. That might not have been the preferred descriptor for a boy, but beautiful was all that came to my mind whenever I saw him.

Droplets clung to thick lashes framing gorgeous silver eyes. One fell and traveled down his sculpted nose until it dropped onto his lip. I followed its path, breath catching when I landed on that smiling mouth.

"You have something."

I jerked. "What?"

"You have some swamp on your face."

"What? Yuck! Get it off."

"I've got it." Chuckling, he reached up and gently brushed something off my cheek. "There. You're perfect."

His finger lingered on my skin as our eyes connected. I don't know who moved first—him or me, but in a blink, his lips were on mine. We clashed in a kiss that spoke to how long we had been waiting. The warm water filling my drawers did not compare to the heat that surged through my body as I threw my arms around him. Everything fell away—our surroundings, the chirping insects, our audience. Nothing existed but Ryder Shea and the crashing, soaring wave of emotions that lifted me higher and higher. I was flying. I was—

"Miss Moon! Mr. Shea!"

We tore apart with a splash to find Patchett towering over us looking less than pleased. Her girlish glee at being in her element was long gone.

"Stop that at once! Where do you think you are?!"

Cheeks flaming, I saw the entire class—including Clancy—was staring at us. Ryder and I scrambled to our feet.

She thrust out her hand, pointing to the path. "I want both of you to go inside and get cleaned up. Don't bother coming back."

"Okay." I peered down at the water sloshing within my waders. "Do you mind if we take half the swamp with us?"

Ryder snorted and it set us off again, cracking up like loons.

"Leave!"

We stumbled out as fast as we could, breathless from laughter. We couldn't have looked more ridiculous waddling down the path with the water weighing us down, and whenever either one of us said something about it, we split our sides.

We made it to the bins, stripped out of the overalls, and abandoned them. Dripping wet, we burst into the hotel and ran up the stairs. My cheeks hurt from laughing so hard, but I couldn't keep the smile off my face.

"See what you did, Moon?" He charged me and attacked my sides with his fingers. "You got us kicked off the tour."

Shrieking, I danced away. "No tickling," I cried. "It's a good thing we were booted. I'd hate to see what kind of rescue you'd pull if I fell in with the alligators."

"As we've seen, I'd fall in with you and we'd die together." He came for me again, but I took off, racing toward my room.

Ryder caught me inches from the door and lifted me up as I squealed. He pressed me against the wall and kissed me again. This time I didn't think of pulling away.

If there were words to describe what it was like kissing Ryder, I did not know them. I only knew that my entire body felt alive. The fingers at the nape of my neck. The hand on my thigh. His chest pressed against mine. I felt them so keenly like my nerves had been dulled before, but now were sparking with life.

I pulled away, breaking our kiss. Ryder looked down at me in confusion as I panted. "We're covered in disgusting water," I explained. "We should do like Patchett said and... get cleaned up."

I gazed into his eyes, hoping he saw what I wanted him to see in mine. "Good idea," he whispered.

Ryder stepped back as I walked up to my room and let myself in. I padded across the carpet as I grabbed the hem of my shirt and lifted it over my head. It fell to the floor with a wet squelch and my jeans soon joined it. I paused before my bed and turned, facing him in silk, white underwear that was now see-through.

My hands shook as they reached for the clasp of my bra. I had done this plenty of times before. There was no reason for me to be nervous, but yet I was. Ryder once said this couldn't happen because of our history. He had done things too terrible to ever be forgiven, but it was that history that made this moment even more miraculous. It took trust and faith the likes of which most people could never reach to bring us to this moment. I was giving Ryder more than my body. I was trusting him with all of me, and as I looked into his eyes, I knew I had no reason to be afraid.

Ryder's eyes darkened as my breasts were freed from their prison. I hooked my thumb through my panties.

"No, wait," he said. "I'll do that."

Still dressed, he crossed the room and knelt at my feet. I held my breath as he grasped my thighs and pressed a kiss to my stomach.

"Don't tease me, Ryder," I whispered.

He tilted his head back and flashed me a grin that made my core throb. "I would never." He moved up my thigh, pinched the fabric between his fingers, and slowly pulled it down. He stood as I stepped out of it and pulled his shirt over his head.

I feasted on the dips and ridges of his chest until I remembered this wasn't a look-but-don't-touch situation. I touched.

I ran my hands all over his body as he undid his belt and pulled down his pants. Then my hands continued their journey down.

Ryder caught my wrist before my fingers could wrap around his member. "Come on."

Giggling, we hurried into the bathroom. I pulled back the frosted doors and flicked on the steamy water.

"Hold on, Val."

I twisted around and saw him heading toward the door. "Ryder, I swear, if you say we can't do this and give me some line about not deserving me, I will *drown* you in that swamp."

He barked a laugh. "I was going to run out and lock the door. Just in case."

"Oh. Well then, carry on."

Ryder stepped out. When he came back, I was in the tub, letting the warm water heat my chilled skin. I gazed at him as he stepped inside. I used to compare Ryder to a Greek statue—timeless, chiseled perfection, but while those nude guys tended to be lacking between the legs, Ryder did not have that problem.

My pulse quickened. *I should have sent him out for a condom.*

You're not going to be with Ryder for the first time on a school trip with Ace outside the door and Markham on the prowl, common sense countered. *When we're finally together, I plan on taking my time.*

I grinned as he stalked toward me, pulling me into his arms and pressing our wet bodies together.

Until then, I'll take advantage of this stolen moment.

Ryder tilted my head back and latched on the sensitive part of my neck. I gasped as the shower rained down on my face.

He kissed a sizzling trail over my collarbone and down through the valley of my breasts. I thought I knew where he was going but suddenly, he came back up. My disappointment was lost when he kissed me.

We had fun sudsy-ing up each other and running our hands over our soapy bodies. I loved him like this—when he held nothing back and was enjoying being with me as much as I was with him.

"Ryder," I said between dropping kisses along his jaw. "For your next labor, let's go to a hotel and spend the weekend together."

"S-sorry," he said huskily. His voice deepened with desire and the effect made me pulse with need. "You don't get to pick your labors."

I didn't pause in kissing him. "I bet I could convince you."

He groaned. "I bet you could too."

I took his hands and moved them off my waist until they rested on my breasts. Ryder let out another tortured groan. "You and me." I kissed him. "Next weekend." Another kiss. "Soft sheets. No interruptions." Kiss. Kiss. Kiss. "How does that sound?"

I kissed him again, but slower this time, taking my time as his heart pounded beneath my hand. He spoke against my lips when we broke apart. "I'd be a fucking idiot to turn that down, and I'm definitely not that."

"So next weekend?"

"Next weekend." He stepped back, flashing me that grin that made my heart race. "But as for right now."

I didn't know what he meant until he got down on his knees. The bubbles returned with a vengeance as Ryder backed me against the frosted glass. Carefully, he lifted one leg on his shoulder and then the other. I stifled a squeak when his mouth found me.

I tried to hold it in, biting my lip so hard it almost bled, but one swipe of his tongue and a moan ripped from my throat. The bubbles expanded out from my stomach and filled me with pleasure that crossed my eyes. My nails dug into Ryder's scalp as the pressure crested and then finally exploded into sunbursts.

Boneless, Ryder slid me down the glass and laid me next to him on the porcelain floor. The shower spray beat against our skin as he draped his arm around me.

"Next weekend," he said softly.

I smiled. "Next weekend."

I don't know how long we lay there, but it was long enough for the water to turn cold. Eventually, we picked ourselves up and stepped out of the tub. We wrapped up in thick, fluffy towels and padded out of the bathroom.

Sofia grinned at us from her bed. "Hey, guys."

A flush crept up my neck as she gave me that knowing look. "How long have you been here?"

"Long enough, my friend. Long enough." Sofia shifted her attention to Ryder. "I got Jaxson to sneak over some dry clothes, but you better go. Markham came by twice looking for you. I told her you went for a walk."

"Got it. Thanks, Sof."

"No problem."

Ryder took up his clothes and went back into the bathroom. I perched myself on the edge of the bed and riffled through my bag. "How was the rest of the tour?"

"It was cool. Clancy took us to see the alligators. Creepy little things. They just sit there staring at you with those dead eyes. I don't know what I'd do if I was splashing around and those beady-eyed devils suddenly popped up next to me."

"Wish I could have seen them."

She raised her brows. "Yeah, right. I think the sightseeing you were doing was way better."

I ducked my head. "Are you trying to see how red you can get my cheeks because it's working."

She laughed. "Not trying to make you blush, but I want every single detail when he's gone."

As if on cue, the bathroom door opened and Ryder stepped out in black jeans and a sweater. He favored me with one last kiss before hurrying out the door.

"He's gone. Spill."

I shrugged out of my towel and got dressed while I spoke. "It's not as juicy as you think. We didn't have sex."

"Is he still going on about not deserving you?"

"No, I threatened his life so hopefully that's over." I pulled my blouse over my head and then stepped into my jeans. "But we both seemed to agree we didn't want our first time to be in a tub with my best friend outside the door." I shot her a look that she accepted with a smile. "We're going to get together over the break."

"That's great, Val. I'm so happy for you." Her grin turned wicked. "Your harem will soon be complete."

"It's *not* a harem!" I cried. I jumped on top of her, pinning her to the bed as she shrieked. "But if it was... hell yeah, it is."

Sofia bucked and flipped me over. I went down laughing, feeling so happy I almost forgot about lurking Spades and Ace.

"We should go to lunch," Sofia said when she let me up. "This is our only free afternoon so Zane and Kai want to catch the movie screening. They even snuck in popcorn."

"I knew there was a reason I kept those twins around."

OVER THE NEXT FEW DAYS, Patchett put us through everything she threatened. We woke up early, scarfed down breakfast, and then headed out to tramp through the swamps collecting samples, learning about water purity, and enduring lectures in rubber outfits while being tortured by the humidity and opportunistic mosquitoes.

Despite all of that, my friends and I managed to have a good time. We made sure to go in the opposite direction every time someone from the other class came our way and we laughed ourselves sick when Kai, Jaxson, Maverick, and Paisley ended up slipping in the swamp too. It was almost like we were regular teenagers on a school trip.

"Regular teenagers don't have to go through this shit!" Kai cried. He flung his pen across the room, narrowly missing Ezra when he came through the door.

"Watch it, man." Ezra set my mug on the coffee table and then joined me on the floor. The original nine—Me, Ryder, Ezra, Maverick, Jaxson, Sofia, Kai, Zane, and Paisley—had taken up a sitting room in the back of the hotel. It was a nice spot with wall-to-wall windows and plenty of comfy couches and chairs for us to spread out and work on our papers.

I thanked Ezra for the tea as he hooked his arm around me and kissed my neck, making goosepimples pop on my skin. That was all he did and all he would do in front of an audience. I had not been able to risk another stolen moment with any of the guys, which made me all the more thankful we would be leaving the next day and going on break.

"I'm serious," Kai continued. "We have to do a paper on what we learned while being eaten alive in a swamp. Other seniors are coasting their way to graduation."

"There's no such thing as coasting in Evergreen," Maverick replied. "Dad told me he dealt with the workload while writing his first program. He was so sleep-deprived he developed a twitch."

"That clearly paid off," said Paisley. "He twitched his way to a billion-dollar company."

He shrugged. "He was under a lot of pressure though. First in the family to graduate from high school and his family depending on him to make something of himself."

Ezra sighed. "We all know that pressure."

"Sup, guys."

I looked around Ezra to the doorway. Eric, Ciara, and Claire stood there with laptops under their arms. "Mind if we join?"

"Sure," I said. "You guys can grab some coffee table."

The three of them came in and sat down around the table. Ciara took the spot on my other side. She pointed at my closed laptop. "Are you done?"

"Yep. Unlike these guys"—I nudged Ezra's shoulder—"I wrote half a page of my paper every night so that I could get the last day off to sit here sipping tea."

I laughed when Kai flipped me off.

"Great minds think alike," Ciara replied. "Do you want to check mine and I'll read yours?"

"Ezra already polished it up for me, but I'll give yours a look."

"Ciara, you can read mine." Claire passed her laptop over. "I'm almost done. Just the conclusion left."

We lapsed into a silence that was only broken by the tapping of keys. Markham poked her head in the room a few times, but we were good about doing our own work, and only helping each other for the final proofread. No one was willing to risk a zero.

Claire typed the final period on her conclusion and stood up. "Since we're finished, do you guys want to hang out while they work?"

"Sure." Ciara got to her feet and both of them looked down at me expectantly.

"Okay." I twisted around to give Ezra a kiss before picking up my things and following them out.

"The dining room is open all day," Ciara said. "Let's get those chocolate biscuits."

I moaned. "I've eaten my weight in those since we got here. I'm going to wake up over break with a dozen zits."

"They will all be worth it."

We busted out laughing. I forgot sometimes how much I liked hanging out with them—which was easy to do considering how often they ditched me.

They also stood up and walked out of that cafeteria. That has to count for something.

The three of us wandered into the dining room and begged the staff for all the chocolate biscuits in the building.

"No one can resist them," the waiter said with a wink. "Most don't try."

"Put me in that category," I said. "I'm embracing the zits."

Claire snorted her laughter. "You crack me up, Val. I miss us hanging out like this."

My smile dimmed as she echoed my earlier thought. The waiter wandered away as my lack of reply hung in the air between us.

Claire lowered her head. "Val, I know there is nothing I can say—"

"Don't."

"But I want to apologize."

"Don't bother, Claire. It's like you said. There's nothing you can say. So let's put it behind us and move on."

I turned away and headed for one of the dining tables. Claire darted into my path. "Okay, you might not need to hear it, but I need to say it. I've never felt this awful in my life."

I clenched my fists. *Fine. If she wants to do this, let's do it.*

"Why do you feel awful, Claire? Because you found out the real reason I was marked? If it turned out I *deserved* to be bullied and humiliated, you'd still be sleeping peacefully."

"That's not true. I've hated ignoring you all these years. We weren't friends before Evergreen, but we became friends, and I never had many of those in my life. It killed me to turn my back on you but—"

"But you had a family depending on you to get them out of Wakefield, and you couldn't risk that over me." I scoffed. "I know, Claire. I've heard it before. The thing is, I had a family counting on me too, but I stayed. I fought. I did the right thing. You had the same choice. I can accept that you're doing the right thing now, but I'll never get how the girl who used to be picked on for being smart and called a freak, would turn around and bully someone else."

I sidestepped her, but her hand flashed out, grabbing my arm. "Because I was a coward."

It was those words, not her hand, that made me stop.

"I was the worst possible coward and I understand why it's harder to forgive me. Of everyone in that school, I was the only person who knew where you were coming from. I knew what it was like to grow up the way we did. I knew what you went through in our middle school because I went through it too. I should have been there for you then, but I want you to know that whether you forgive me or not, I will be here for you now."

I was quiet for a long time. When I finally spoke, my voice was soft. "Even if another card shows up in my locker?"

"I'll rip it up myself."

I bobbed my head. "Even if I break out in massive pimples and give you bullying ammunition?"

She cracked the barest smile. "It'll be hard, but I'll hold myself back."

I smiled too. "Okay, then let's put this behind us."

Claire held out her hands and enfolded me in a hug. A cough behind me broke into the moment. Ciara gave me an awkward smile when I turned to her.

"I don't know if I can say it as well as Claire, but I want to apologize too." She closed the distance between us as Claire backed away to give us space. "Do you remember freshman year? Natalie tripped you, and when I took you to the nurse, I said that no one wants to hurt you. This was just how things had to be." She shook her head. "You rejected that for the bullshit it was and said that everyone had a choice. After you told me that, I decided I wouldn't join in anymore. I would stay out of it, and whatever happened to you, at least I wouldn't be part of it.

"I thought at the time it was enough to keep my conscience clear until... you told us about Professor LeBlanc. You were innocent the whole time and we were all used by a monster—even me. Staying silent was just as bad and I won't do that anymore. I won't ask you to forgive me either, but if it comes down to it, I'll be next in line to sucker punch Natalie."

I laughed.

"Seriously," she insisted, smiling too. "Damn, that girl takes bitch to the next level. The best day of my life was when Sofia knocked her out."

I pulled her in for a hug before she finished. "We're hoping to keep this thing from getting physical, but I'll keep that in mind if people start throwing hands."

The next thing I knew, Claire was hugging the both of us. It got even more embarrassing when we started crying. The hug fest didn't stop until the waiter came out with our biscuits and then we were busy stuffing our faces.

We moved off the heavy stuff and started talking about life after Evergreen, where we wanted to go to college, what we wanted to study, and things like that. After the food, we moved the party to the game room and converged on the pool table.

"I could see you as a psychologist, Val," Claire said as she rescued the balls. "You're no-nonsense, but you're also patient and forgiving."

"Thanks." I hung back and let Ciara and Claire get the first round. "I can see you as a lawyer too. What about you, Ciara?"

She sighed. "Don't tell my parents, but I think after four years of killing myself at the academy, I want some time off. I'm planning to go backpacking around the world."

"Amazing," Claire said. "I'm so jealous."

We talked more about her trip and where she wanted to go while Claire destroyed her in a game of pool.

"Your turn to be humiliated, Val," she said as she passed me the cue.

I played, lost, and then we moved on to a game of cards. We were yukking it up in the game room for so long that the others found us in there when they finished their papers.

Maverick, Ryder, Jaxson, and Ezra took over our card game while Sofia and I went up against Claire and Ciara in another game of pool. We cheered when we won.

Ciara threw up her hands. "Obviously my suckiness is dragging down Claire's skills. Eric, you take over."

"Sure. I'll play."

"I could use a break too," Claire said. "I have to go to the bathroom."

Kai slid in and took her spot. "I'll play with you guys, but how about we make things interesting?"

I lifted my brow. "What did you have in mind?"

"Strip pool," he replied without a lick of shame. He twisted around and glanced over to where Paisley was playing a board game with Zane. "Paisley, come play with us."

I shook the eight ball at him. "I would throw this at you if I wouldn't get in trouble for denting that fool head."

He threw his head back laughing while we set up the table. I loved that guy, but he was incorrigible. Although, according to Paisley, she had never dated anyone sweeter or more sensitive.

"I'm kidding," Kai said. "How about the losers pay the winner ten bucks?"

Sofia and I shrugged. "Okay. Sounds good."

We played teams for the first game and won thanks to Sofia. For the next round, I went up against Eric one on one.

"You ready for me, Eden?"

He looked up from his phone to shoot me a grin. "I've seen you play. I'm not worried."

Those were fighting words. Ten minutes later, we were locked in a heated game. You would have thought the stakes were higher than ten bucks from the intensity on our faces as we lined up our shots.

"This is it, Val," Sofia said. "Sink this ball and you win."

I nodded. The orange ball became the center of my universe as my eyes narrowed.

Eric is looking nervous. Show him he should be.

I tapped the ball and it went whizzing across the felt, heading straight for the black ball and... missed. The groan was half out of my throat when it bounced off the edge and came roaring back. It glanced off the ball and knocked it into the hole.

"Whooo!" Sofia and I jumped up and down, cheering and whooping it up. Ryder looked over from his card game.

"Be honest, Moon," he said. "That was an accident."

I leveled a finger at him. "You mind your business. I sank that shot."

"Nah. She gets this one," Eric said. "She won fair and square. She's a true match for me."

I beamed. "Thank you, Eric. I'll take my winnings now."

"One more game," Kai replied. "Double or nothing."

"Nope."

Eric was already reaching into his pocket. "Here you go, but let's call it quits, guys. It's almost dinner and I'm starved."

I moved over to the window and pulled back the curtain. It was true. The sun had set on the Rayonner Hotel and outside was pitch black. Untouched nature meant no cars or streetlights. I could barely see the outline of the trees.

"I didn't realize it was so late," I said. "But I could use a bite too."

"Good." Eric came up and hooked an arm through mine. "Let's sit together. We can talk winter break."

Sofia gave us a funny look like she was shocked to see Eric in her position, walking me out the door. That was until Zane came up behind her and wrapped his arms around her waist. She was giggling at the kisses he peppered on her neck as Eric and I left ahead of everyone. We didn't talk much these days, but Eric had finally come through for me with the yearbook. He had proven he was on my side.

Rapidly approaching footsteps warned me that someone was coming up behind us. Hands settled on my hips before I could turn around. "I haven't gotten any time with you," a deep voice breathed into my ear. "Any chance I could steal you away for dinner? We could take it back to an empty room and have it just be you and me."

That was incredibly tempting. "Eric got in there first. We're catching up over dinner."

Jaxson rested his chin on my shoulder as he peered at him. "Do the honorable thing, Eden. Step aside."

He chuckled. "What happens if I—"

A roar of laughter cut him off. The main living room loomed in front of us, just before the dining room. We were steps away when a figure streaked out of the door, making me jump.

Clutching my chest, I cried, "Claire? What's wrong?"

Claire's face was deathly pale. She looked at me with huge eyes as the noise behind me said the rest of my friends and boyfriends were coming. "Don't go in there."

"What? What are you talking about?" I took a step forward and her hand flashed out, blocking me.

"Do *not* go in there! I'm going to get Professor Markham, she'll stop them."

"Claire, what are—" She spun around and raced off. "What is going on?!"

Another roar of laughter followed my shout.

"Stop it!" someone screamed. "You've gone too far!"

Dread curdled my blood as I recognized that voice. It was Juliet Cochran.

I surged forward, but Jaxson's grip held me fast. "Wait, Val. Let me go first."

He ran around me before I could argue.

"What's up?" Sofia asked. "Is something going on in—"

I darted after Jaxson and burst into the living room. Skidding to a stop behind him, I took in the scene before me. The senior class—both sides were in the living room. I could see a fight was brewing as people from our side rushed the group standing in front of the entertainment center, but it was the television above their heads that claimed my attention.

Pictures flashed across the screen too fast for my sluggish mind to make sense of them. As they slowed, a voice came through the speakers.

"Valentina Moon has turned this school upside down."

My hair stood on end at the creepy, high-pitched voice. It was fake. No one could sound like that.

"She wants you to believe the Spades can't be trusted," the voice said as a picture of me came on the screen. It was me on the sidewalk outside the gates coming back from my weekend with Ezra.

I shivered. *Someone had been watching me.*

"Her and her little friends have painted themselves as the good guys and told you all to follow them, but do they look like people you can trust?"

"What is this?" Sofia whispered. I hadn't heard the rest of them come in. Horror had frozen me to the spot.

The pictures flashed across the screen again, but this time they were slow enough for me to see—for everyone to see.

Paisley's bare breasts were the first thing my eyes latched on to. There was a seductive smile on her face as she straddled Kai. Both of them were naked and spread out on a blanket. The backdrop told me it was the forest of the academy.

"Turn that off!" Paisley screamed. "Turn it off!"

"Motherfuckers!" I was knocked aside when a hard body ran past me and charged the blockade in front of the DVD player. Darren shoved him back. Kai fell, landing on the coffee table, but he flew back up swinging. He landed a punch square on Darren's jaw and the two fell to the floor, grappling viciously.

"Kai!" Zane ran to his brother's aid as Paisley burst into tears. She ran crying from the room as the awful slideshow continued.

"Pills," that hideous voice hissed. Claire came onto the screen. She was ducked behind the fountain in the courtyard, putting what looked like a red-and-blue pill into her mouth.

"Drugs."

Ciara was next. She was in the forest too. The sandy-haired girl was leaning against a tree smoking something that was not a cigarette.

"Come on, Kai," Zane cried as he struggled to pull him off.

"Cheating," said the voice.

My mouth fell open as the next picture lit up the television. It squeezed my heart when I heard the gasp behind me.

"Paisley needs you! Go to..." Zane trailed off as he took in what we were all seeing—him standing beneath the arch, kissing Penelope Madlow. "Wha— That's not—" He whipped around as retreating footsteps told me Sofia bolted from the room. "Sofia, wait! It's not what you think!"

Zane was forced to abandon his twin as he ran after her. Jaxson sprung to take his place. I was knocked to the side again as Maverick, Ryder, and Ezra went to help, but the video wasn't over.

Pictures of me returned but I wasn't alone. Me kissing Ezra on the porch. Me walking hand in hand with Jaxson. Me snuggling in Maverick's arms. Me sharing a kiss with Ryder outside this very hotel.

The voice spoke as violation churned my stomach. "The Spades have no desire to hurt the innocent. We only want to keep students like this from dragging us all down. Valentina Moon had the choice all marked have which was to pack her bags and go to another school where no one would bother her. Instead, she turned Evergreen into a national joke, seduced our Knights until they lost their position, accused a woman who isn't here to defend herself of being a pedophile, and then ripped the school apart when she and her boyfriends were questioned.

"Lying and scheming is what this girl does. She'd have you believe Evergreen is better off without the Spades, but we have existed since the school began and brought nothing but order and peace."

"Except for Walter fucking McMillian!" I screamed; the words yanked from my throat. "Fear is not peace!"

The video carried on unheeding of my outburst. "Since Valentina Moon has set foot on these grounds, there has been nothing but drama, fighting, scandals, and now war. Think about it, everyone. It is not the Spades that need to go. It's Valentina Moon."

The screen went dark for a second, but then the picture returned. The video was playing on a loop.

Fury rattled my bones the likes of which I had never felt before. One word roared in my mind.

Ace.

I knew I should go after Sofia and Paisley, but I couldn't get myself to move. Sharp, stinging pain warned me of the nails digging into my palms.

Ace did this. That cold, fucking bastard stalked and hurt my friends for standing up to them! When I find them—

"That's enough!" Ryder bellowed. He ripped Darren off Kai as Maverick and Jaxson pulled the twin away. The boys fought in their hold, trying to get at each other. They both looked horrible. A cut over Darren's eye wept blood and made him look even more frightening. Kai had a split lip, torn clothes, and an eye that was starting to swell.

An arm brushed against me as Eric stepped forward. "Get Kai out of here. Claire ran to get Professor Markham and if she finds out they got into a death match, they're both in trouble."

I went rigid. *Wait... What did he say?*

The warning banged around in my head until it knocked something loose.

Match. Match, I thought. *In the game room Eric said...*

"*She's a true match for me.*"

Slowly, painstakingly, I reached into my pocket and took out my phone. My fingers were stiff as I tapped the screen. It took me a few tries to open my inbox, but as the boys hauled Kai out of the room, Ace's messages laid out before my eyes. I scrolled up until I found it. Seven black words stark on a white background revealing everything that I did not want to be true.

Ace: You are a true match for me.

"Turn that fucking video off," Eric cried. "Do you want Markham to flip shit on all of us?"

"It's you," I whispered.

"What, Val?" He turned around. His handsome features were the picture of innocence—so reminiscent of the boy I met four years ago. The Eric who became one of my first friends. "What's wrong?"

"It's you," I repeated through numb lips. "You're Ace."

Eric gazed at me, trimmed eyebrows together, until his face smoothed out...

...and he smirked.

"You!" I screamed. White-hot anger exploded in me and I lunged at him.

Eric's eyes popped as the smirk disappeared. He ducked my swipe and ran under my arms. I raced after him.

Our feet thundered on the squeaky floorboards. Eric was quick, pulling ahead of me as he ran past the dining room.

"Eric?" Jaxson stuck his head out and immediately jumped back with a shout when I shot past him. "Val?! What's going on?"

There was no time to answer him. Eric rounded a corner and disappeared.

"Heavens!" someone cried. "No running in—"

Bang!

I burst into the front room and saw the entrance was wide open. I didn't hesitate. I followed Eric out into the night.

The chilling air smacked me in the face as I searched for a figure in the darkness.

There.

"Eric, stop!" I took off after him. "Face me!"

Eric didn't slow. The figure kept running for the trees and I was hot on his heels. Putting on a burst of speed, I closed the distance between us until he was inches from my grasping hand.

"Tell me why!" I cried. I swiped and my fingers brushed his collar just as he broke through the trees.

Branches ripped and tore at me as I gave chase. This wasn't the clear, smooth path we took every day to our patch of swamp. I did not recognize the gnarled roots that reached for me in the darkness. The creatures that chittered and screamed at me, I couldn't identify.

Still, I ran. Spurred on by betrayal that burned my throat with the heat of a red-hot poker. How could he do this to me? We weren't always friends, but I never saw him as this. Ace hated me. Ace was obsessed with the Knights and seeing me broken. Ace tormented me, made me cut my hair, forced me to kiss Kai, announced that my son was the result of statutory rape, and turned the school against me more times than I could count. What could I have done to ignite that kind of loathing in my old friend?

"What did I do?!" I jumped and tackled him.

Eric cried out as we went down hard, landing in the wet, sticky grass. "Val, stop!" He struggled, trying to scramble away from me, but I grabbed his flailing wrist and yanked it up his back.

"You're Ace," I shouted as he cried out. "You blackmailed me! You forced me to do those horrible things. Why?!" I viciously tugged his arm higher and he bellowed.

"S-stop! You'll break my arm!"

"Tell me why!"

"It— It w-wasn't me," he cried, voice laced with pain. "It wasn't me. I didn't do it. I swear."

"Liar!" I released his arm and took hold of his shoulder. Eric didn't have time to recover. I flipped him onto his back and clutched his collar. I twisted until he let out a choked gasp. "You said I was your perfect match! You—"

"A-Ace t-told me to," he rasped. "Ace made me say it. I can... prove it. Look at my phone!" Eric beat desperately at my hands. "Please, V-Val. The texts are on my phone."

Breathing hard, I gazed at the huge, staring whiteness of his eyes.

This is another trick. He's fooled me for years. I can't believe anything he says.

His nails dug half-moons into my wrist. "Look at the phone and you'll see. I'll tell you everything, Val. I promise."

My hand shook on his neck as his pleas tore at my resolve. It couldn't hurt to look. Now that I knew who he was, he wasn't getting away from me.

"Shit! Fine." I smacked at his pockets until I found his cell.

"Under AOS," he said as I stabbed at the screen. "It's all there."

I found the name at the top of his inbox. My grip was tight on his neck as I opened the messages, but it loosened as I read.

AOS: Tell her she's a true match for you.

Eric: Why?

AOS: Just fucking do it. Tonight. Before the video.

Eric: What's the point of all of this? It's too much.

AOS: None of this would be necessary if she left in freshman year like she was supposed to. I didn't start this shit, but you better believe I will end it. Tell her she is your perfect match, and then smile at her after she watches the video.

Eric: And if I don't?

AOS: There have been rumors your dad isn't fit enough to run the company after his little heart attack. I'd hate to see

the rumors confirmed and him forced out. But that will be nothing compared to what I'll put you through if you don't do as I say.

The phone slipped from my hand as I fell off Eric. What did this mean? Was this for real?

I gaped at him as he staggered to his feet. "What the fuck is going on?" I croaked.

"...Val..."

I whipped around as a cry pierced the gloom. It sounded like Maverick. The guys were looking for me, but I wasn't sure where I was. We had run so deep into the bayou; I heard the squelching of the wet marsh beneath my feet louder than his calls.

"You know what's going on, Val." I spun back to Eric as he righted himself. It was so dark, even with my vision adjusted to the night, his face was cloaked in shadows. "You don't know how close to this you really are."

"What do you mean?"

He went on like I hadn't spoken. "You've got most of it figured out. That's why Ace stalled me."

"Stalled you?" I stepped closer. "What the hell are you talking about? What do I have figured out? I'm trying to find Ace. If that's not you, then who is it?"

There was no reply and his silence enraged me.

"I'm not doing this anymore, Eric!" I surged forward and grasped his forearms. "Tell me what you know about the Spades! Why did Ace choose you?"

Eric did not try to pull away. He was still in my hold. "Because, Val... I am a Spade."

"W-what?" Shock stole my breath.

That can't be true. It can't!

"Valentina…" A voice broke through, closer but still faint.

"You can thank my grandmother for telling you more than you were supposed to know," he continued. The pain and fear were gone from his voice. He just sounded blank. "To be fair, she didn't know who she was talking to."

"Your grandmother?" I whispered. "But she didn't tell me anything."

"She told you that it was all about legacy—one that went way back to the first class at Evergreen Academy. You thought that if family had to do with who was chosen as a Knight, then maybe that had something to do with the Spades too. You were right, which is why Ace wouldn't let me give you those yearbooks."

I tossed my head. "Eric, I'm not understanding any of this. What does the first class have to do with anything?"

Now he grabbed me. His hands flashed out and yanked me in. "Thirteen students. Thirteen families. Some of us become Knights. Some of us become Spades, but all of us have to protect Evergreen Academy."

"Why?" I tugged at his hold, but he held me fast. "Why do you have to do that?"

He scoffed. "Why does anyone do anything? Money."

"Money?" I ripped myself away, breaking free. "Someone is paying you to do this?"

"We're all getting paid. Think about it, Valentina. After all you've been put through, why did you stay at this school instead of transferring?"

"I wasn't going to be run out," I spat. "Evergreen is the best school in the country. I had to think of my future."

He snapped his fingers. "There it is. You'd do anything to be there because it's not just the best school in the country; it's the best school in the world. People will do anything—pay anything to get their little geniuses into Evergreen Academy, and that's what it's all about.

"Have you ever wondered why there are no limits on scholarships? Evergreen doesn't only want spoiled, rich brats. They need the best and brightest."

"The Spades need them? Need them for what?"

"They need us to be geniuses. They need us to fight and compete among each other to be the best so that when the time comes, they'll be the first one to pounce."

My head was spinning. All of this was barely making sense.

"I heard you guys in the sitting room," he continued. "Maverick told you his dad came from a poor family of people who never graduated high school, but then Marcus gets into Evergreen Academy and wows his professors with lines of code the government can't crack. When he inevitably starts talking of opening his own company, the right people are waiting to invest."

"So... Evergreen is some kind of brain farm," I replied, "and you Spades are lurking in the shadows, waiting for the next big thing so you can ride them to success. All of this for *that*?!"

"You make it sound like that isn't enough. People kill over fifty dollars. Do you think they wouldn't do worse for fifty billion? August Eden became one of the first African-American millionaires in history when he took a chance on Judah Shea and gave him the money to help start Shea Industries."

"Shea Industries? But—"

"Sofia Richards." Eric was on a roll and didn't seem to be slowing down. "At thirteen years old, she invented a shampoo that penetrates the hair shaft better than anything else on the market. I wonder if her mother told her that single product has made them millions. Whether she takes over Honey Hair or starts her own company, there are people standing by more than willing to invest in whatever her brilliant mind comes up with next."

"Valentina! Where are you?"

"Eric, can you hear me?"

We heard the faint shouts of the searchers, but we didn't call back. We were locked in our own world as the truth finally came out.

"In this world, there are the people with ideas and the people with the money to make them reality. The thirteen families have the money, and the Knights and the Spades make sure the kids with ideas keep coming through the gates."

I threw out my hands. "By doing what? Marking people? Bullying and intimidating them? That's insane!"

"That's a last resort," he shot back. "What don't you get? The marked are supposed to leave. Nothing happens to them if they walk away—which all of them did, until you and..."

"Walter and Nora," I finished.

"Exactly." He stepped closer to me, lowering his voice. "It's not supposed to get that far." I could hear something creeping into his voice. Anxiety was breaking through the coldness. "None of this was supposed to happen. They told me I was chosen to be a Spade. They said what was expected of me, but they didn't prepare me for turning on my friends, following a pedophile's orders, or dealing with that psychotic *tyrant*!"

I stiffened. "What tyrant? Who are you talking about?"

"Who else but Ace?!"

"Do you know who they are? Who is Ace, Eric?"

Eric roughly shook his head. It was like he hadn't heard me. "You have to understand. It made sense when Grandma told me. She said that people don't send their kids to schools with bad reputations. If news came out tomorrow that a human-trafficking ring was running out of an Ivy League school, admissions would drop to nothing no matter how prestigious it was. It's all about perception, and we made sure Evergreen's was perfect."

I could practically hear Wilhelmina Eden speaking through Eric's mouth.

"The problem of every boarding school are the students who go there," he continued. "No rules will stop them all from sleeping around, getting their hands on drugs, finding a way to cheat, the list goes on. We make sure no one outside the gates hears of that stuff and we mark the ones who are scandals waiting to fucking happen."

I latched on to something he said. "You make sure? Knights and Spades? Teenagers. You're the ones who are supposed to police the damn school? That's what the professors and the headmaster are for."

"No, no, no, Val!" he exploded. "Stop pretending you don't understand."

I edged back. He reminded me of Roundtree—disappointed in me for letting him down. Why didn't I understand what was so perfectly reasonable in the kingdom of Evergreen?

"If a professor gets involved, then they have to report it. People have to be notified. Parents called and the harder it is to contain, but not if the students handle it themselves. It's all legal that way."

"Legal?" I repeated.

"Yes. You and I didn't sign any contracts saying we have to report bad students. If we take care of it, no one is in a position of having to cover things up, and they like it that way. That's why Evergreen hasn't changed and never will. We make everything so simple."

"We police ourselves. We punish ourselves. We expel ourselves," I stated. Eric was right. It makes a twisted sort of sense. "All so Evergreen remains a shining beacon of perfection, drawing in the brightest kids of our time so the thirteen families can keep investing in them and getting richer."

"That's..." Eric trailed off. Through the gloom, I saw him frown.

"Eric?"

Suddenly, he spun around. "What is that?" he hissed. "Did you hear that?"

I pricked my ear to the sound of desperate shouts, calling our names. "Of course, I hear them. They're looking for us. We can get out of here sooner if you talk to me." I grasped his shoulder and spun him to face me. "Who are the thirteen families?"

"Well, there's the... Edens," he began. He sounded distracted as his head turned this way and that. "And there's... uh..." He tried to turn around again.

I gripped him harder. "Eric, look at me. You said Shea, but the Sheas weren't one of you, right? They were just one of the people your family used."

"No. How do you think August and Judah met? They were both in the first class. The Sheas are one of the thirteen."

"But that's not..." Shock gripped my throat. *Ryder is one of them? He's been playing me this whole time? How could he do this? How—*

"But Ryder doesn't know." Those four words halted my downward spiral.

"How do you know that?"

Eric wasn't looking at me as he answered. "My dad told me. Benjamin told him Ryder wasn't to have anything to do with this. He said this wasn't his legacy and he had no right to claim the honor—whatever that means. None of us were allowed to tell him after his father disappeared, but of course, he became a Knight anyway."

"Baby, please!" Jaxson's voice found me through the swamp. "Tell me you're okay!"

It killed me hearing his panic, but I was finally learning the truth.

"But if you're right," Eric continued. "The reason why Scarlett chose him... wasn't because of his father."

"No," I replied, voice hard. "That was entirely because of her."

"I still can't believe it," he breathed.

"She was one of you, wasn't she?"

"She was more than that." Eric stopped looking around and looked me in the eyes. "She was Ace. She was Ace when she went to school at Evergreen, and then she took over again when she became a professor. Of course, no one questioned her when she marked you, and I'm sorry for that. None of this should have— Val, look out!"

There was no time for me to react as hands seized me from behind. A hard blow to the back of my knees made me buckle, and I collapsed to the ground. I screamed as my head was shoved down into the marsh. Water rushed into my airway as I frantically kicked and twisted.

Yanking my head to the side, I sucked in air before a hand clamped down over my eyes.

"Guys, stop! I didn't— *Ugh.*"

"Eric!"

A thud shook the ground. Through the space between the fingers, I saw one thing clearly—Eric's wide, unblinking eyes. In the next moment, they were replaced by feet.

"Deal with him," said a familiar high-pitched voice.

My blood ran cold. *Who the hell is that?*

"As for you, it's time to end this."

I cried out when my hands were roughly yanked behind my back. Something wrapped around my wrists, binding them together. I tried to buck them off, but a knee pressed on my back, keeping me still. There was more than one person here. This was not just Ace.

The hand over my eyes vanished for one blessed second only to be replaced by a dark cloth. "Stop! Let me go!"

I bucked again as the hands slipped under me and lifted me up. I was being moved.

"I'm here!" I screamed. "The Spades have me! Help!"

Jaxson. Ryder. Maverick. Ezra. Where are you? Why can't I hear your voices? Why can't you hear me?

I could not hear anyone, not even the voices of my captors. Their silence made me even more afraid. If they were arguing, shouting, panicking over whatever they were going to do next, that would have been better than the cold, efficient way they took me and Eric out. They knew what they were going to do next, and there was no hesitation about it.

"W-who are you?!" The tight band I had not felt in so long constricted my chest. I thought I knew fear, but nothing compared to the terror that shook me and tore my lungs. I couldn't breathe. I couldn't think about anything other than what Eric said.

"People kill over fifty dollars. Do you think they wouldn't do worse for fifty billion?"

Were these faceless monsters going to kill me?

"Let me go!"

"Valentina?!" The tiniest thread of hope broke through when I heard him.

"Jaxson? Jaxson! I'm here!"

The cry was barely out of my mouth before they stopped.

"Untie me, you crazy—"

"Let me make something very clear." That dreadful, unnatural voice stopped me cold. "It's been fun playing this little game, but it's over now. You're done at Evergreen Academy. You do not come back next semester. If you do, you'll go the same way as Walter McMillian. Goodbye, Valentina Moon."

I opened my mouth to curse them when the hands reared up and sent me flying through the air. I screamed as I splashed down into the bayou. Water rushed into my mouth and nose, choking me as I sank below the depths.

I scrambled to get my feet under me. My knees found purchase on something hard and I burst from the water in time to hear him.

"Valentina, where are you?!" Twigs snapped as he crashed through the brush. "Talk to me!"

"I'm over here! I'm in the—"

I cut off as I felt something brush against me.

"Jaxson! Jaxson!" Terror brought my screams to an inhuman pitch. I scrambled up and tried to run. I made it one step and slipped, sinking into the murky depths.

Something clamped down on my hands and hauled me out of the water. "Baby, it's me. I've got you." He ripped the cover off and I buried my face in his chest, sobbing my eyes out as he held me. "It's okay," he crooned. "I've got you. You're safe now."

Chapter Eight

The clock read three a.m. but sleep was a far cry. In five hours, we would be getting on the bus that would take us home.

A bus with the people who did this to me.

The pillow crumpled in my fist. If I was in my room, I would have gotten up and crawled into Sofia's bed. We both had one hell of a night, and enduring it together was infinitely better than being here alone.

Eek.

I shot up when a sliver of light escaped through the opening door. "Who's there?!"

"Shh. It's me. We don't want to wake her."

I relaxed as Jaxson eased the door shut and padded across the room in the dark. The bed dipped as he slid in next to me. "What are you doing here?"

"You know why I'm here." He put his arm around me and I burrowed into him, clutching him tightly.

"You'll get in trouble," I whispered into his chest.

"It's worth it." Jaxson gently stroked the shell of my ear. "I understand why Markham moved you into her room and posted herself outside the door, but you shouldn't be alone—not tonight."

228

I squeezed my eyes shut as tears threatened to leak out. "Is she still there?"

"She's sleeping on a cot in front of the door. I had to step over her to get in." He laughed. "Not so great as a bodyguard, but that's why I'm here. I'll protect you, baby. You can get some sleep."

I don't know how he knew I was sitting in the dark, too afraid to close my eyes, but that it worried him enough to bring him here broke me. The tears spilled out hot and fast.

"I was s-so scared."

"I wouldn't have let anything happen to you." Jaxson kissed along my forehead and down my cheek. "I'll always be there when you need me."

"Who did this? Markham rushed me inside and made me shower and go to bed after I told her what happened. Please tell me you caught them."

"I want to, but the entire class ran out looking for you. It was chaos with all of us tromping around in the dark. Ryder and I separated from Maverick and Ezra. We ended up on our own. Markham and Patchett freaked, of course. They shouted at us all to go back inside and then I finally heard you, but when we came back, there was no telling who came from where."

"What about Eric? Is he okay? It sounded like they hurt him."

His grip on me tightened. "The last I heard... they still hadn't found him."

I choked on a sob. "I was so stupid. I never should have followed him out there. If I had responded when you were calling to me, you would have gotten to us before they could."

"This is not your fault."

"Yes, it is. I'm a fucking idiot who thought she could take down a psychotic secret society that's existed for over a hundred years. They were ready for me."

"You're not an idiot. They are the idiots because they've made their last mistake. I'll make them pay for what they did to you tonight."

"If you hadn't saved me—"

"I'll always save you."

"There was something in the water," I cried. "I thought I was going to die, Jaxson. Alone in the dark with no one to help me like I've dreamed so many times before."

Jaxson pulled back until he was looking me in the eyes. Gently, he brushed away my tears. "Next time, I'll be there sooner. But I'm hoping there won't be a next time. I can't stand the thought of anything hurting or scaring you. I... love you, Valentina. I love you so much."

Those beautiful words reached deep inside of me and ignited a place fear couldn't touch. "I love you too."

My tears had stopped when our lips met. Our clothes came off beneath the sheets, and I gave myself over to him completely. Jaxson made love to me slow and passionate and soon I drifted to sleep in his arms.

Hours later, the sun woke me. A beam of light cast directly over my eyes, blinding me as I squinted at the clock.

10:45

I shot up like the bed was electrified. After ten meant the bus left over two hours ago.

How could they leave me? The boys and Sofia wouldn't just ride off without me.

I hurried into my clothes, shoved my feet into my shoes, and threw open the door.

Markham blinked at me with her hand poised to knock. "Ah, you're awake. Do you feel up to some breakfast?"

"Breakfast? But the bus—"

"The bus left hours ago. There were loud protests, but I sent them on ahead. I did not think you would be able to handle the ride back after what happened." She held up a hand when I opened my mouth. "Don't worry, your mother has been contacted. She knows you will be late and why."

I slumped against the doorframe. Markham was right. The last thing I wanted to do was get on a bus I knew was filled with my attackers, but how would I explain this to Mom?

"Come. We are the only ones left in the hotel and Mrs. Fountaine made you a special breakfast."

"Um, okay. That sounds nice."

I followed her out into the hall and fell in step beside her. I asked her the question plaguing my mind. "How's Eric? Did you find him?"

She kept her gaze ahead, but I noticed the tightening of her jaw. "Mr. Eden is still missing."

I swallowed hard. Visions of my old friend floating facedown among the things that lurked in the swamp flooded my mind until tears threatened to fall again.

"That is another reason I stayed behind," she continued. "The police and Mr. Eden's parents are on the way."

"Is he the only one missing? You know they took him. They—"

"Everyone else was accounted for."

"Why did you let them leave?" I demanded. "They all need to be questioned."

"You told me last night that you could not identify the people who took him. If I tried to keep those students here, I would have a million parents and their high-priced lawyers threatening to sue me."

"So you just—"

"I know what you are going to say, and you're right." There was a hard edge to her voice that quieted me. "I do not like this either. I'm trying to keep my students safe and... I'm not doing a good job."

No more passed between us on the way to the dining room. My thoughts were spinning through my head too fast for me to hold on to one of them. What had they done to Eric? Ace used him for a pawn and then attacked him when he tried to tell me the truth. They couldn't have killed him. He never got a chance to tell me anything that I could use against them. He—

I stopped dead on the polished hardwood as one thought slowed down enough to penetrate. *He didn't get a chance to tell me, but he did bring the yearbook. No wonder he was acting so squirrelly. He did not want to risk his Spade friends finding out he was giving it to me. He truly turned on them.*

And he paid for it, another voice countered.

But it doesn't have to be in vain if I find out what he was trying to tell me.

"Professor Markham."

She glanced over at me as she took her seat at the dining table. A lovely spread had been laid out for us—complete with a plate of chocolate biscuits. This charming scene was so out of place with the horrors that went on last night.

"Yes, Miss Moon."

"Eric's things. Are they still here?"

"Of course. The police will no doubt want to go over everything. His room hasn't been disturbed."

"Okay, okay," I mumbled as I took a seat. This was good news. He took the yearbooks off the bus. They would be in his room and I would get them the minute we were done here.

"Please, eat." Markham reached for the teapot and tipped the steaming hot water into my mug. "And drink this. Irish Breakfast tea is very strong. It'll help."

I gazed at her while she fussed over me. There was a kindness in the lines of her face—often hidden under disapproving scowls and furrowed brows. I could believe in that moment that she truly cared about me. Maybe that was why I said what I did next.

"Professor, tell me about Nora."

The hand stirring the tea stilled. "Excuse me?"

"Nora Wheatly. Tell me what happened to her and Walter. There's no reason to hide anymore. I know about the Spades and the thirteen families—"

Her eyes bugged. "Don't say that. You—"

"We're alone. It's just you and me so let's stop this already. Tell me why he was killed."

She looked away, lips pinched. "What does it matter? It was over thirty years ago."

"It matters for the very fact that people keep trying to pretend it *didn't* matter. Why will no one face this? I know you were there, Elizabeth Fairchild." Her head whipped around at the name. "You were in their class. You must know why this started."

She lifted her chin. "It seems like you know quite a bit yourself. How?"

"I saw your yearbook at Eric's house. It was also the day Wilhelmina Eden told me Nora was a common slut. Why would she say that?"

Her lips twisted. "Of course she would say that. Harsh woman."

I sat back, waiting. Markham looked from me to her cup and then back to me. She seemed to be trying to make up her mind.

"Nora was my friend," she finally said. "Even though she was everything I wasn't. Wild, free, bold, and beautiful. She sat down next to me during assembly and that was it."

"Why was she marked?"

Markham gazed into the depths of her cup. She didn't look at me as she spoke. "I told you, Nora was wild and beautiful. Guys fell at her feet and she was happy to pick a few of them up. By sophomore year, she was dating multiple guys, but unlike your case, they did not know about each other.

"The grades were just as separate as they are now. It was easy to keep them apart and she used to brag to me about having lovers in every grade. Her biggest catch was the Knight: Andrew Eden."

I sat up in my seat. "Eric's father was with Nora? Was he the one who—"

"Please, Valentina. Let me finish."

Slowly, I nodded and settled back down.

"As I was saying, she had many boyfriends, but the one she truly came to care for was Walter. He was kind to her. Sweet and charming while one of the others wasn't."

"One of the others?"

She bobbed her head. "She wouldn't tell me who, but things turned sour with one of her boyfriends. They became possessive, mean, and on occasion, violent. She showed up to class one morning with a black eye."

"Oh no," I breathed.

"I wanted her to go to the headmaster, but she refused. She promised me she ended things with him and that everything was fine. She had bigger things to worry about after discovering she was pregnant."

My mouth fell open. "Pregnant? Was that why...?"

"Yes, that was why she was marked. She kept it quiet for as long as she could, but then the baby began to show and the card appeared in her locker soon after she confirmed it."

I shook my head. Disbelief colored my tone. "Of course it did. Pregnancy may not be an expellable offense, but it sure doesn't look good to parents to find out kids are running around getting knocked up at Evergreen."

"Precisely."

It all made sense. It all made perfect sense. "So Walter stood up for her and paid for it. Was he the father?"

"No." Markham paused to take a steadying sip of tea. "She would not tell me who it was, but she assured me it wasn't Walter. They were together for the first time weeks after the baby was conceived."

"But do you have any idea who it was?"

"I have ideas. I suspect Nora ended up in the bed of someone with the power to make her go away."

"A Spade."

"Yes. That seems almost certain now."

"The same guy who hit Nora. The same guy who killed Walter."

She inclined her head. "You do not know how Walter died, do you?"

"No."

"He had asthma—a very bad case. He was found on the floor of his room, clearly having suffered an attack, but his inhaler lay inches from him. It might have been declared an accident if it wasn't for the clear signs that there was a struggle and he had been pinned down."

"How awful," I hissed. "He was only trying to do the right thing."

"His loss broke Nora. She left the school without a fight and we lost touch."

"So you never found out who fathered the baby or marked Nora?"

"Never."

"What about the baby? Did she have a boy or girl? Where—"

"I know nothing about the child. Nora's parents would not give her the phone when I called, and one day, I found the number disconnected. I have no idea what happened to her or the baby."

I shook my head. "Why would you come back and teach at that school after everything that happened? You know that nothing has changed. The Spades are still free to destroy lives and Eric told me it's even bigger than a few students." The words were tumbling from my lips. "They are backed up by their parents, and money, and maybe the headmaster himself! That's why he does nothing but sit in his office all day—"

"Valentina."

"You know the school is some kind of brain farm. They're looking at all of us as the beings who will turn around and make them money one day."

"Valentina."

"They made Maverick Technologies a reality, and what does a grateful Marcus do? He moves in down the street, fits the school with the best computer system, and then sends his genius son there. It's a vicious cycle and no one sees it for what it is because they haven't broken any laws. They let their children handle everything and then step in on graduation day saying 'let's talk about your future.'"

"Valentina," she broke in. "Take a breath."

I tried but my breathing was shallow. I couldn't take it all the way in. "It's just wrong. It's painted as kids being kids, and bullying that normally crops up in schools, but it's actually an organized system to make the rich get richer."

"That is what all things are about in the end."

"I'm going to stop it," I announced. "They can't do this to people."

"So you will be returning to Evergreen next semester?"

"I—" My reply lodged in my throat.

"You're done at Evergreen Academy. You do not come back next semester. If you do, you'll go the same way as Walter McMillian."

Tears prickled behind my eyes. "They'll just keep doing this. They'll never stop."

"We don't know who they are. We can't fight an enemy we can't see."

"Someone has to try."

"That someone does not have to be you." Markham reached across and laid her cold hand on mine. "You must stop now. The Spades have destroyed too many good people. I could not stand to lose you too."

I said nothing. I couldn't. I did not know what to say. I knew even less what to do. After a few minutes, I went back to sipping my tea.

"THANK YOU FOR SPEAKING with us, Miss Moon."

I rose with the officers. "You'll find him, won't you?"

"We're organizing a search party as we speak. We'll find him." The uniformed women in front of me sported stern, but confident faces. I wished I shared that confidence.

"I wish I could do more to help."

"You've done all you can. You should go. I believe your teacher is waiting to take you back home."

"Okay." I shook their hands one last time and left the room. I didn't go outside to the waiting car.

This is my chance before they search his room.

I thought this hotel cute and charming when I arrived. Now the eerie silence roared in my ears. The creak of the floors beneath my feet ratcheted up my heartbeat. I needed to hurry, get those yearbooks, and get out of this place.

Eric's room was at the end of a short hallway. I quietly let myself in and went over to the bed with the green backpack. I knew that was Eric's.

I gazed around the room. *Now to find the brown duffle bag.*

I peeked under the bed, looked in the closet, searched the bathroom, and even took the cushions off the couch. After scouring the place twice, I accepted it.

The duffle bag was gone.

DUSK HAD FALLEN OVER Evergreen when the car pulled up to the gates. Markham parked behind a beat-up four-seater. Mom climbed out of the car as she turned off the engine.

"Thank you," I said softly.

"Goodbye, Valentina."

I stepped out and Mom burst into a run. She enfolded me in a hug that I returned just as fiercely.

"My baby. Are you okay?"

"I am now." I buried my nose in her neck, breathing in the scent of love and safety. "Please, let's get out of here. I don't want to be near this place."

"Don't have to ask me twice."

We piled into the car and I instantly saw someone was missing. "Where's Adam?"

"He's at home with the babysitter. I didn't know how long you would be or how you'd feel when you came back."

I accepted that as the best move, although I ached to see him. "Let's go home."

"Leaving right now, baby, but on the way, I want you to tell me everything that's been going on."

"Mom—"

"Everything." This was a tone I didn't hear often. This was serious, not-messing-around Olivia. "Afterward, I'll decide if you're going back to that school."

I might have argued, but at that moment, there wasn't a speck of fight left in me. "Okay."

We made the ride back, but not in silence. I told Mom everything that had happened in the last four years. There was yelling, shouting, and even more crying. She cycled between distress at all I had kept from her and rage at what had been allowed to happen to me. When we pulled up to our tiny house, the both of us had been put through the emotional wringer.

Mom pulled me into her arms when we reached the doorstep and kissed my forehead. "Just go inside and get some sleep. We'll talk in the morning."

"Yes, Mom."

We stepped inside to a dim house. The soft glow from the living room drew me to the babysitter. She smiled at us when we walked in.

"The little angel is sleeping."

"Thank you," I said. I veered off and went into Adam's room. The nightlight cast swirling stars on his sweet face, and I felt my tension ebb away as I gathered him in my arms. The toddler didn't wake as I carried him to my bed and snuggled under the covers with him. I slipped away, feeling truly safe for the first time in a while.

"WHAT DID YOUR MOM SAY?"

"She was mad as you can imagine," I replied. "She doesn't want me to go back."

"Do you want to go back?" Sofia asked.

I didn't answer. My eyes drifted down to the open envelope on my bed. The letter resting on top of it carried the embossed logo of Somerset University.

"Congratulations, you have been accepted to..."

"How are you?" I asked. "Did you talk to Zane?"

Her sigh came through the phone. "I did. He promised me that he didn't kiss her. He said Penelope ran up to him under the arch, crying about something flying into her eye, and when he bent to see, she planted a kiss on him and then ran off."

I shook my head. "She's certainly evil enough to set him up."

"I know," she said softly. "It's not that I don't believe him, but when I saw that photo... It was like someone punched my heart out. It was just so c-cruel, Val." Her voice became choked. "And Paisley and Kai? Everyone saw that photo. Paisley has been crying all week."

I crumpled the sheets in my fist. It was hard to believe a week had passed since that awful night.

"Ciara and Claire will probably be expelled for the weed and pills. I knew they would hit us hard, but this..."

"It's like you said: Cruel."

There was a lull as it sunk in. I looked around at Adam, happily playing with his toys on the carpet of my room. I tried to picture raising him on a legacy of deception and deceit, and then sending him to the academy to continue the tradition. My mind rejected the very thought.

"I've been thinking about what you said for the past few days," Sofia said. "Thirteen families. People watching me—marking me to see what I'll invent next like I'm some betting horse they're waiting to see perform. I haven't slept properly since that day."

"You and me both."

"Mom is freaked out too."

"You told Madeline?"

"Yes. Dad too. We actually had a good talk the other night. I told them what I was feeling. It was weird." She let out a soft laugh. "But they opened up too and apologized to me."

"I'm glad, Sof."

"Yeah. But the thing is, they don't have a clue who the other eleven families could be. They've heard of the Spades, but never thought it went so far as some kind of mafia organization. They're thinking of pulling me out of school too."

"Can't blame them."

"Have you talked to the boys?"

"Yes. I told them everything that went down in the bayou when I got home the next day. Ryder didn't say much. I don't think he knew what to say, but I'm going to see him today so we'll talk properly."

"I'm happy you guys are still doing it. You need this after everything you went through."

"You all loving me and supporting me is everything right now. Just like I'll love and support you whatever you decide to do."

"Thank you."

"I hope I see you after Christmas."

"I'm not sure if you will. Mom and Dad have been talking about going on a family vacation—get away for a bit. I'll call you every day if we do."

"Perfect."

"Just don't put that kid on Santa's lap this year," she continued.

I laughed. "He's older. He should be able to handle it, right?"

"Or he'll give him another wallop and get you really banned this time."

We chuckled, enjoying a rare, light moment. "No Santa. I got it."

"I have to go, but I'll call you tomorrow."

"Bye."

I set my phone down on the bed and got up to play with Adam. I was tickling him into submission when Mom knocked on the door to tell me Ryder had arrived. I picked my laughing baby up, peppered him with kisses, then handed him to Mom.

Ryder stood on the front porch waiting for me. He looked great in a pair of loose jeans and a wooly sweater that strained to contain him. His raven locks curled at the nape like they did when he let the air dry them after a shower. "Hi, Val."

"Hi."

We kissed—just a soft peck—but it warmed me through. I had missed him over the last week.

"You ready to go?"

"More than ready."

He took my hand and led me to the car. I waited until we were inside to grill him. "Will you tell me about the hotel we'll be staying at? What will we do this weekend? It's before Christmas so we can see the lights, go shopping, watch movies."

"We'll do any and everything you want, but first, there's somewhere I want to take you."

"Is this about your final labor?"

"Yes."

"Will you tell me what it is?"

"Not yet, but you can trust me."

I did trust him. Ryder reached across the dash and laced our fingers together. We talked on the drive. The topics started out light, but naturally drifted to the one hanging over our heads.

"I never knew about Benjamin and the thirteen families," he said. "Mom was just as shocked as me when I told her."

"That's no surprise. Eric said he wanted you denied of that legacy too."

"I've thought it many times before, but again, I am glad to not be his son."

"I just wish we knew who the other eleven were." I gripped his hand harder. "We would know... if the yearbooks hadn't been taken."

"The yearbooks?"

"Yes. I've been thinking of nothing but since I found that duffel bag gone. It's why Eric brought all of them instead of the one I asked for. If I had seen them all, I would have discovered the secret for myself. I would have noted the thirteen last names that popped up over and over throughout the years going back to the first class."

"Of course." He smacked the dash. "Fucking hell! That makes sense." He took his eyes off the road to look at me. "But there are other ways to find that out. We can check public records for families who have lived in Evergreen since it was founded."

"That includes too many people. Sofia's mother's family have lived there for years too. Not to mention there are no guarantees they live near the academy. It's a boarding school. The students don't have to commute."

"Shit. You're right."

"Plus," I went on. "Even if we got around that, there's no way we'd get access to students' records to confirm they went back to the first class. The easiest way was to look at those yearbooks, which is why Eric tried to sneak them to me and why they were taken. We have to find other copies."

"There aren't any at my house. I mean, there's one from Mom and Benjamin's senior year, but only that one. I've never seen any others."

"There has to be more. Maybe in the school."

"But you're not going back to school, are you? Not after..."

My throat clenched as I remembered the choking water and the foreign thing that brushed against my hand.

"I don't— I don't know."

"You don't have to," he whispered. "Even if you don't come back, I'll never give up finding the Spades and making them pay for what they did. They won't get away with it if I have to beat the truth out of everyone in that school."

I chuckled softly as I wiped away a tear. "I know you won't give up."

I said no more about it and thankfully Ryder changed the subject. I relaxed as the next hour passed. I didn't know where we were going, but I trusted him.

Eventually, anonymous highway gave way to cute shops and general stores. Ryder turned down a cul-de-sac and pulled the car up to the curb.

"Ryder? Where are we?"

He didn't answer. Instead, he leaned over me and pointed through the window. My eyes lit upon a two-story house with a small blue fence. There were two cars in the driveway and a pink bike abandoned behind them.

"Who lives here?" I asked.

"Val." Something in his voice made me turn to look at him. There was an expression on his face that I couldn't read. "I said that you couldn't choose your labors, but this one you can. If you want, I'll start the car, drive away, and we'll never talk about this again, but..."

"What? Ryder, what are you talking about? Where are we?"

"We're outside your father's house."

I froze. My eyes grew as that sentence penetrated. "My... father?"

He nodded. "I wasn't lying about the private investigator in freshman year. They did track him down and this is where he lives. If you want to meet him, he's there."

"How do you know?" I whispered. "He might not be home."

"He works nights. He's home during the day."

Slowly, I turned to the house. "Home... with whoever owns that pink bike."

"He has a daughter," he confirmed, "and a wife."

A fist clamped down on my heart and squeezed. *He has another family. One he didn't run out on.*

"What's his name?" I croaked.

"It's Conrad Smalling. He's home, Valentina. They all are if you want to meet them. This time, it's truly your choice."

"My choice..."

I never had a choice. Olivia refused to utter one word about him my entire life. All I knew of the man who fathered me was that he rejected his college girlfriend when he found out she was carrying his kid.

I could meet him. I could see his face for the first time. And my sister. I have a sister. Does she have the pointed chin I didn't get from

Mom? Does she know I exist? Has she been wishing I would knock on that door one day?

Has he? Does Conrad regret leaving me? Has he spared one thought for the daughter he never knew?

I sat there for a long time. Ryder didn't speak or rush me. He gave me my space as I looked out at that pretty house and the promise of a happy family it contained.

I turned away. "Let's go."

"Are you sure?"

"Yes. The man in there isn't my father. They aren't my family. He's just... a stranger."

Ryder started the car and pulled away. I didn't look at the house as it faded in the rearview. There was nothing for me there.

We turned out of the cul-de-sac and paused at a red light. Ryder leaned over and kissed my cheek. "I hope I didn't upset you. It's just felt wrong all of these years to know where he was when you didn't."

I stroked his cheek. "No, Ryder. I'm not upset. I'm glad you brought me here. You reminded me of something I forgot for a moment."

"Reminded you of what?"

The hand stroking his cheek stopped. "You reminded me I have a choice and that no one but me should decide what happens in my life. I chose to go to Evergreen to make a better life for my son and my reason hasn't changed. I'm going to finish what I started... and I will take down the shits who tried to get in my way."

To my surprise, the corner of his mouth tugged up into a grin. "You know, you're really sexy when you plot vengeance."

"Oh yeah?" I replied, laughing. "Did you remember there was something else we had planned for tonight?"

"I couldn't forget that. The hotel room is booked and waiting for us."

"Let's go now. I don't want to wait any longer."

Ryder zoomed off when the light turned green. It was lucky he had the foresight to book a place near our destination. It would have been awful to have to go all the way back to Wakefield when I was itching to tear his clothes off now.

"It's right there." Ryder pointed through the window at a grand hotel towering in the sky. My mouth fell open seeing the luxury resort. Christmas had arrived at the property. String lights wrapped around the trees and garlands hung over the doors. It was even more magnificent on the inside. White Christmas trees twinkled throughout the lobby.

Ryder checked us in and took my hand on the way to the elevator. "I got us the honeymoon suite."

"Oh?" I pulled him inside when the doors slid open and pressed him against the wall. "Is there something you need to ask me?"

His cheeks reddened. "Not tonight, but I thought you would appreciate the extras included with the room. I want tonight to be special."

"It will be." I rested my head on his chest as we were whisked twelve floors up. Ryder and I stepped out and made for room 1201—the final door at the end of the hall.

He opened the door, but stepped aside so I could go in first. I took two steps and gasped.

I had been expecting cheesy touches like rose petals scattered on the floor and a heart-shaped bed. What I walked into was a gorgeous winter paradise. The lights were dimmed to give the Christmas tree the chance to shine. This one was green and perfectly matched the dark green covers on the bed that took up the raised platform. Fairy lights cast a gentle glow over the space and onto the small table for two and the meal resting on it.

Ryder stepped out into the middle of the room. "I made sure dinner would be waiting for us in case you were hungry. You mentioned Christmas movies? There are plenty on the TV. We can watch while we eat."

"I'd love th-that," I said, voice cracking. I was in serious danger of crying, but I didn't want to do that. Words couldn't describe how perfect this was, but tonight, actions would. "We had our first date over Christmas. It's right that this is happening now."

"A date to remember." Ryder picked up our plates and moved them to the coffee table. "Adam beat up Santa, we ran away like fugitives, and the elves made fun of us."

"Get used to it, Shea. That is the kind of trouble you're in for if you stick with the Moons."

He smiled at me over the champagne flutes. "I can definitely get used to it."

Ryder held the glass out to me. "It's apple cider."

I took it. A thrill went through me just thinking of what else the night would bring. Together, we snuggled up on the couch as Ryder put on the movie. Watching, giggling, feeding each other bites, I was content in his arms as we relaxed and let this unfold without rushing.

When the credits rolled up the screen, I tilted my head back to look at him. "Want to watch another movie?"

"Nope."

"Want more room service?"

Ryder trailed his finger down my cheek and traced the curve of my lips. "Nope."

"So what do you want to do?" I whispered.

"I'll give you a hint."

I was still smiling when he bent down and claimed my lips. The kiss was slow and sweet—all the things I once thought Ryder could never be. Slow though it was, it sparked electricity in my body that surged through me and curled my toes.

I was breathing hard when we broke apart. "I didn't quite catch the hint. Can you tell me again?"

His laughed warmed my lips. Ryder's answer was to stand and hoist me into his arms. He carried me to the bed and set me down gently on the sheets. Our eyes locked as he reached for the edge of his shirt and pulled it over his head. I reached for the buttons of my dress as he pulled at his belt. My pulse quickened as we undressed for each other. We weren't touching each other, but the anticipation made me pulse with need.

Why had we waited a week? Why did we wait at all?

Only when we were naked did I turn over and crawl to the pillows. The mattress dipped as he followed me. Heart racing, I faced him and sank into the bed.

Ryder pressed his lips to my forehead. "Are you sure about this?" he asked.

"Yes."

He kissed my head, then the tip of my nose, then down to my lips where he lingered. I draped my arms around his neck, but he slipped out of them as he continued his journey. He kissed down my body as my heart rattled in my chest. I bit my lip as he kissed my belly button.

Ryder's head sank between my legs. The next thing I felt was his soft lips against my inner thighs.

"We talked about the teasing," I gasped.

His chuckle reverberated through me. "I told you I was going to take my time. We have all night, Valentina. I'm going to spend it exploring every inch of you."

That sounded like such exquisite torture. I didn't want to wait, but I also didn't want to stop his exploration. His touch tingled on my skin long after he moved on, and soon I felt him everywhere.

Ryder kissed and licked every inch of my body until my core wept for him. "Ryder," I panted. "Please."

"Please, what?" He put his arms on either side of my head, grinning down at me.

I groaned. "There's no ridding you of that evil streak, is there? You know what I want."

"But I'm not finished." He bent until our noses brushed together. "There are a few parts of you I haven't tasted yet. Like... here."

I sucked in a breath as he closed his mouth over my nipple. They were hard as pebbles, but so sensitive he pulled moan after moan from my throat as he worshiped it with his tongue.

"Then there's this one."

He moved to the other breast and I almost ripped my nails off as my hands clutched the bed. He put the other nipple through the same treatment as beads of sweat broke out onto my body. I had imagined sex with Ryder more times than I admitted, but I had never pictured making love with him, because this was what it was.

Ryder lifted his head and gave me a kiss that seared my blood. Our tongues danced as our hands roamed each other.

His breath was ragged when we came up for air and it thrilled me. I loved the effect I had on him.

"I'll be right back," he whispered into my ear.

All I could do was nod as he slid down my body. Black spots popped along my vision as he put his mouth to my core. His tongue probed, licked, and tantalized me as I contorted with pleasure. A cry escaped my lips when he slipped a finger inside of me and found that spot that drove me crazy. I came screaming. My back arched so far off the bed, the top of my head touched the sheets.

Ryder put his arms under me and pulled me up, pressing our chests together. As I watched, he swiped his tongue across his lips, tasting every last drop on his lips. We kissed again before he reached around me and grabbed a condom.

His eyes appeared almost black in the fairy lights. I could see his need for me as clearly as my reflection.

"Turn around," he whispered.

I didn't hesitate. I turned over and settled on my hands and knees, offering myself to him completely. My excitement rose as I listened to the crinkle of the condom unwrapping.

Ryder put his hands on my waist, but surprised me by pulling me back up. I molded to his chest, feeling his heart pound against my shoulder.

"There's something I want to tell you before we do this."

"What's that?"

His hands moved up my thighs and cupped my breasts. "You're so fucking beautiful."

I laughed breathlessly. "You said that the first time you kissed me—minus the cursing. Do you remember?"

"Of course, I do. We were twelve. You came over to my house and snuck me away from my tennis lesson. We hid behind a palm tree and in the middle of giggling like we did something really bad, I kissed you. Then I found out about the affair and everything changed. If I could go back and do things differently, I would."

"I wouldn't. If things had been different, I wouldn't have Adam. I wouldn't have gone to the academy. I wouldn't have fallen for you, Jaxson, Maverick, and Ezra. All that matters is that we are here together now."

"That reminds me of the other thing I want to tell you."

"What, baby?"

"I want to tell you that I love you."

Holding my breath, my eyes fluttered shut. I held still as I tried to capture everything about this moment. The feel of his hands, the sound of his breathing, the pounding of his heart, and the emotions swirling inside of me.

"I love you too."

Ryder's hands made a slow journey down to my thighs and no more words passed between us. I gasped when he pushed into me and my exclamations only got louder as he moved. Every thrust brought me closer to the edge until I tipped over and the black spots exploded in my mind. Collapsing on the bed, I rode the aftermath down as Ryder lay on top of me.

"I love you," he whispered.

I would never get tired of hearing him say that.

Chapter Nine

The rest of my winter break was perfect. Ryder and I spent an amazing weekend watching movies, Christmas shopping, and exploring the resort. At night, we made love until we fell into an exhausted sleep.

I thought things couldn't get any better until we went to Maverick's house for Christmas dinner. Our families had such a great time, the Beaumonts invited us back for another year. I could picture us all around the fireplace year after year, laughing and eating as a family, and it was a picture I liked.

As the night wound down, Maverick and I snuck away for a private moment in his room. It wasn't until we dressed that I told him about my decision to go back to school. He took it as well as Ezra did—as in not at all.

"They threatened your life, Val. This isn't a game anymore."

"It was never a game. It's bigger than me now. Eric is still missing. The Spades turned on their own. They showed that there is nothing they wouldn't do, and that they have no intention of stopping. I have to stop them for all the innocent students like me who passed through the gates looking for a dream and ended up with a nightmare."

"But why you?" He came around the bed and grasped my arms. "Let's tell the police."

"Tell them what? Who would they haul in for questioning?"

He tossed his head. "I don't know—the Edens. They have to know who the other families are."

"If that was enough to get their son back, Sofia wouldn't be texting me about visiting their manor and finding Mrs. Eden won't get out of bed. She's been a wreck since it happened."

"This is crazy," he burst out, throwing up his hands. "All of this is crazy."

"I know it is, but unlike anyone else, I know how to end it." I grabbed his chin and made him look me in the eyes. "I have a plan."

"What plan?"

"One you can help me with so that this can all be over for good, and we can go back to planning our future in that tiny apartment with my mischievous three-year-old."

A smile graced his lips as he enfolded me in his arms. "Who said anything about tiny?"

Convincing the men I loved that I had to go back was the easy part. Then there was Mom.

"Val, I don't understand this. Why would you go back there after what happened?"

"It's my last semester," I said as I packed my bag. Adam sat amid the pile of clothes, watching television while he ate his snack. "How would it look to Somerset if I changed schools?"

"Who cares how it looks? They would understand if you explained the situation."

"They might, but it's more than that. I don't want to leave. You didn't raise me to run away when things get tough. I'm not going to start now."

"Valentina." Mom pulled the sweater out of my hand and spun me around. "This is bigger than tough. You were attacked and thrown blindfolded and bound into a swamp!"

I looked over at Adam. He was no longer watching the screen. A frown marred his face as he looked at us.

"Mom, please, don't scare him. I promise you; I'll be fine."

"No."

"But I have to go back," I argued. "You know what's going on there. I have to put a stop to this because it's clear no one else will."

Folding her arms, she shrugged. "That's Evergreen's problem—the school and the headmaster. If he's happy to churn out a graduation class full of sneaks and felons, that's for the authorities to sort out, not you. You're not going back to that school."

"I'm eighteen. I don't need permission." The words were out of my mouth before I could stop them.

Mom's brows shot up her head. "Oh, you want to play that card?"

"No." I backed down immediately. "I didn't mean it like that. I just meant that this is important to me. I've gone through a lot to graduate from this school."

"Things that I am only just hearing about. I'm your mother, Valentina. How can you keep so much from me?"

"It wasn't because I didn't want to talk to you. I was afraid you'd pull me out of school."

"You're right; I would have. Just like I'm doing now."

She spun on her heels and marched toward the door.

"Will you at least listen to my plan?" I burst out. "I have a way to get through this safely. I can take everyone down and end this once and for all."

"It does not matter what your plan is. I have to think of your safety."

"Please, just listen."

"No." The door swung shut behind her.

It took me pleading and cajoling for most of the day before she finally sat down and listened to my plan. Then there was another hour of explaining it backward and forward until she grudgingly agreed it was a good one. The result was that I got to return to Evergreen, but I had to call her three times a day and assure her I was okay. If I missed a call, she was driving up to the school and yanking me out.

Cresting the lone road that led to Evergreen wasn't like all the times before. I had felt so many things during the moments I topped the hill and saw those gates—joy, eagerness, dread, sorrow, resignation. None of those emotions felt close to what I was feeling, but maybe it was because it was hard to think with Mom's steady stream of warnings.

"Do not go anywhere alone."

"I won't."

"Don't go chasing anyone into the woods in the middle of the night."

"I've learned that lesson."

"You know you can trust Sofia and the boys. Stick with them."

"I will, Mom."

"Call me every single day. I mean it."

"I know. I promise, I'll call."

When she pulled up to the curb, I climbed out and got in the back seat to give Adam a hug and kiss goodbye. Mom's kiss and hug goodbye for me was ten times more strangling.

"I love you. Be safe, not stupid."

I chuckled. "Yes, Olivia."

"Mom, baby. Always Mom."

I gave her an extra squeeze. "I love you."

"Love you too."

She let me go with obvious reluctance and got back in the car. I waved them off until their car disappeared, and then I turned and faced the gates.

Four figures were staring back at me. I steeled myself as I walked up to them.

"Are you ready?" Jaxson asked.

"I'm ready."

Together, we turned and passed through the gates. Every eye latched onto us from the seniors to the returning freshmen, and I read the question in their gaze.

What is she doing back?

I expected their surprise. I expected Ace's anger for defying them, but no one would be expecting what I would do next.

"First things first," I said as we crossed the lawn for the dorm. "We find those yearbooks."

"YOU WOULDN'T THINK that this would be so hard." Sofia flipped through her mother's yearbook for the fifth time. She was propped up on my bed next to the stack of yearbooks the boys had brought from home. "But none of us have books farther than when our parents went to school. I'm pretty sure the Edens only did because they're obsessed with this legacy stuff."

I shook my head. "I can't believe I lost Eric's books. They were right there and it took me so long to figure it out."

The book dropped onto Sofia's lap. "I can't believe we lost Eric."

I turned away. It was still hard to think of that night. It was even harder to comprehend how we were a month into the new semester and Eric was still missing.

"Do you think he's dead?" Sofia asked.

"I can't let myself go there, Sof. It's too much."

"It's all been too much."

I couldn't deny that. I was right about Ace not being pleased about me returning to school. The first few days of classes, I received wave after wave of threatening texts.

Ace: You'll regret coming back.

Ace: I will get you out of this school if it's the last thing I do.

Ace: Drowning in that alligator swamp was too good for you. I'll have to think of something better.

It continued in that vein until I finally blocked their number. It might not have been the best idea, but I couldn't take it anymore. I didn't need their poison leaking into my life anymore. The next thing Ace wanted to say to me, they could say it to my face.

That was a meeting I was sure would be soon, but as the weeks ticked down and we didn't manage to find more yearbooks, I grew less confident.

"If only we could just ask people for them," Sofia said.

"We don't want Ace to know we're still looking. They think they've beaten me by whisking the duffle bag away. I want them to keep thinking that."

"They might not find out. We barely see the second class nowadays."

I snorted. Less than barely was more accurate. I hadn't so much as laid eyes on Natalie in two weeks. The first week of the new semester started out like our new normal. We were on the fourth floor enduring our second classroom and mealtimes, but it turned out, we couldn't handle sharing the same hallway either.

Our group was heading to English on the fourth day of class, when the new Knights passed by. Darren smirked at Paisley and said "nice tits," and the spark lit the match. Paisley hauled off and smacked him across the face. He stumbled back and had no time to recover before Kai was on him. They went down fists flying, and within minutes, we were all fighting.

It was terrible. More people jumped into the fray, letting months of frustration bring them to the boiling point. Penelope clawed Sofia's arm causing deep, bleeding gouges and she responded by ripping out a handful of her hair. Two guys jumped Maverick and he knocked them clear across the hall. They came back, refusing to give up, and then Jaxson, Ryder, and Ezra got involved.

Natalie came for the person that had been the object of her hatred for years: me. She grabbed my head and smacked it into the locker. Head pounding, I whipped around and hit her in the face with my backpack. There was still a bloodstain on it from where I broke her nose.

It took five teachers and four security guards to break us up. The next day, Evergreen yelled at us in the auditorium until he was blue in the face. No one tried to haul him off this time. Despite the haranguing, no one was punished. Much like no one was punished for the video at the hotel. That was good news for Claire, Ciara, Kai, and Paisley, but it didn't satisfy their need for retribution. Maybe Evergreen sensed that because when he brought us in for a second assembly, it was to tell us the two classes were being separated indefinitely.

My class was now on the first floor while the freshmen had been moved to the second. We shared nothing with the other seniors and had no reason to see them. This cut way down on the harassment, but deep down, I knew it wasn't over.

"We don't see them, but there could still be Spades hiding out in our class. We can't tell anyone we're looking for the yearbooks."

"We have to do something, Val, because it's been weeks and we're nowhere. Your mom cheered you on for breaking that bitch's nose, but what if the next fight makes her pull you out of school."

"What else can I do?"

Sighing, she let her head fall against the headboard. "I don't know. How about asking the one other person who could have copies going back that far?"

"Like who?"

"Headmaster Seamus Evergreen."

"JUST ASK EVERGREEN?" Jaxson repeated. "That's the plan?"

"It couldn't hurt," I said the next day. It was a crisp February morning, but we stuck to our decision to spend the Saturday having breakfast by the fountain. The wind whipped up a chill, but I was warm by Ezra's side. "She's right that he's the one most likely to have a pile of school yearbooks around. They could be in administration."

"He has no reason to let you see them if he does."

"I'm just going to ask. If it doesn't work, I'll think of something else."

"Okay," said Jaxson. "You're right, it can't hurt to ask. I'll go with you to talk to him."

"*We* will go," Ryder corrected.

I laughed. "For what? To protect me from his steepled-fingers and disappointed glare? He's not going to do anything to me."

Ryder shrugged. "And yet, we're still going with you."

I rolled my eyes, but let it go. I was dating four highly protective guys. This was my fate.

"Can we get back to what we were talking about before?" Ezra cut in. He peered over my head at Maverick. "Ryder and I got into Somerset too, Rick, so I don't know why you think you're going to be the one who gets an apartment with Valentina."

"Because I asked her first."

"The fuck does that have to do with anything." Ezra put his finger under my chin and lifted until I was looking into those eyes. "Don't you want to live with me?"

A smile curled my lips. "Of course, I do."

"Stop seducing her with your devil eyes, Ezra," Jaxson protested. "Baby, what about me? The studio isn't far from campus. We can get a nice place, fill it with records, and go to the beach every weekend."

"Really, man?" Maverick said. "You're resorting to bribes?"

"I don't have to bribe her. I've got this"—he gestured to his body—"and she can't resist it."

I couldn't help but giggle. "It's true, I can't."

Ezra glanced at Ryder. He was busy eating his eggs while the battle raged around him. "Why aren't you saying anything, Shea?"

He lifted his shoulders. "Because the solution is obvious, isn't it?"

We all stared at him blankly.

He set down his fork. "Okay, four of us need to go to Somerset, one of us needs to go to the studio, one of us needs a good preschool, one of us has to stay home and be there for my mom, and all of us want to live with Valentina. The only thing that solves all of those problems is if the five of you come and live in Shea Manor with us." He picked up his fork again and speared a bit of egg. "I've already asked Mom and she's excited. She said the manor was meant to be filled with people."

The four of us gaped at him open-mouthed. I didn't know what the other boys were thinking, but I couldn't believe that Ryder had gone so far as to ask his mom to let us live with them.

He truly wants this—us.

"I think that's a great idea," I said. "Somerset is only thirty minutes from the manor, I can see Mom as often as I want, and there are some of the best preschools in this area." I looked between Ezra, Jaxson, and Maverick. "What do you guys think?"

"That's cool with me," Jaxson said. "I practically live at Eugene's house as it is."

Ezra and Maverick were slower to answer. "There's plenty of room and I'd be close to my mom too. I'm down."

I slipped out from under Ezra's arm and scooted up to Maverick. Taking his face in my hands, I placed a soft kiss on his lips. "What do you think?"

He smiled down at me. "Let's do it." Maverick kissed me once more. "But there's one condition: you and I share a bedroom."

The protests were immediate. I laughed as Maverick smirked triumphantly at the others. I would be settling this battle later, but right then, I had something I needed to do.

"I have to go, guys. I'm going to ask Evergreen about the yearbooks. You don't have to"—the four of them got to their feet, breakfast forgotten—"come."

The boys trailed me as I headed through the courtyard and pushed through the main doors. It was Saturday, but Mrs. Khan and the headmaster kept normal office hours while the rest of the admin staff were off for the weekend.

"Wait here, please," I told them. "It'll look strange if we all roll up on him for some yearbooks."

"Fine," Ezra agreed.

The boys hung back, but they didn't go far. I went inside and Mrs. Khan looked up from her desk. The door to Evergreen's office was open. As I crossed to the counter, I saw him hunched over paperwork, scribbling away.

"What can I do for you, Val?"

"Morning, Mrs. Khan," I greeted. I was careful not to let my voice carry. "Sorry to bother you, but I was wondering about the school yearbooks."

"Yearbooks?"

I nodded. "A friend of mine lost their copies. They had almost all of them going back years. Is there any way they could get new ones? Could they buy replacements from the school?"

She tsked. "How sad. I wish we could help, but it's not that simple. We order them from the printer and only get as much as we are paid for. If a student loses their copy, there are no extras left."

"That sucks. They were hoping to use it while they documented their family tree."

"Oh, what a fun project. Maybe there is something I can do..." Mrs. Khan scrunched up her nose as she thought. "You know, they could speak to the headmaster. He has copies of all the yearbooks in his office. I'm sure he'd be happy to let your friend have a look." She rose from her desk. "Do you want me to ask him now?"

I shifted to gaze at Evergreen. He hadn't moved from his earlier position, bent over his work. I opened my mouth and said, "No. That's okay. I'm sure my friend wouldn't want to bother him."

"Alright. If you're sure."

"Bye, Mrs. Khan."

The boys were right where I left them when I stepped outside. "So what did he say?" Ryder asked.

"Sofia was right. Bless her for the genius she is."

"He has them?"

"He's got copies in his office."

Maverick stepped forward. "Is he going to let you see them?"

"I didn't ask."

"Uhh," Jaxson sounded. "Why not?"

"Because I realized it's no good to have him staring over my shoulder while I flipped through every book writing down names. That's if he even lets me see them in the first place. I have to come back on my own and check them out."

"What does that mean?" Ryder asked.

"It means... I'm breaking into the headmaster's office." With that, I turned and marched toward the doors. I was out in the courtyard before I heard them running up behind me.

"What did you just say?" asked Maverick.

"I said I'm breaking into his office. I'm getting the stuff now."

"The stuff? What stuff?! Your handy breaking-and-entering kit?!"

"It's not a kit. It's just a hammer."

"Val." Ryder ran out in front of me and pulled me up short. "Stop and talk to us."

"What do we need to talk about? This is the only thing that makes sense."

"None of this makes sense," Ezra retorted. "This is insane. You could get expelled."

"What's insane about it? I won't get caught." I flapped a hand. There are cameras in the courtyard and around our dorm, but there are none in the main building and I've been in Evergreen's office enough times to know there are none in there. I'll put what I need in my bag and walk around with it for the rest of the day.

"When it hits five o'clock, weekend office hours are over and Mrs. Khan will go home while Evergreen retreats to wherever he comes from. The office will be empty, but it will still be early enough that when I get back, I won't look like a prowler creeping in after dark." I shrugged. "You see? It's perfect."

The guys shared incredulous looks like they couldn't believe all four of them had fallen in love with a lunatic.

Jaxson was the one to break first. "At least let me do it," he offered. "It doesn't matter if I get expelled. I don't have Somerset to look forward to."

"Jaxson, no. I appreciate that"—my hands balled into fists—"but I need to do this myself. After what they did to me, I won't sit on the sidelines."

"But—"

"No one is sitting on the sidelines," Ryder broke in calmly. "We all go."

The denial was hot on my lips. "Guys, no way. I'm not risking you getting in trouble too."

"If the plan is as foolproof as you say, then there is no risk."

"I want to get in and out quickly," I tried again.

Ezra nudged my shoulder. "You can't be quick going over all those names and faces by yourself. You'll need our help anyway."

Damn, that's a good point. It would be much easier with the five of us.

I looked around at their handsome, and determined, faces. They would come with me if they had to stalk me.

"Okay. Let's do it."

I SAID IT WOULD BE easy, but it surprised me how much. I returned to the dorm to get the hammer and then the five of us went into the quad and found a quiet spot to sit and watch the hours tick by. Five o'clock came and went, but we stayed. We did not move until the clock struck thirty minutes past.

"Ready?" I asked.

They answered by getting to their feet. Together, we entered the main building. I tried the handle for the admin door and it didn't budge.

"Stand back."

"Do we have to do it like this?" Ezra asked. "Everyone will know someone broke in."

"I told you I don't have a breaking-and-entering kit. I can't pick the lock so I have to break it." I waved them back. "Go on, guys."

Reluctantly, they stepped aside. I didn't waste the precious time we had. I raised the hammer in the air.

Smash! Smash! Smash! Clang!

The handle clattered to my feet. I kicked it aside as I shoved the door open and padded across the room to the headmaster's office. I gave it the same treatment as the boys followed behind.

The headmaster's lock was made of sturdier stuff. It took eight hits to finally get the thing off.

"We're in," I whispered. "Search everywhere."

"Why are you whispering?" Ryder asked in a normal tone. "We're the only ones here."

"Just hush," I snapped as the others snickered. "Find the year-books."

"I did say I liked them bossy," Ezra mumbled as he passed by me.

My cheeks warmed as memories of our night in the hotel flooded my mind.

Now isn't the time.

The guys fanned out. Ryder took his desk. Ezra scanned the bookshelves. Maverick and Jaxson began opening file cabinets. "Maverick, let's switch. Listen to make sure no one comes. If they do, they'll notice the broken door."

"Okay."

Maverick moved outside and I took his position. The four of us were quiet while we searched. My cabinet was full of student files, but I checked each one thoroughly to be sure. I was reaching for the final cabinet when I heard—

"Here they are." Jaxson stuck both hands into the cabinet and pulled out as many as he could lift. Different colors, styles, and sizes, but all of them said Evergreen Academy Class Of. We found them.

Ryder and Ezra crouched on the floor as Jaxson took out the rest.

"As quick as you can." I reached into my bag and pulled out notepads and pens. I passed them out to the guys. "Write the names that keep coming up. We'll compare them after."

I pulled the recent years to me and we got to work. We didn't speak as we searched, but one by one, I saw the boys write down names. My own pad was still blank by the time I reached Shaun Roundtree. My former professor was no less handsome as a young senior. His toothy smile glittered on the page.

I kept flipping. Carefully, I scanned over the names until I found one. Then another. My eyes were beginning to cross by the '90s, but I forced myself to focus.

Almost done. This is it. We're so close.

I reached for the second-to-last book on the stack and started with the seniors. The pages whispered in my hands as I revealed row after row of grungy clothes and old-fashioned haircuts. My eyes had reached the bottom of the fifty-third page when I stopped.

Wait.

"That's the last one, Val. Let's put these away and get out of here."

I jerked my head up. "What? Oh, right. Here. I'm done too."

I passed over the books as Jaxson hurriedly put them back in order. He reached for another stack in my hand when the door flew open.

We jumped as Maverick appeared in the doorway. "We have to get out of here. Now!"

"Hey! What happened to this door?!" The shout was muffled, but there was no mistaking Gus. "Who's in there?!"

Jaxson snatched the books out of my hand and threw them in. Maverick slammed the drawer shut as we scrambled to our feet, looking for a way out.

"Quick," Ezra cried. "Out the window."

We didn't spend another second thinking about it. Ezra practically ripped off the latch and threw the window open as the admin door banged against the wall.

"Who's in here!?" Gus bellowed.

Ryder and Maverick grabbed me and tossed me unceremoniously out the window. I landed in a heap on the grass, coming down hard on my elbow, but I ignored the pain as I scrambled out of the way. The boys leaped out and we bolted as Gus burst into the headmaster's office.

We ran and didn't stop until we reached our fountain. I practically collapsed on the rim of the basin, willing my heart to slow. "I'm not cut out for the life of a burglar," I wheezed.

"Let's see if it was worth it," said Ryder.

Ezra, Ryder, and Jaxson pulled out their note papers and handed them to me. I calmed as I took them. Finally, we would end this.

The boys sat down at my feet as I read, cross-checked, and marked out names. They had come up with over sixty, but the further I went through time, the more I was able to eliminate. I set the pen down after writing the last name.

"One, two, three..." I counted until I hit upon the number. "Thirteen."

My hands shook as I handed over the paper. "This is it. These are the Spades."

"Not all of them," Ryder said. "Not Shea."

"No, not you," I agreed.

"But look at these other names," said Ezra. The sun was beginning to set. It cast a dusky light on his harshly pale skin. "This can't be true, can it? They can't all be Spades."

"I'll find out if it's true. I know everything now. The Spades don't know it yet, but they're done."

"ARE YOU SURE, VAL?"

"As sure as I can be." I picked up two apples and put one on her plate. The sun had dawned on Monday morning like it was another normal day, but nothing could ever be normal again. "There are no yearbooks of the actual first class, but these same thirteen names appear in most of the yearbooks. Thirteen, Sof. That's not a coincidence."

We accepted our breakfast plates and moved off the line. We had gotten up early and beaten most of the dorm to the cafeteria. It gave us a chance to talk without being overheard.

"What are you going to do now?" she asked. Her hand tremored as she picked up her milk. I took it from her and gripped her fingers. She squeezed tight.

"You know what I'm going to do," I said. "You know the plan. Everyone knows the plan. I'm not going to deviate."

"What if *they* deviate? You can't predict what they're going to do? No one in their wildest dreams would have imagined they would attack you and leave you in the bayou."

"Maybe I can't predict their every move, but I know Ace is no idiot. I'm thinking like them and this is what I would do if I were Ace."

"Okay, okay, I just—" She took a shuddering breath. "I wish there was more I could do."

"We're always a team, Sof. No matter what happens."

She gave me a smile that wobbled, but a smile it was. After a minute, we picked up our forks and dug into our roasted pear and quinoa porridge. The cafeteria filled up as we ate. Soon, Kai, Zane, and the boys were setting down their trays.

Zane pulled Sofia's chair closer to him and gave her a kiss that heated up the lunchroom. The two had been hotter and heavier since the video almost broke them up. I think Zane realized what he could have lost.

Paisley was the last to arrive. She had just dipped into her porridge when the cafeteria doors flew open.

"Attention, class," Evergreen announced. Markham trailed him as he crossed to the center of the room. "There will be an emergency assembly in ten minutes. Finish your breakfast and go straight there. Is that clear?"

"Yes, sir."

"What's that about?" Paisley asked after he left. "What did we do now?"

Ryder and I shared a look. We picked up the pace and finished breakfast. As a group, the second senior class walked the short distance to the hall and filled in the back rows. The other class came in behind minutes later.

Whispers echoed through the hall. "What did we do now?" was on every tongue. Evergreen stepped up to the podium with an expression that said it wasn't good.

"Good morning, seniors. I will be speaking to all grades to make clear that the student or students who broke into my office..."

I tuned the headmaster and his promises of severe punishments out. Our immediate summons to the hall meant that I still had my phone. I took it out of my pocket and pulled up my contacts. No more waiting. It was time to face Ace.

My phone buzzed like crazy when I unblocked their number and the flood of texts poured in. I ignored their hateful words as I typed in my own.

Thirteen last names.

Burned as they were in my memory, I did not need to look at the list as I spelled out the final name and hit send.

I put the phone back in my pocket. I didn't need to say more. Ace knew that I knew. It was their move now.

Chapter Ten

"The guy finally decides to punish us all and it's the one time we're innocent." Kai roughly stabbed at a piece of trash. "Why do we have to pick up garbage because some jokers broke into his office?"

"We're taking over as janitors every week until the people involved confess," said Zane. "Anyone have something to say?"

He was joking, but I kept my head down as we moved across the lawn. I felt bad that everyone was being punished for what we did, but it had to be done. I sent that message and then went to class after leaving the assembly. All day my thoughts returned to the phone box until finally the bell rang, but when I took it out, the phone didn't buzz.

It did not buzz while I did my homework. It didn't buzz while I changed for trash duty, and it didn't buzz while I tromped through the grass. There was no reply from Ace and the guys threw me worried looks that night as we readied for bed.

"Why haven't they replied?" Maverick asked.

"They will," I said.

Jaxson took my arm and drew me in. His hand was warm on my back as he trailed his fingers up my pajama buttons. "When they do, tell us immediately. No repeats of last year and the almost strip show."

"We're long past the point of hiding things." I rose up on tip-toes and kissed him. "Night. I love you."

I said good night to each of them and then headed up to bed. The covers enfolded me in their cool embrace and I welcomed sleep.

Ezra awaited me in my dreams. He was naked as Dream Ezra tended to be and doing things to my body that he'd done to me in reality as well.

"I love you more than strawberry root beer and peanut butter brownies."

"I love you too. More than—"

"Wake up!"

Rough hands seized me and dragged me out of the dream and my bed. I tumbled from the sheets and fell to the floor. Figures that were only blurs in my vision gripped my shoulders and held me down.

Benjamin!

I screamed as fear flooded my mind and overwhelmed all reason. A hand clapped over my mouth.

"Quiet," a voice hissed. It was impossible to make them out in the dark room, but I knew that voice. "You know who we are, yes?"

Breathing hard through my nose, I nodded as my sense returned. *It's not Benjamin. He's dead. He can't hurt you.*

"Then you know why we're here. You're not going to scream. You're not going to run. You will walk calmly out the door and follow us so the cameras don't pick up anything wrong. Got it?"

I nodded again.

"Good. Let's go."

Just like that, they released me and I sucked in lungfuls of air, trying to slow my panic enough to give them the calm they wanted.

"Get up."

I stood on knees that wobbled. They let me stumble to the other side of the room and jam my shoes on, then I followed them to the door. They pulled it open and the hallway lights revealed what I didn't want to be true: the Spades hiding among us.

Juliet Cochran poked me in the back. "Go on."

I did as she said, falling in behind Genesis as she led the way downstairs. Both of these girls had walked out of the lunchroom with me. They both cried and said they couldn't stomach the evil of the Spades. They both lied to my face.

I kept my expression clear as we made our way out of the dorm. On the second-floor landing, I chanced a look at Ryder's closed door.

"Don't even think about it, Moon," Genesis hissed.

I turned away and continued walking.

The night air chilled my cheeks when we stepped outside. The pajamas I chose were thick, but not thick enough to keep out the cold. They led me across the lawn with one in front and one behind. The three of us had rounded the main building and entered the quad when I spoke.

"Where are we going?"

"Where do you think?" Genesis replied.

I bristled. I never much liked her but I bought her change of heart. It was good to know my first instinct about her was right. "That's not an answer."

"That's all you're getting."

I let it go. I would find out where we were going soon enough. As we walked soundless through the quad, I flashed back to the night in the swamp.

It was them. They tied me up. They threw me in that water. They—

"Eric," I cried. "Where is Eric? What did you do to him?!"

Juliet scoffed. "You should be worrying about yourself right now."

"If you've hurt him—"

"You'll what?" Genesis asked. She peered at me over her shoulder. "Please, tell me. Amuse us."

My lips curled into a snarl. "You're a twisted bitch, you know that?"

She laughed. It was a harsh, mirthless sound. "Yeah. I know."

I had no reply for that. I quieted again as the sports complex loomed in front of us. I assumed we were going inside, but at the last second Genesis veered off and we went around the back. I realized where we were going before she grabbed the door handle.

"Why are you taking me to the roof?"

"We like hanging here," Genesis said. "Ezra did a great job fixing it up for us."

"That wasn't for your crazy ass."

"All of this is for us, Moon. I'd have thought you'd realize that by now." Genesis yanked open the door and pointed up. I went in without argument.

I had climbed these stairs so many times before—nights laughing with Sofia, connecting with Ezra, or breaking through walls with Ryder. Something else entirely awaited me up there.

I reached the roof entrance and went through without prompting from Genesis. Eight pairs of eyes fell on me as I slowly strode before the group. They were everywhere—on the couch, sitting on the ledge, standing by the coffee table. I met each of their gazes in turn.

They're here. They're all here except one.

No one spoke, so I decided to be first. "Hey, guys. Nice of you to drag yourselves out of bed to see me, but we haven't all met. How about introductions?"

They didn't so much as twitch.

"Don't all jump up at once. I made a list so I'll go through it for you." I shifted around and leveled a finger on a familiar face. "Let's start on this side and work our way around. Natalie Bard, Darren Rosewood, Penelope Madlow." I turned to the people on the couch and by the table. "You must be the underclassmen Spades. That would be Barbara Williams, Timothy Davis, Rebecca Chang, Reed Morris, and Victor Cinco." I clapped. "How did I do?"

"You're not impressing anyone," Juliet said as she stepped around me. "We know that you know who we are."

"Not all of you," I shot back. "There are ten of you, but we're missing three. There's Eric Eden and Ryder Shea, but there was also a final name to show up over and over again in the history of the academy. The most obvious name: Evergreen."

Stoic faces looked back at me.

"Twelve Spades have walked the halls of this school led by Ace. In the end, I didn't have to find Scarlett's father in the yearbook because I found Scarlett herself under her maiden name: Scarlett Evergreen."

I thought that would get a response, but still they stared at me. Anger lit a fire in my gut. Why were they just sitting there? What were they waiting for?

"I know she was Ace," I pressed on. "Eric told me so there's no point in denying it. She was Ace, but now she's gone, and was taken over by the psycho tormenting me. I want to know which one of you it is." I narrowed my eyes on them as my fists clenched. "Which one of you fuckers blackmailed me, marked me, and threatened me. Who is Ace?!"

"I'm afraid it's none of them."

I went rigid as a voice sounded behind me. *Wait. Is that...*

"None of them could be Ace, Val. That right belongs to me and me alone."

I couldn't move—couldn't breathe as horrible realization washed over me.

"N-no."

Ciara walked out in front of me, a pleasant smile on her face. "After big sis *left*, it was up to me to take over as Ace."

"Big sis?" I repeated, although the words did not make sense.

"That's right. I guess it's my turn for introductions." She stuck out her hand. "Nice to meet you. My name is Ciara O'Bri-an-Evergreen."

I made no move to shake. "But— But that— That can't be right."

She dropped her hand, but not the smile. "Why not? Because you fell for my little performance at the hotel?" She adopted a high-pitched tone. "*Staying silent was just as bad and I won't do that anymore. I won't ask you to forgive me either, but...* blah blah blah."

"No," I rasped. Shaking my head, I backed away until I was stopped by the door. "You were in the video. They outed you for smoking. Why—"

"I put that in there so you wouldn't suspect me." She shrugged. "It's not like Daddy would expel me."

"Daddy?" I repeated. "Daddy!?" Suddenly I was shouting. "The headmaster doesn't pay a lick of fucking attention to you! He's not your father! What the hell kind of game are you playing right now?!"

Ciara's face remained neutral through my outburst. "He is my father. Can't you see the resemblance?"

My glare was my response. They both had sandy-colored hair, but so did a dozen other people in the school. They looked nothing alike.

She heaved a sigh. "Oh, well. Everyone always said I looked like Mom, but I don't need to inherit his looks to inherit his title. You're so damn smart, Moon, think about this. Ace leads the Spades. They choose the Knights. They deliver the marks. Who besides the Evergreens would have the right to decide who does or doesn't belong in Evergreen Academy?"

"But it can't be you. How can it be you?" I whispered. My mind recalled every minute I had spent with Ciara. "The junior winter trip. You— You were in the hot tub when Ace attacked me with the ski."

"But I wasn't."

My head whipped around at the voice. Penelope smirked at me from her spot on the wall. "Ciara sent the text to get you out. I dropped a little lesson on your head."

I turned back to Ciara, gazing at her as my denials faded. "But... you were my friend."

There wasn't a flicker of emotion in Ciara's brown eyes.

"How could y-you—" I stuttered to a stop.

Big sis, I recalled.

She watched her sister struggle with me before flying over a cliff. Of course, she hates me, but...

I swallowed thickly as I glanced at the others. *Do they all know what happened with me and Scarlett? Do they know what really drives this crusade?*

I can't go there, I reminded myself. *If there is a chance they're still in the dark, then they need to stay that way.*

"How could you let it get this far?" I amended. I was staying far away from the topic of Scarlett. "You marked the real Knights and turned the school on its head. Aren't you supposed to be about maintaining the status quo? You've wrecked this place!"

Her eyes flashed. A spark of anger broke through her cold mask. "Me? I turned the school on its head? That wasn't me. That was *you*," she hissed. "*You* forced me to mark the Knights. *You* turned them against me."

"You did that, crazy! You blackmailed their girlfriend."

Ciara's lips peeled back into a snarl. "I'm not crazy. I tried to get them to see you for the worthless slut you were. I gave them a chance to do the right thing. Their loyalty is to me, not you."

I scoffed. "You guys are really full of yourselves, aren't you?" I swept over all of them. "This school isn't here for you. The students don't exist to make you rich and no one owes you loyalty."

"That's where you're wrong. My grandad made it clear to me." Ciara threw out her hands. "All of this is mine, Moon. The Evergreens built this place. We own it. We *allow* you to walk our halls. We grant you permission to be among the best. If I don't want someone here, then I can make them go. The Knights are chosen by an Evergreen. If they won't obey me, I'll choose Knights who will."

My fists clenched. "Like Eric? He wouldn't obey any longer so you got rid of him?" I turned my attention on the others. "Are you hearing this? She doesn't care about you. She blackmailed, threatened, and had you attack one of your own. You're all expendable to her."

Silence followed my statement and it buoyed me. "This isn't how it's supposed to be, is it? When you learned about the history of the Spades and the thirteen families, did anyone tell you it would involve assault, lies, and murder?"

The Spades looked at me, faces blank, until a noise sounded on my right. Disbelief killed the rest of my speech in my throat as Natalie laughed. The others soon joined in. All of them were laughing... at me.

"Murder?" she cried. "What are you talking about? No one killed anyone, idiot."

"But Eric—"

"Eric isn't dead." Natalie peeled herself off the wall and came to stand at Ciara's side. The look on her face told me how much she was enjoying this. "The plan that night was he was supposed to lead you off into the swamp. Get you away from your *boyfriends*. It worked until we followed and found out he hadn't brought you to the spot we arranged."

Darren picked up the thread. "It took longer to find you guys and when we did, we heard Eden spilling everything. He betrayed us."

"We had to think fast," Natalie continued. "We got him out of the way and Darren and Genesis snuck him back to the hotel while everyone was frantically running around looking for you. Once we got him in Darren's room, we called his grandmother."

"His grandmother?"

"That's right. She raced down and took him away, but not before getting out of him his little plan to give you the yearbooks."

My breaths grew shallow as they spoke. What the hell were they saying? "You mean Eric isn't missing?"

"He's taking a little... time out while he remembers what his priorities are," Natalie replied. "We're not freaking murderers, Moon."

Anger twisted my gut. I shot off the door, advancing on her. "Sorry if I don't know where you draw the line. You all bound and blindfolded me. You threw me in water and left me alone in the dark. I can't swim! There could have been alligators in there."

"Ugh," Penelope groaned. "Do you ever stop bitching? You're fine, aren't you?"

I bristled at the nastiness in her tone. She didn't give a flying fuck about how terrified I was that night.

"It was to teach you a lesson," she went on. "One that you still haven't learned. Why the hell did you come back to the academy after that?"

"I—"

"And I was so clear too." Ciara brought my eyes back to her. Her phone was in her hand and when I looked, she tapped the screen.

"*You're done at Evergreen Academy.*" The creepy high-pitched voice that haunted my dreams filled the night air. "*You do not come back next semester. If you do, you'll go the same way as Walter McMillian. Goodbye, Valentina Moon.*"

She ended the recording and her hands fell to her sides. "You shouldn't have come back," Ciara repeated.

I swallowed hard. "But I did come back. I'm here and I'm not leaving." My lips quirked up in a smile that trembled at first, but held as determination broke through. "There are only a few more months until graduation. I've stood up against everything you've thrown at me for years. I can hold out for a little longer." My smile widened into a smirk. "And now, I know who you are. I know your names. I know about the thirteen families. I know everything. Something tells me things are going to be a lot easier from here on out."

Genesis stomped toward me. "I wouldn't listen to that 'something' because it's dead wrong."

"Why not? You think I won't tell everyone what I know?"

"You won't," Ciara stated. There was a surety in her voice that rattled me but I didn't let it show on my face.

"How do you think you're going to stop me? I'll tell everyone if you don't leave me and the people I care about alone. Unless you are planning to do to me what was done to Walter McMillian, there's nothing you can do to stop me."

Natalie laughed again. "Will you get over yourself? No one is risking prison over you. We told you we're not murderers."

"That's right, Val." Darren picked himself up and walked over to us. I tensed when he passed behind me. "No need to go through all of that when there are easier ways to keep you quiet." Darren pressed his nose to my neck and inhaled deeply. My skin crawled as his lips brushed against me. "We'll go through your friends and fucks."

"We'll have Evergreen expel Claire for the pills," Genesis announced. "She'll end up right back in your slum where she belongs with the other drug dealers. Which is what we'll say she is when we tell the headmaster she offered to supply us."

"The twins too." Darren moved around me and slung his arm over my shoulder. "They'll find drugs in their lockers and both will be shipped back to Africa where they came from."

Horror filled me, chilling my blood. "Y-you can't—"

"Then there are your boyfriends." Penelope continued. "No one sued Interstellar Records after the leak, but we're sure for the right amount of money, we can convince a band to."

"And Ezra," Genesis said. "They didn't kick him out when he knocked you around in sophomore year, but they will when I tell them he hit me."

"But Ezra didn't—"

"Maverick Technologies might be hard to go after," said Natalie, ignoring my interruption. "But Maverick Beaumont isn't. When I start telling everyone how the giant, hulking quarterback pushed me into the locker room and forced me to have sex with him—"

Red descended on my vision. "You wouldn't fucking dare!" I surged forward, claws extended, and jerked to a halt gasping as Darren's arm tightened around my throat.

He hauled me back, keeping my swiping hands away from Natalie. "Easy, Moon. You haven't heard what we're going to do to *Ryder Shea*," he growled. "I thought of something perfect for him while I was sitting at home with my jaw wired shut."

"G-get off!"

"No one ever found out what happened to his old man," he continued. Although he loosened his grip slightly, letting me breathe. "But we always suspected his mental patient of a mother. She must have gotten tired of his dad running out on her and sleeping with every slut he saw, so she had him *taken care of*. We'll be sure to pass that along to the police."

"Leave them alone!" I struggled in Darren's hold. "You can't do this!"

"We won't do it," Natalie said, voice hard. "If you go back to your dorm, pack your shit, and don't tell anyone what you know. Understand?"

I bobbed my head rapidly, bouncing on Darren's arm. "I won't. I won't tell anyone."

"And you'll *leave*," she pressed.

"I'll leave. I'll be gone tomorrow."

She closed the distance between us, putting her face in mine. "You'll be gone before the sun comes up or I'll go crying to the headmaster."

"Okay," I whispered. I stopped fighting Darren. "I'll leave before they wake up."

"Good. I'm glad we understand each other."

Just like that, Darren released me. I stumbled away from him, furious tears burning behind my eyes. I held them back. I wouldn't let them see me cry.

Natalie smirked at me all the same, reveling in her victory. It took everything in me not to lunge at her again.

"We're done here, guys," Ciara spoke up. "Go back to bed. No reason to lose more sleep over her."

"Can't disagree with that," said Natalie.

One by one, the Spades filed out until only Ciara and I remained. I glared daggers at her as fury made my limbs tremble. Ciara strolled up to me, looking completely unconcerned.

"You won't get away with this forever! Someone else will discover your secret. I—"

Ciara reeled back.

I didn't have time to react as the punch connected with my face and snapped my head around. I went flying, crashing onto the coffee table. Dazed, all I could do was wheeze as the air rushed out of me.

"That was for my sister, bitch." Nails dug into my shoulder and hauled me up.

"Ciara, wait—"

The next punch was even more brutal. Cartilage snapped under her fist as blood spurted from my nose.

"And that's for everything else."

I staggered back and tipped onto the sofa, clutching my face. Through the tears, I could see Ciara lean over me. The pain scrambled my mind, but I forced myself to speak.

"Ciara," I croaked. "Listen to me."

"What? You going to beg and say how sorry you are? That you never meant to spread those lies about my family?"

Slowly, I shook my head. "No. I was going to say... your sister is a sick, twisted monster that got exactly what she deserved."

I was ready for the next one. When Ciara swung, I threw myself to the side and her fist went sailing through the spot where I was. I took my chance and ran.

The roof's ledge loomed in front of me, but if I could double back around the couch, I could make it to the door before—

Hands seized me and pulled me back. I crashed onto Ciara and flailed as she got me into a chokehold like Darren's.

"Let me go, you psychotic piece of shit! You've made your point!"

Ciara's arm constricted until my screaming was cut off with a gasp. "I haven't begun to make my point," she hissed into my ear.

"Those idiots may be too weak to get rid of you, but I don't have that problem."

Suddenly, the arm choking me was gone. Ciara put her hands on my back and shoved. I careened forward and fell a foot from the ledge. She was on me before I could get up.

Ciara's nails dug into my neck as she raised my head off the ground. "I can't say I liked Scarlett. She grew up with her mother and never gave enough of a fuck about me to come around. It definitely pissed me off when I came to the academy and she refused to let me take over as Ace, but no matter how I felt about her. You can't get away with—"

"I'm innocent!" I bellowed. "I never wanted any of this to happen. She came after me. She marked me. She dropped the planter. She set my room on fire."

I spun around, arm up, and knocked her hand off me. Quickly, I scrambled to my feet and we faced each other.

Ciara didn't look pissed at my escape. On the contrary, she was smiling. "Actually, about that last one. It wasn't Scarlett who started the fire; it was me."

I gaped at her, genuinely stunned. "You what?"

She lifted her shoulders. "I told you Scarlett wouldn't let me take over. I had to do something to prove I could be Ace so I took my chance to get rid of the mark that just wouldn't leave. Then Daddy moved you to that dorm and I couldn't try again." Her smile widened. "Don't have to worry about those cameras now."

I could barely hear her over the roaring in my ears. *It was Ciara. She was the dark figure that escaped into the night. She tried to burn me alive.*

My chest felt so tight it hurt. A thin layer of sweat covered my body and made me shiver as the cool air ripped through my pajamas. *I thought this girl was my friend and she tried to kill me.*

"How could you?" I asked, voice rising. "What the fuck is wrong with you?! Who would try to kill someone because they won't obey a stupid card?!"

Ciara's face twisted. "It's more than a card, Val. That's what you never understood. That is why you never belonged here. Quae sequenda traditio. Tradition is everything.

"It's the traditions of this school that have made it the best in the world. You think the thirteen families are using the students, but what they're really doing is helping them make a difference. No one gives a fuck about the person who had the idea. It's the ones who make it a reality that end up in the history books."

Ciara took a step toward me and I resisted the urge to move back. I wasn't getting any closer to that ledge.

"My grandfather explained it all to me." She took another step and was only inches away. "We do good. Not just for the students, but for the future. We make sure that people with the potential to be something, achieve that potential. The very least we can ask in return is that people don't ruin our good name." She swept out her arms. "All of this is mine, and everyone here has to obey me—whether they know it or not."

I lifted my chin and looked her directly in the eyes. "I won't."

She laughed—a sharp, mirthless sound. "You don't have that option anymore." Her eyes flicked over my shoulder. "Go ahead. Jump. Make it easier on both of us."

I held her gaze steadily. "No."

"Fine." In the time it took for me to blink, she lunged.

I screamed as Ciara shoved my shoulders and sent me flying. Reacting fast, my hand flashed out and grabbed her before she could pull back. We both fell hard and I cried out when my back hit the ledge.

Snarling, she pulled away and grabbed the sleeves of my pajamas, readying to shove me over for good.

"Wait!" I cried. "Ciara, listen—"

"Shut the fuck up!" She heaved me to my feet. It was terrifying how strong she was. "I'm done with you, Mo—"

"It's about Scarlett! I need to tell you something about Scarlett." Ciara jerked, coming to a standstill.

"What about Scarlett?" she asked through gritted teeth. "You going to admit you and your boyfriends lied about her?"

My breaths came out in rapid pants. "I w-will admit something." I yanked an arm out of her grasp and straightened. She let me, but the other arm was secure in her grip. "You need to know that your sister"—I grabbed the collar of my nightshirt and ripped—"fell for the same damn trick. Say hello to the camera, bitch."

Ciara's eyes popped open. Her grip slackened in the moment of surprise and that split second was all I needed. I swung at her jaw and connected with a blow that knocked her back. Ciara tripped over her feet and crumpled to the floor. I jumped on top of her before she could get up.

I plucked her phone out of her pocket and flung it with all my might. It smashed against the roof door and splintered into satisfying pieces.

"That was to get rid of any *videos* you might be holding on to," I hissed into her pale face. "But just in case you've gotten it saved somewhere else, my handsome, computer genius boyfriend who has been watching the whole thing as it streamed to his laptop, has also sent every single electronic device you own a nice virus."

The blood from my nose dripped onto her cheek and ran down, looking eerily like a teardrop. "Try running this place from jail, psycho, because the police are on their way."

As if they heard me, the sound of sirens pierced the air.

Chapter Eleven

"Are you sure you're okay?"

Kiss. Kiss. Kiss, kiss, kiss.

"I'm fine, Mom," I wheezed. She was squeezing me hard enough to crack a rib. "The nurse even said I could leave."

"How can you be fine?" She kissed my cheek again. "I almost had a heart attack when I saw that video. I agreed to your plan, but *you*"—Mom promptly dropped me and spun on Maverick—"were not supposed to wait so long to call the police! That girl almost threw her off the roof."

Maverick didn't try to defend himself. "I'm sorry, Miss Moon."

"Mom, don't blame him." I tugged her arm and pulled her back to me. "I made him promise to wait until Ace— I mean, Ciara said something that would nail her. She admitted to setting my room on fire. She's going away for a long time."

"She admitted to more than that," said Sofia. She leaned over and took my hand. "I still can't believe this stuff about the families and the Evergreens thinking they have the right to rule us like this is their kingdom." She shuddered. "You once called this place a haunted house horror show. You were right."

All of us were squeezed into the nurse's office. It was hard to believe only hours ago I was on that roof with Ace, but dawn brought a swarm of police and all the people I loved. Maverick,

Jaxson, Ryder, Ezra, Sofia, Mom, and of course, my Adam. Adam twisted out of Ryder's hold and reached for me. I took my baby and let him snuggle into my side.

"The horror show is over," I said. "I knew once I texted Ace those names that the Spades would try to get me alone to threaten me. I've been wearing that button cam night and day—which turned out to be smart because I wasn't really expecting them to kidnap me from bed." I shook my head. "But it's okay. The Spades are exposed, we know where Eric is, and Ace is going down hard." I let my head fall back onto the pillows. "It's finally over."

Ryder came up to me and stroked my cheek. I leaned into his touch. "If the nurse said you could leave, let's get out of here. I have a feeling classes are canceled today. I want to get you away from this place."

Mom patted Ryder's shoulder. "The best thing I've heard all day. Come on, baby. I'm getting you out of here and you're not coming back until those awful people have been handled."

I opened my mouth to argue but the look on Mom's face made me think better of it. "Okay." I picked up Adam and climbed out of bed. Ezra took my hand as we headed out of the door and my boys fell in around me.

Adam put his arms around my neck and rested his head on my shoulder. My heart swelled as I kissed his curls. "It's over," I whispered. "Everything is going to be okay."

One Week Later

I SAT ON MY BED, STARING at an unseen spot on the wall. Around me, my room was a chaotic mess of strewn clothes, open suitcases, and upturned textbooks.

"...down to the car." I heard his voice before he stepped into the doorway. "Hey, baby. Do you need help?"

"No, Jaxson. I'm fine."

"Are you sure?" He came fully into the room, not worrying about the rules. No one had to worry about the rules now. "Doesn't look like you started."

"No, I..." At that second, I made up my mind. "I have to do something first. I'll be right back."

I stood and made for the door. Jaxson stopped me at the threshold. "Hold on. Where are you going?"

"I need to talk to someone."

"Who? I'll go with you."

I cupped his cheek. "You don't need to be so protective of me anymore. I'll be right back. I promise."

I sidestepped him and slipped out of the door. The dorm was a mess of noise, shouting, and chaos, but I passed through it and stepped outside. The sun shone fiercely on the academy, heating up my skin as I crossed the lawn and stepped into the courtyard.

If I thought too hard about it, I might talk myself out of what I was going to do, so I trusted the part of me that spurred me on.

Mrs. Khan's desk was empty when I walked inside, but Evergreen's wasn't. He looked up at my footsteps. "Miss Moon." He set down the stack of papers in his hands. "What can I do for you?"

I walked inside and closed the door behind me. "I thought we could talk."

Only the slight wrinkle between his brows gave a hint to his feelings. "What about? As you can see, I'm very busy right now." He stood and crossed to the bookshelf. He began emptying the shelf and moving the books to a box at his feet.

"I wanted to talk about Nora Wheatly and Walter McMillian."

Evergreen stilled. A book dangled from the tips of his fingers over the box, but he made no move to let it go. He made no move at all.

"You don't have to worry," I continued. "I don't have any cameras. I'm not recording you. I just want the truth."

"The truth about what, Miss Moon?"

"You know I broke into your office and looked through the yearbooks. I found Scarlett's yearbook with your last name, and put the pieces together. I realized I was wrong about her age. If you were her father, then she was born when you were seventeen, and there was one other person I know who became a teenage parent at that time: Nora Wheatly."

The book finally fell into the box. Evergreen turned to me, his face tight. "If you want me to confirm that Nora is Scarlett's mother, then the answer is yes." He gestured to the door. "Now is that all? I am busy—"

"Why did you mark her?" I demanded. "Ciara said all Evergreens are Ace. *You* were Ace. You marked the person carrying your child. Why? Was it to punish her for cheating on you?"

Evergreen's face crumpled into a scowl. "It was a punishment, but it certainly did not come from me."

"What does that—"

"It was my father." Evergreen sighed and the exhalation of breath seemed to take his strength with it. He slumped against

the bookshelf. "It was bad enough that I had sullied the Evergreen name by getting a girl pregnant, but when she came clean
to her other boyfriends about me and the baby, word got back to
him. He told me to push her aside and deny the child. It could
be Andrew's or Walter's or who knew who else. I couldn't let her
ruin my life. I refused him and the next day, a card appeared in
her locker."

"Your father sounds like a hard man."

"Yes, he was." Evergreen slowly returned to his desk. He sat
down, turning his chair a bit away from me. "It was impossible growing up under his shadow. He suffocated me with his ex-
pectations, and though I tried to spare Scarlett the same pressure, just bearing my name meant people expected more of her. I
thought it would be easier for Ciara if no one knew she was my
daughter, but I underestimated my father's influence."

He tossed his head. "No, I cannot blame him. I should have
seen what was going on." His face was turned away, but I read the
agony in his stiff jaw and the lines around his eyes. "I've failed my
daughters in every way."

"And Walter?" I pressed when the silence grew unbearable.
"What did you do to him?"

"Nothing." Evergreen shifted, shrouding his face in shadows.
"Not what you're imagining."

"Then tell me what happened."

"There is no purpose. Nora passed away five years ago. Walter
is long gone, and his killer can never be brought to justice."

"Is that because he went missing years ago too?"

Evergreen's head jerked up. "What did you say?"

My hands shook in my lap. I clasped them together to still
them. "I had a good look at your yearbook. I never checked the

junior class which is where I finally found him: Benjamin Shea."
The name tasted bad on my tongue, but I forced it out and kept
going. "I know now that he was a Spade. I also know that he
doesn't take it well when he discovers that he's been cheated on."
My gaze bore into Evergreen. "Nora had a boyfriend in every
grade. Was he one of them?"

Stricken, Evergreen seemed to age before my eyes. The lines
on his face became more pronounced as he paled. "Yes," he whispered.

"He was the violent, possessive boyfriend." It was a statement, not a question. "He gave her the black eye."

He nodded without speaking.

"And he killed Walter when the boy she chose over him took
it a step further and tried to turn the school against the Spades."

Evergreen sat unmoving for so long, but I waited him out.
"He didn't tell me that was what he wanted to do." The words
came slow, as though they were being pulled out of him. "He said
that we had to do something. If I wanted to prove to my father I
was worthy of being Ace and not a useless embarrassment, I had
to step up." Evergreen's eyes were unfocused as he gazed at a spot
on his desk. "He was good at that—getting right to your weak-
nesses and using them against you."

I found myself nodding.

"We went to Walter's room that night," he continued. "We
were only going to rough him up, scare him a little and tell him
to back down, but..."

"But Shea took it too far," I finished.

"Walter had an asthma attack and Ben snatched the inhaler
away from him. I told him to stop messing around and give it
back, but he wouldn't. I tried to take it from him, but he turned

on me. Benjamin knocked me out and when I woke up... Walter was dead."

"And you never told anyone."

He shook his head. "Ben made it clear he'd deny it and say it was me. Nora was carrying my child. It would look like I was the one with the real motive to hate her boyfriend, and I couldn't reveal the Spades. So I... told no one."

I nodded, letting that sink in. "I guess that explains it."

"Explains what, Miss Moon?"

"Why you've been so accommodating to Caroline Shea. Why you gave in to her request for late admission for a fifteen-year-old mother, and everything else she has asked you over the years. It wasn't because of how much money she's given the school; it's because of your guilt." I knew how harsh I sounded, but I could not hold back. "If you had told the truth, she never would have ended up married to that violent brute."

Evergreen tried to hold my gaze, but in the end, looked away. "You may be right."

"You don't have to protect the secret of the Spades anymore and Benjamin is not here to throw the blame on you," I said. "I know you'll tell the truth now."

"Why do you believe that?"

"Because I saw it in your eyes when I told you what Scarlett had done and you apologized for failing me and the students she assaulted. Your remorse was real, and I realized then that even though you are a terrible headmaster, you're not a bad person."

He pinched the bridge of his nose, squeezing his eyes shut. "How can you say that? You were correct that day. You were marked and I did nothing to help you."

"No, you didn't, but I can understand that you were caught up in what you were raised to believe." I glanced around. "Plus, I've already seen justice done to you and this school. I'm not angry at you anymore, but I hope that you will tell the truth. I couldn't find anything on Nora, but I did learn Walter has elderly parents that retired to Florida. I'm sure they would like to finally know the truth of what happened to their son."

Evergreen shifted around and looked me in the eyes. "I'm sure they would. You are right, Mis— Valentina. It's time to tell the truth."

I nodded and left it at that. I shut Evergreen's door and walked out of administration. Four boys were standing in the hall when I stepped out.

A smile tugged at my lips as I looked at Jaxson. "I told you to turn the protectiveness down, playboy."

"Not a chance, mama. Why would you speak to Evergreen alone?"

"We had some things we needed to clear up. Everything is fine now."

Shaking his head, Ryder took hold of my wrist and pulled me to him. "So you just had a nice chat after you got his daughter arrested, outed his secret society, and got the school closed down?"

It had been a crazy week. Ciara was arrested and the Spades hauled in for questioning. The police were very interested in their elaborate plans to frame and blackmail. As well as the influence of the thirteen families that drove them to it. A lot of well-known, wealthy people were in hot water.

"Yes," I replied. "It turns out Seamus Evergreen knows where the blame truly lies."

"Still," said Maverick. "Let's get out of here. Your mom and Adam are at the dorm packing away your things. It's time to go."

I moved out of Ryder's hug but held tight to his hand. Ezra came up to my side and took the other one. "Even after everything that's happened," I said, "it's hard to believe the five of us won't be at Evergreen anymore."

Ezra snorted. "Booted in the middle of our last semester too. All of the students are being sent to other high schools."

"I'll have to re-enroll at Joe Young High," I said as we stepped out into the courtyard. "I'll be hours away from you guys."

"Not if we go to the same high school," said Ezra. "Another academy. All four of us will apply."

"What other academy?" Jaxson asked. "Who would even accept us this late?"

"I've been looking up schools since they announced this place was closing. I found one close by called Breakbattle Academy."

"Breakbattle?" I repeated.

"Yeah." Ezra lifted his arm and draped it over my shoulder. "It's a weird place, but as long as I'm with you, I don't care."

I rested my head on his shoulder, grinning as his spicy sweet scent enveloped me. Ryder's hand was warm in my grasp, soothing me like the presence of Maverick and Jaxson at my back. Things had been tough, but all of it had gotten me here to this moment with these amazing guys. I would go to Breakbattle, or anywhere else if it meant we would be together. Then fall would see us all living in Ryder's home with Adam.

I came here to create a future for my family, and as I walked away from Evergreen Academy surrounded by my loves, I knew we were headed for one even better than I imagined.

"I love you, Jaxson. I love you, Maverick. I love you, Ezra." I squeezed Ryder's hand. "And I love you."

"We love you too," Ryder said. He stroked the inside of my palm the way he knew made me shiver. "Now, let's go home. We have to start on those applications."

Ruthless

Valentina

Evergreen Academy was supposed to be my fresh start...

...and Somerset University my second chance.

All I wanted was normal. Normal classes. Normal professors. Normal sorority.

I wanted the Somerset Sallys to be like every other Greek house.

I wanted the pretty, fun, sweet sisters to be genuine. I wanted the smile of their enigmatic leader not to conceal a secret.

And I wanted the story they told me to be true.

I should have known that was too much to ask.

Ezra

Somerset University was the first step.

I'd make excellent grades, better connections, and take over the Media Maven's empire.

Joining a fraternity wasn't part of the plan. Neither was stumbling into a disturbing plot, witnessing a kidnapping, and having the world think I'm delusional.

The Somerset Sams are not what they seem, and when they struck, they brought me to my knees.

But I am not what I appear to be either. Beneath the charming persona is the man who'll protect the woman he loves at all costs.

For Valentina Moon, I will be what I have to be.

Ruthless.

Mailing List

Join my mailing list for info about new releases and treats. No spam ever.

Mailing list: https://www.subscribepage.com/rubyvincent-page

ABOUT THE AUTHOR

Ruby Vincent is a published author with many novels under her belt but now she's taking a fun foray into contemporary romance. She loves saucy heroines, bold alpha males, and weaving a tale where both get their happy ever after.

Made in the USA
Coppell, TX
08 April 2021